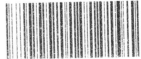

B E N   P I C

# FREIHEIT

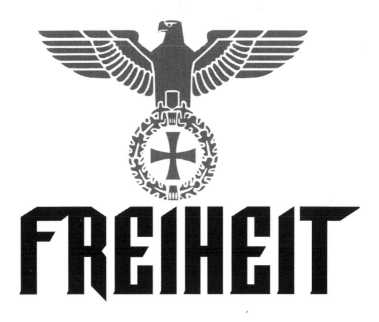

**WHAT IF HITLER
HAD NEVER LIVED?**

Jericho Lane Publishing Limited
7 Bell Yard
London
WC2A 2JR

Printed in the United Kingdom



This book is a work of fiction. Names, places, characters and incidents are the product of the author's imagination or are used fictitiously. Any resemblance to events, locales, persons living or dead is coincidental or they are used fictitiously.

Cover design and layout by www.spiffingcovers.com

# CONTENTS

Based on an original screenplay by
Darren Ripley and Ben Pickering
and a screen story by Darren Ripley

Platinum Winner of the
Koestler Award for Longer Fiction

**frei•heit** | ˈfraihait | ▸**n.** 1. freedom. 2. liberty.

# PROLOGUE

Janek Przygonski never knew his birthday.

He never knew his age.

Or where he was born.

He never knew his nationality.

He knew his parents as a young child. Until one day they were carted off to Auschwitz-Birkenau, the notorious concentration camp in occupied Poland and one of the many death factories in the Third Reich.

He watched helplessly as the SS guard murdered his father as he sat beside him.

He never saw his mother again.

Janek escaped from the camp, only to be recaptured and escape again, this time with his own life as the brainchild of Heinrich Himmler and Reinhard Heydrich – the Final Solution – drew to its barbaric and shocking conclusion.

He made his way to France, slowly but surely slipping from Adolf Hitler's grasp as his manufactured war on the twin evils of "international Jewry" and Bolshevism brought the full might of the British, Americans and Russians into the heart of his beloved Mitteleuropa.

After the war ended, Janek made his way to England, where many Poles – which by now he presumed himself to be (he never knew for sure) – settled after the Yalta Conference yielded his homeland, a pawn traded in international statecraft since Bismarck, resulting in more than fifty years of oppressive communist puppet governments acting for successive occupants of the Kremlin.

Post-war England often struggled to understand why it was necessary to continue to support émigrés like Janek. Late Forties austerity soon bit and bit hard, generating animosity and resentment amongst a kind-hearted but war-weary indigenous population. It was not unlike that which had afflicted the German people in the aftermath of their humiliation with the Treaty of Versailles after the First World War, known simply as the Great War until the Nazis deliberately provoked its rerun.

So in order to fit in and to avoid any racial or ethnic stigma for his future family, he changed his name to an English one.

John Stevens.

As John, he lived a quiet but productive life, fathering two children with his British wife and living to see all five of his grandchildren born. He died in 2001.

He was my children's great-grandfather.

As a gesture to his bravery and good fortune, without which my children would not be here today, we gave the middle name of Przygonski to our firstborn. It was our small contribution to keeping our family's link to its long and predominantly lost past alive for future generations.

Much has been written and said about Hitler and the Nazis since the fall of Berlin brought the Allies' total war to its conclusion in April 1945.

The roots of the Second World War – which began on September 1st 1939 with the German invasion of Poland – lie in the aftermath of the First.

The first half of the 20th Century saw the bloodlust of mankind combine for the first time with the technological means to achieve it. Many would perish as the family squabble in the palaces of Europe spilt over into rain-sodden trenches on the Western Front.

It was the war to end all wars, a conflict between the competing ambitions of dynastic monarchies – all of whom were related – at the helm of decadent empires in their sunset years.

Sparked seemingly by the assassination of an unloved heir to the throne of a dying empire, it was used as a pretext for a conflict lasting over four years, costing almost ten million soldiers their lives alongside millions of men, women and children, innocent and ignorant of their roles as pawns in a sick family game of chess.

It cost three rulers their thrones.

And one of them his life, along with those of his family and closest aides.

In early 1918 the advantage rested with the German Army. The Russians, having toppled and murdered their Tsar and installed the Bolsheviks in his place, had sued for peace. The terms demanded by the Kaiser were punitive but the new Russian government had a more pressing civil war, pitting "red" and "white" Russians against each other, to worry about.

This left the Triple Entente without the very country they had gone to war to support in the first place, shedding blood on the battlefields of northern France and Belgium for ever-diminishing returns.

Victory was within the Kaiser's grasp.

But a German decision earlier in the war – to starve the British of the resources of its Empire by disrupting its shipping – would have disastrous consequences for his enterprise.

The sinking of the Lusitania in May 1915 was the most notable of many German U-boat victories. But they were ultimately pyrrhic as the German Navy's indiscriminate campaign eventually brought fresh American legs into what was until then a European war.

A short window of opportunity had presented itself in the spring of 1918 for the Germans to overwhelm the tired British and French forces before the Americans could fully mobilise on the other side of the globe.

Had all five of their offensives – from Michael through to Blücher – been successful, the outcome of the Great War could have been quite different.

The German Army had incredible self-belief, even after four long years of war. They felt that "might made them right".

Which was what made the armistice that followed just a few months later so unbearable for the German infantry, the frontschwein.

They felt betrayed by their own government.

It was an anger that had to manifest itself in another form.

It wasn't so much the punitive nature of reparations in the Treaty of Versailles that they despised and resented. That was a fig leaf, albeit at $420 billion in today's money an expensive one. It was the despondency of an unexpected and unnecessary defeat, of a war they felt was unfinished, of the "poor bloody infantry" who had shed blood for what they thought was a just cause only to be let down by weak political leadership.

In this febrile atmosphere, the lack of trust in the political establishment combined with the fear of socialism

Russian-style – of the very Slavic takeover that the Germans had gone to war to avert – inevitably led to the popular surge and growing acceptability of the Deutsche Arbeiterpartei (the DAP or German Workers' Party) formed in 1919 by Anton Drexler.

Within two years, it would be led by Adolf Hitler.

In the decade that followed, Germany was in turmoil, torn between competing visions of communism and social democracy on the one side and the working class right on the other.

The DAP started out on the far left but by the time it entered government it had transformed unashamedly into a party of the far right – the Nationalsozialistiche Deutsche Arbeiterpartei.

The Nazi Party.

Hitler and his devoted acolytes unleashed little short of Armageddon on the world, plunging it back into a war that for Germany had never really ended.

The consequences for political opponents, homosexuals, the disabled and infirm, gypsies and Roma and of course Jews were deadly.

Hitler was a gifted orator, political strategist and propagandist.

Through *Mein Kampf* (*My Struggle*) he grappled with what many of his contemporaries felt were the pressing issues of the day, blaming international Jewry and Bolshevism for stifling the rise of the mythical Aryan race.

A hubristic and petty man who believed his own spin, Hitler was "King of the Wimps" with a victim mentality to boot. Rejected by the Austrian army in February 1914 as "unfit due to inadequate physical vigour", he later enacted cold-blooded revenge by conspiring in the assassination of the Austrian Chancellor twenty years later before forcing its union (the Anschluss) with Germany, one of many land grabs after taking power in 1933.

It was his stated objective in *Mein Kampf* to wipe out international Jewry, followed by the Slavs. War with a Bolshevik Russia was for him inevitable.

And as for the Kaiser before him, desirable.

But this deep-seated obsession was not wholly shared by the other senior Nazis, those that would have led the party in his absence.

The NSDAP was not a "one-man band".

Hitler was merely first among equals.

Joseph Goebbels, his "loyal Joe" until the grisly end in the Berlin bunker in April 1945, backed Hitler in his power struggle with the left-leaning Gregor Strasser in the early 1920s, even though like Strasser he was a socialist, not a fascist.

There was much about Bolshevism that the younger Goebbels admired. There is every reason to believe that had he led the Nazis, a second front with Russia would have been avoided.

War hero Hermann Göring, by far the most popular member of the NSDAP in its earlier years and one of its first elected MPs in 1928, was more interested in fine art, finer wine and morphine – not always in that order. As a former military man himself, war for war's sake was not in his DNA.

Party Secretary Martin Bormann, SS Chief Heinrich Himmler and his charismatic deputy Reinhard Heydrich all shared other priorities.

Picking an unnecessary and unwinnable fight with the Bolshevik bear was not one of them.

And then there was Rudolf Hess, Deputy Führer and second in line after Göring in the succession.

Hess's naïve peace mission to Britain in May 1941 – widely derided as a last-ditch attempt to restore his flagging prestige at home – was a failure because it was unsanctioned by Hitler and due to lamentable poor timing. While he was crash-landing in the Scottish countryside, the House of Commons was being firebombed in a significant upscaling of the Luftwaffe's blitz of London.

Many have speculated about whether the Second World War – or World War One, Part Two – could have been averted if Hitler hadn't existed.

Surely the world would have been spared the deaths of sixty million people and the horror of the Holocaust.

Others regard him as a blessing in disguise.

For had a different Führer – Göring, Himmler, Goebbels, Bormann or Hess even – sought war in the west and not taken on Russia too, the history of the 20th Century could have been quite, quite different.

Ben Pickering
London, September 1st 2019

To John Stevens

*'Why remove a madman only to replace him with a lunatic?'*

Dr. Karl Goerdeler
German politician
Born July 31st 1884
Executed February 2nd 1945

# 1
# THE SPANDAU ONE

**August 1987**

As the gates cranked open, the asphalt crackled gently in the midday sun.

It was no day to be wearing a uniform.

But they were used to it. This was a soldier's life that they had chosen, in a cold war without battles.

Only casualties.

Today's casualty in this baking Berlin August: comfort.

Even with his light cotton shirt and shorts allowing his bare legs to breathe, the little boy felt the prickly heat. His grandmother's hand, so often cold to touch, felt unusally clammy as it pulled him across the road, one jolt almost losing him his precious wooden biplane in his other hand. He thought it was the heat too. Little did he know of the somersaults in her own nervous stomach as they edged ever closer.

There was no traffic on this road. Only soldiers peppered the route to the gates of the notorious Spandau prison, their gaze fixed blankly on anything but the little boy and his grandmother.

Its tranquillity hid a torrid past.

Within the walls of this relic of a bygone era had resided the last remnants of the Third Reich, those without the courage to spare a bullet from their own pistol or who dodged the short drop from a hangman's noose at Nürnberg.

*

In the eerie surrounds beyond the prison's foreboding iron gates sat a summerhouse, like a fungal mushroom in a factory, completely alien to its locale.

As the little boy and his grandmother stepped inside, the musty smell engulfed their nostrils. The acrid smell of old. The Berlin sun bathed the study, for a moment less summerhouse and more greenhouse, seemingly illuminating every flake of dust as they slowly percolated through the air. Time certainly felt like it went slower there.

A well-stocked bookshelf flanked the wall, with Günter Grass' *The Rat* the most recent addition.

On the arm of the rocking chair, with somewhat futile illumination from a nearby reading lamp, sat the mottled hand of Spandau's last remaining resident. Formerly chiselled good looks had given way, over a century, to a skin etched hard against the man's skull.

'Papa Rudi?' the grandmother asked softly in perfect German. 'Wie gehts du?'

Rudolf Hess barely flinched. He sat quietly awake, mouse-like for an old airman, his eyes contemplative yet simultaneously vacant.

*

Situated on the river Havel at the mouth of the Spree, Spandau had originally been the site of a Wendish fortress. The Wends were a group of Slavic tribes that had settled the lands between the rivers Elbe and Saale in the west and the river Oder in the east by the 5th Century. After sporadic wars between the Wends and their archrivals the Franks, by the 9th Century the Franks began a campaign of religious subjugation under Charlemagne to forcibly convert them to Christianity.

German annexation of the territories began under Henry I in 929 but their control collapsed in 983 during a Wendish rebellion. The German expansion eastwards resumed under Emperor Lothar II in 1125, with a German crusade led by Henry the Lion against the Wends sanctioned by the Roman Catholic Church. The crusade decimated the Wends, spilling much blood and leading to German colonisation of the area by 1230.

Though civic rights were granted by 1232, the Wends themselves were enserfed and gradually assimilated by their German masters, as former Wendish areas formed an important commercial and industrial centre in northern Germany.

Originally built in 1876 as a military detention centre under Bismarck, Spandau's old brick prison was enclosed by three perimeter walls – the tallest reaching thirty feet – topped by electrified wire.

With its capacity for six hundred inmates and widespread civil unrest after the Armistice, from 1919 the prison also became home to civilians. In the aftermath of the Reichstag fire of 1933, journalists as well as opponents of the new government led by Adolf Hitler as Chancellor under President Paul von Hindenburg were held there in so-called "protective custody". While in theory run by the Prussian Ministry of Justice, the fledgling Geheime Staatpolizei – better known as the Gestapo – abused and tortured inmates held there, making the prison something of a forerunner of the first concentration camps that opened later that year.

By the end of 1933, all remaining prisoners held in state prisons had been transferred to concentration camps at Dachau, Esterwegen, Lichtenburg, Oranienburg, Osthofen and Sonnenburg.

The Allied Powers – Britain, France, the Soviet Union and the United States of America – had requisitioned Spandau prison in late 1946 to house convicted war criminals following the numerous trials taking place, starting with the International Military Tribunal (IMT) at Nürnburg.

Two hundred German war crimes defendants were tried at Nürnberg – symbolically chosen as it was the ceremonial birthplace of National Socialism, lending its name to the controversial Race Laws as well as hosting the Nazi Party's annual rallies – with a further sixteen hundred tried through other channels of military justice.

But with the Werl prison housing scores of former officers and other lower-ranking Nazis, it fell to Spandau to house just seven.

The Spandau Seven.

Had the Soviet Union had its way at Nürnberg, they would have been the Spandau None, pushing for the execution of all of the condemned men as a totem of the de-nazification of post-war German society under the Morgenthau Plan.

In private Winston Churchill himself advocated a policy of summary execution, presumably for the higher echelons of the Nazi regime who he rightly expected wouldn't go quietly.

As it turned out, most of them didn't go at all.

At the Tehran Conference in 1943, Soviet Premier Josef Stalin had proposed executing 50,000 to 100,000 staff officers (not his own this time). US President Franklin D. Roosevelt joked that maybe 49,000 would do.

Believing them both to be serious, Churchill denounced the idea of executing soldiers fighting for their country, fearing it made the Allies no better than the Nazis in their brutality. He said he would rather be taken out into the courtyard and shot himself than agree to it.

Had the British and the Americans lost nineteen million civilians, perhaps they too would have thought differently.

However the court was limited to violations of the laws of war. Restricted by the London Charter of 1945 to punishing the major war criminals of the European Axis, saving embarrassment for Soviet complicity prior to the invasion of Russia in 1941, the IMT only tried crimes committed after the outbreak of war in the respective countries.

With Hitler, Himmler and Goebbels already dead, a diminished group of twenty-four leading Nazis – including Bormann, who was then thought to be alive and on the run, only for his remains to be found by construction workers twenty-seven years later – went on trial on up to four charges apiece.

The charges included participation in a common plan or conspiracy for the accomplishment of a crime against peace; planning, initiating and waging wars of aggression and other crimes against peace; war crimes and crimes against humanity.

After Robert Ley, one of the founders of the DAP, committed suicide a week into the trial, no verdict was entered against him. But of the remaining twenty-two, twelve – the original Dirty Dozen – were sentenced to hang, including Reichskommissar Göring, Foreign Minister Joachim von Ribbentrop, the head of the OBW (Oberkommando der Wehrmacht) Wilhelm Keitel, his deputy Alfred Jodl and SS leader Ernst Haltenbrunner.

Two – radio commentator Hans Fritsche and former Chancellor Franz von Papen – were acquitted while one, the ailing industrialist Gustav Krupp, had all charges dropped as he had been indicted in error instead of his son Alfred.

Of the seven spared the noose, Kriegsmarine chief Karl Dönitz was sentenced to ten years' imprisonment while his predecessor Erich Raeder got life, the Protector of Bohemia and Moravia Baron Konstantin von Neurath fifteen years and the Gauleiter of Vienna and former head of the Hitlerjugend Baldur von Schirach twenty, as did Hitler's favourite architect and Minister for Armaments Albert Speer. Walther Funk, the Reich's Economics Minister and head of the Reichsbank, also got life.

Along with former Deputy Führer Rudolf Hess.

Hess would have hanged with the Dirty Dozen were it not for his absence from the country following his misguided but doomed flight to Britain in May 1941.

It was a flight that saved his life at the cost of his soul.

The Four Powers alternated control of the prison on a monthly basis, bringing with them their own teams of professional civilian wardens, prison directors and their deputies, army medical officers, cooks, translators, waiters, porters and others.

Sixty soldiers stood guard of the prison complex, its

guard towers containing up to six machine gun placements manned 24/7.

Visits were sparse and brief, memoirs and journals prohibited and during Soviet months food bordered on Medieval gruel.

Once in prison, the seven were no longer known by their names, only their number. Baldur von Schirach was Number One, Rudolf Hess Number Seven. Given the vast capacity of the prison, an empty cell was left between each inmate for fear they would try to communicate in Morse code. To what realistic end was never clear.

The cells were spacious, with ceilings reaching thirteen feet high and almost square in shape, leading to one being converted into a prison library and another into a chapel.

But the highlight of the prison, given the lack of other prisoners, was its garden.

Initially divided into plots for growing vegetables by the inmates, as old age crept up rapidly on almost all of them it became the private purview of Speer. The architect with such grand plans to reshape post-war Berlin into a new capital of the Reich – Germania – found himself demoted to cultivating a complex garden with floral beds punctuated by paths and rockery.

The war may have been over but that didn't mean an end to their petty rivalries and disputes. Hitler had maintained his absolute power by pitting his subservients against each other, giving them overlapping briefs and leaving them solely responsible for very little.

While von Schirach and Funk were inseparable and the diplomat von Neurath naturally got on with everybody, Speer and Hess were dubbed the loners, disliked and distrusted by the others. Speer had disowned Hitler during the trial, admitting his own guilt and probably saving his life in the process, while Hess had long been regarded as mentally unstable with delusions of grandeur.

The two former Grand Admirals, Raeder and his replacement Dönitz – who, after Göring and Himmler's respective falls from grace in the final days of the siege of Berlin, had been anointed as Hitler's successor (an honour for which he blamed Speer until his dying days) – ran the library. Despite preferring each other's company as military men, "The Admiralty" returned to the old order, with Raeder designating himself Chief Librarian and Dönitz his deputy. They continued their wartime feud, arguing over whether Raeder's battleships or Dönitz's U-boats had lost Germany the war.

Of the seven, three were released early, including two of the lifers. Von Neurath was released seven years early in 1954, dying two years later, while Raeder and Funk served nine and eleven years of their life sentences before walking out the gate early in 1955 and 1957 respectively. Dönitz followed the other half of The Admiralty beyond the wall in 1956 after his ten years were up, followed a decade later by Speer and von Schirach at the end of their twenty-year tariffs.

Of the Spandau Seven, by 1966, just one remained.

The one who hadn't even been around for most of the war.

Hess.

It needn't necessarily have been so.

In March 1952, Hess was temporarily released from his cell at a time when the Soviets were in charge of Spandau. He was secretly squirreled away to a clandestine meeting with senior officials of the German Democratic Republic, by then a fully-fledged client state of Moscow.

An increasingly ill Stalin had an offer.

Hess's freedom, and a leading role in the East German government, provided Hess endorsed the GDR as realising the socialist ideal to which he had aspired since the heady early days of the DAP.

Stalin's offer fell on deaf ears as Hess remained loyal and true to Hitler – a relationship that Churchill later described charitably as "abnormal" – even though it meant that, unlike the other lifers at Spandau, he would never taste freedom.

Number Seven had been by far the prison's most demanding inmate. Avoiding all of the work that he regarded as beneath his dignity, in particular tending to the gardens, he was dubbed "the laziest man in Spandau" or, more disparagingly, "His Imprisoned Lordship".

A hypochondriac ever since his brushes with death in the Caucasus during the First World War, he constantly complained of illness. He was also paranoid, taking the plate of food furthest away as a precaution against poisoning.

His behaviour was dismissed with scorn by The Admiralty and von Schirach as attention-seeking, but both Speer and Funk found a kindness for Hess, realising the likely psychosomatic origins of his illness. Speer often tended to Hess's needs, bringing him a coat to keep him warm and covering for him when he feigned illness to avoid work.

But after Speer departed in 1966, Hess's only companion was the warden, Eugene K. Bird. He soon became a close friend.

With the release of Speer and von Schirach, fearing for his mental state and that death was imminent, the prison directors all agreed to a slacker regime for the last inmate. Hess was moved to the more spacious former chapel space, with a water heater to make coffee and tea whenever he liked. His quarters were permanently unlocked so that he could freely access the prison's bathing facilities or the library.

As the West Berlin government was in the chair for the bill for running Spandau, the perception of the prison being a grotesque misallocation of resources and nothing more than a symbol of victors' justice grew as the months became years and the years became decades.

The continuation of Hess's incarceration as the sole occupant of Spandau prison drew the West to conclude that the Soviets had ulterior motives for keeping the prison open, using the changeover to their rule for espionage purposes during the Cold War.

It made Hess the conflict's only known casualty.

*

The little boy played with the wooden biplane. It was far and away his favourite toy.

In the background the state-sponsored television news from TASS was barely audibly, offering an incompatible soundtrack to the little boy's imagined dogfight.

Behind him his grandmother held a vase, placing fresh sweet peas in one at a time as she admired the little boy conquering the world.

The smile deserted her face as her skin turned ashen.

The newscaster on the television behind the little boy was solemn.

'Rudolf Hess, the last remaining Nazi leader imprisoned after the Nürnberg trials, has been found dead in his prison cell in the German Democratic Republic. He was 93. The Four Powers have issued a joint communiqué saying that a post-mortem examination will be carried out but that they have no reason to suspect foul play.'

The vase shattered into a thousand shards, the grandmother's hand immediately suppressing the shriek of a heartbroken woman. The little boy took his eye off the ball, crashing his wooden biplane into his nearby Lego castle.

*

## Four years later

The funeral cortege inched slowly into the Wunsiedel cemetery before coming to a dignified halt. From the black Mercedes stepped the nearest and dearest of the recently departed, resting on his back in his own oak-panelled mausoleum in the rear of the front car. Around him lay lettered floral tributes to "Papi".

The elderly widow to "Papi" rose slowly from the back seat of the car, with a granddaughter soon at her side to steady her walk. Friends and well-wishers followed behind her.

In the far distance a different grandmother and her young grandson, both older and dressed for winter, stepped daintily across sunken graves before coming to an abrupt halt in front of one in particular.

RUDOLF HESS
1893-1987

Taken from the German Reformation scholar Ulrich von Hutten, the inscription beneath read simply: "Ich hab's gewagt."

I have dared.

The grandmother suppressed a tear and a whimper as she placed the wreath against the headstone of the combined family grave.

'In a different life,' the grandmother sniffled, 'things will be different.'

She kissed the middle fingers of her left hand before resting them tenderly on top of the headstone.

'I promise.'

# 2
# STOLEN TREASURES

**Thirty years later**

The picturesque country pile befitted an oligarch. Set deep in the wilderness, surrounded on all sides by northern pine trees as far as the eye could see, yet within a stone's throw of Moscow, this was the equivalent of Sloane Square for a successful Londoner or the Hamptons for an American.

Grigor Ivanovich had done well from the collapse of the Soviet Union. In the disorder and chaos that followed the disintegration of communism in 1992, Ivanovich and his friends within the KGB and the GRU had capitalised on the opportunity to feather their nests.

Capitalism for the few.

It afforded him a lifestyle that others would jealously crave yet never be able to achieve. All they could hope for were scraps from the table.

His Christmas party had long been a fixture in the diaries of the great, the good and the not so good. Politicians and film stars, along with their coterie, travelled from near and far to mingle with Ivanovich and other members of the self-perpetuating elite that now owned Russia.

It would be no exaggeration to say that it was the society event of the year.

This year's party had the theme of a masquerade ball. The band could be heard as far away as the gatehouse. A seemingly never-ending succession of limousines crept forward as an over-officious security guard checked their invitations against a list.

A very long list.

Once past the gatehouse, limousines made the mile-long journey up to the snow-drizzled main house, passing security guards patrolling the perimeter. They were heavily armed and accompanied by Caucasian Shepherd Dogs.

To the trained eye, they could pass for a private army.

On the steps to the house, Ivanovich stood in wait for his guests. He was a typically portly Russian businessman, stocky bordering on overweight and with a perfect face for radio. Only an ugly man of his wealth could have ensnared a wife of the calibre of Anna Ivanovich.

Anna was everything Ivanovich wasn't. Slender and glamorous, naturally radiating personality and charm. An English rose. And at thirty-five one of the oldest women present, with the hotchpotch of male guests punching remarkably above their weight with women as young as their granddaughters.

The latest limousine pulled up. A footman opened the passenger door to legs that seemed to go on for miles and miles. As she stepped out of the back of the car to reveal her provocative cocktail dress, this young woman epitomised male attitudes towards women in modern Russia.

'Vladimir!' boomed Ivanovich.

After the young alpha woman came the inevitably older beta male.

Vladimir Kuchev was a senior member of the Russian government. A contemporary of the host, Vladimir had drunk from the same trough like all the other little pigs.

'Grigor…' Kuchev's gravelly voice had been fashioned from smoking Cohiba Behike cigars over many years. Unlike in the United States, Cuban cigars were legal in Russia.

The two men embraced in robust backslapping. For a moment Anna thought they should get a room. As they disentangled, Kuchev turned his attentions to her, planting wet kisses on both of her porcelain cheeks.

'Anna…' Kuchev dribbled over his heavily accented English. 'You look remarkable.'

'Why thank you, Vladimir.' Anna smiled respectfully, a woman aware of her own beauty and never short of compliments, before turning mischievously to Kuchev's female companion. 'And this must be the daughter that I've heard so many lovely things about?'

Kuchev laughed almost uncontrollably as the two women observed each other. They were almost a time travelling mirror image: Christmas past and Christmas future.

Kuchev reverted to Russian for Ivanovic's benefit. 'My daughter is a big fat mule. She's so big she has her own gravitational field!'

'Wherever you're standing in the room,' Ivanovich joined in, 'you're standing next to her!'

The two old friends laughed raucously. Anna didn't speak Russian but, from the uncouth hourglass hand gestures of the two men, she got the gist.

'I am Angel.' Kuchev's young companion introduced herself, extending her hand to Ivanovich.

'I'm sure you are.' Anna's reply was thinly disguised. Her eyes didn't leave Angel's as her husband fawned over her.

'Lovely to meet you, Angel.' Ivanovich took little time to grasp her soft hand and an eternity to kiss it tenderly.

The minister and his Angel awkwardly shuffled off into the now teaming party behind their hosts, leaving Ivanovich to look thunderously upon his wife. It was a glare worth a thousand words.

'Just saying…' she protested.

Her husband was brusque and biting. 'Remember, you were young. Once.'

Despite the withering putdown, fake smiles returned to them both as their next guests arrived, following the minister into the party.

The party was a boudoir of decadence and loose morals, so far removed from the lives of ordinary Russian citizens. It was no wonder that the oligarchs were so widely reviled, even with a willing patron in the Kremlin. It may have been a masquerade ball but the only masquerade was that any of these women were any of these men's wives. The inevitable combination of beauties and their beasts was a recurring theme.

The live band played heavily accented American Fifties rock 'n' roll. Badly. Some of the guests danced but the more raucous partygoers were gambling at the tables. Two younger girls, clearly hookers, seductively licked the Amaretto that a playboy poured down an ice-sculpted luge. Their tongues occasionally touched, as did roaming hands.

Amongst this sea of hedonistic degradation, one guest didn't quite look like he fitted in. A little geekish, with his sheep curl hair and a dinner suit that looked like it belonged to his father, he stepped off alone towards the bathroom carrying two champagne flutes.

*

With all of the guests now safely within the main house, a security shield had dropped around the compound. Security guards patrolled, their boots scrunching the recently fallen snow beneath the clog-hopped feet of their owners. One, replete with snarling shepherd dog on an extendable leash, stopped at a clearing. Puffing away at his fire-cracking cigarette, he raised his hand to his earpiece.

'Area four clear. Over.'

The security guard took a long drag of his cigarette – always the sign of a real smoker – before flicking it into the ether.

He was clearly very cold.

As he stepped off, the paws of the shepherd dog trampled over the manhole cover.

*

Beneath the manhole cover, hidden from the frozen world above ground, lay a succession of service tunnels. Connecting a range of rural properties, they predated the Second World War, when this area outside of Moscow would have been a flurry of industrial activity before being bombarded by the Luftwaffe in the opening salvo of Operation Barbarossa.

The pressure of travelling water and clunking of pipes added to a febrile atmosphere. It was punctuated only by the emergence from a large drainage outlet of a man in a wet suit, his face obscured by breathing apparatus.

Dropping down from the large outlet, he removed the breathing apparatus and the wet suit, placing them in a neat pile nearby. By now in his dinner suit, he clambered up the ladder towards the air conditioning system that serviced Grigor Ivanovich's sprawling country pile.

*

The young man from the party was sat in the cubicle, humming to himself. But the toilet seat was down and the young man's trousers were not around his ankles. Opened in his hands was a worn paperback, bordering on vintage, with folded corners and brittle paper: *Unexplained Mysteries of the Universe* by the late Professor Arlo Greene. As he turned a page, clasped fingers reached through the air ventilation grille above. The young man was seemingly oblivious as the fingers silently pushed out the grille from its socket, laying it flat inside the shaft. From the darkness emerged the face of the man in the wet suit.

'You're late James.'

The young man was expecting him.

James Curtis clambered down from the ventilation shaft, using the cistern and his friend's shoulder as stepping-stones.

'I've been busy.' Curtis dusted himself down before seeing his friend's book. 'Brushing up on your homework Luka?'

Luka Rothstein dropped the book to his lap, putting it away into his jacket pocket. He sighed. 'I hope this won't take all night. You wouldn't believe what we're missing downstairs. This Russian knows how to throw a party.'

Rothstein stood and replaced the grille hastily, before placing a small, magnetised device onto the fire detector above them.

Curtis tied his bow tie, in the full knowledge that Rothstein's was a clip-on. One of the many lost arts of being a man, he thought. 'My invitation must have got lost in the post.'

'Either that or Mr Ivanovich found out about you playing doctors and nurses with Mrs Ivanovich...'

Curtis smiled, reminiscing. 'She was more partial to poker.'

Their repartee was interrupted by three guests filing abruptly into the bathroom. The first two headed for the two empty cubicles on either side of Curtis and Rothstein, leaving the third waiting impatiently at their cubicle door. He started to bang against the middle cubicle door, muttering obscenities in Russian. He was clearly feeling unwell and time wasn't on his side.

A few seconds later, the lock unlatched and Curtis and Rothstein emerged, holding a champagne flute apiece in hand. Curtis zipped up his trousers as he passed without a hint of shame, while Rothstein wiped his moistened lips with the back of his somewhat limp hand. The guest looked on, thoroughly disgusted but his increasingly urgent need for the toilet trumped everything.

Curtis and Rothstein emerged from the bathroom, walking away with faux nonchalance.

Curtis necked the champagne. 'For an allegedly straight man, you do camp very well.'

'I wonder if he wiped the toilet seat after us?'

Curtis stepped towards the edge of the balcony. From their elevated position above the party, he scanned the melee. Downstairs in the ballroom, he could see Ivanovich discretely taking the two young kissing hookers into a private room. A bodyguard, almost as wide as the closing door, blocked it from view as the door slowly latched behind him.

At the opposite end of the ballroom, he saw Anna shimmering in her Hollie de Keyser number and in full knowledge of her husband's impending infidelities. She took a long sip from her flute, her face inscrutable as she checked the time on her 18 karat Limelight Gala watch from Piaget, with its sixty-two individual diamonds.

A guilty purchase no doubt.

Curtis smiled, in fond memory as much as in present admiration. 'Time to go to work.'

Curtis and Rothstein placed their empty champagne flutes simultaneously on a passing waiter's tray. The coast clear, they sidestepped into another doorway, closing the door silently behind them.

The door led to an ornately furnished bedroom suite, subdued by mood lighting. Rothstein reached to turn the main light on. Curtis's hand shot out to stop him.

'I'm sorry,' Rothstein noted sarcastically, 'in the rush I forgot to bring my night vision goggles.'

Curtis headed towards a small library in the far end of the bedroom suite, with no reference to his accomplice.

Rothstein was put out. 'How am I supposed to see what I'm doing?' he asked intemperately.

'You're only here for the back-up plan,' Curtis replied blithely as he ran his fingers along the shelves before identifying a book, barely illuminated in the diffused mood lighting: Dickens' *Oliver Twist.*

Rothstein looked on the book choice. 'Please sir, can I have some light?'

Curtis shot Rothstein an apathetic look while he turned the book onto its spine. To Rothstein's surprise but Curtis's expectation, this triggered an opening in the bookcase, revealing the entrance to a panic room.

The panic room was resplendent in its uncharacteristic simplicity. Other than a chair, a monitor with a real-time view of the bedroom, a drinks cabinet not so modestly stocked and a loaded gun on a side table, its walls were bare – aside from the painting hanging on the wall in solitary confinement.

Rothstein was perplexed. 'How did you know?'

Curtis removed his dinner jacket, placing it on the back of the chair. 'She told me.'

'Wow,' fawned Rothstein in awe as he minced gingerly across the threshold.

Having been there before, Curtis knew there was a step down. 'Mind the…'

Too late. Rothstein stumbled to Curtis's amusement.

'Shut the door, there's a draught.'

Rothstein pulled the bookcase door back, confining them. 'I hope she told you how to get out?'

Plunder and pillage may have been part of all conflict since time immemorial, but Hitler's Germany had turned it into an art form all of its own.

It began almost as soon as he became Chancellor in 1933. An unsuccessful artist himself, having been rejected by the Vienna Academy of Fine Arts, nevertheless Hitler regarded himself as an expert, a connoisseur of the arts. In *Mein Kampf*, he had decried the development of art in the 20th Century, while venerating classical portraits and landscapes by the Old Masters, especially those of German origin.

Once in office, he could do something about it.

Modern art was soon labelled degenerate and all German state museums showcasing it were ordered to either sell their stock or destroy it.

By 1937, Hitler and Reichskommissar Göring had amassed a collection of almost 16,000 paintings and sculptures removed from the walls of German museums. After putting them on display in Munich's Haus der Kunst, to the mockery of two million indoctrinated visitors as well as the Nazi leadership, the art dealers Hildebrand Gurlitt, Karl Buchholz, Ferdinand Moeller and Bernhard Boehmer set out to sell the condemned art, with the proceeds intended to fund Hitler's proposed European Art Museum in Linz, the so-called Führermuzeum he planned for his Austrian hometown.

Having dismissed the art as rubbish, the art dealers curiously struggled to realise sales from their shop in Schloss Niederschonhausen on the outskirts of Berlin.

So they put the torch to over a thousand paintings and sculptures along with nearly four thousand watercolours, drawings and prints.

Courting condemnation from the world akin to that which followed the infamous public mass book burnings, stunned art lovers were provoked into buying, starting with the arrival of the Swiss Basel Museum with 50,000 Swiss Francs to spend.

The dealers had made a fortune for the Reich, as well as squirreling away an unknown number of paintings for their own future personal gain.

But they were far from the only ones partaking in such blatant graft, with the outbreak of war providing the perfect opportunity for both Göring and Foreign Minister Joachim von Ribbentrop to add to their own private art collections.

In 1940, the key Nazi ideologue Reichsleiter Alfred Rosenberg established the eponymous Einsatzstab Reichsleiter Rosenberg für die Besetzen Gebiete (the Reichsleiter Rosenberg Institute for the Occupied Territories). The ERR's original purpose was to collect books and documents belonging to Jews and Freemasons from its base in the Museum Jeu de Paume in Paris.

However later that year Göring, who ultimately controlled the ERR, changed its mission to seize so-called "Jewish" art collections and other items of cultural significance.

By the end of the war, the Third Reich had stolen or destroyed art and cultural objects running into the millions. Poland alone saw over half a million individual art pieces looted while Russian museums were unable to account for more than 1.1 million lost artworks.

Paul Rosenberg and his brother Léonce were the sons of antique dealer Alexandre Rosenberg. They were no relation to the Reichsleiter, who shared their surname but little else. A noted dealer of impressionist and post-impressionist art, he educated his sons in their future trade through a grand tour of London, Berlin, Vienna and New York at the turn of the century. By 1910, Paul had proven a chip off the old block, establishing his own art gallery on Paris's Rue La Boétie, where he became a champion of Cubism as well as a major dealer in modern art in general. Within a decade his gallery was indisputably the most active and influential in the world, leading him to represent the likes of Henri Matisse and Pablo Picasso.

As well as buying many of his works for himself, Rosenberg befriended Picasso, their families holidaying together in the south of France every summer with contemporaries including F. Scott Fitzgerald and Somerset Maugham.

With the likelihood of war growing, Rosenberg acted quietly to distribute his art collection outside of mainland Europe, using the London branch of his gallery run by his brother-in-law Jacques Helft as well as storage in the USA, Australia and South America.

Nonetheless, when the Panzers rolled in the summer of 1940, Rosenberg and his family may have escaped the Nazis' clutches but over two thousand pieces held in his gallery and in storage in France remained behind.

Spending the rest of the war in exile in New York, where he established a new gallery on East 57$^{th}$ Street, Rosenberg plotted the reclamation of his lost collection from afar. On his first trip to Paris after the end of hostilities, he managed to reclaim Picasso's portrait of his wife Elaine and his daughter Micheline – painted in 1918 and drily renamed the anonymous *Mother and Child* by Göring – from a small Parisian museum.

But with the rest of his collection scattered across Europe, some seventy of his paintings remained missing. They included seven works by Matisse, the *Portrait of Gabrielle Diot* by Degas and Picasso's watercolour *Naked Woman on the Beach.*

The same naked woman that now hung before Curtis and Rothstein.

Curtis and Rothstein gently dropped the painting down from its wall mounting. Flicking open a weighty penknife, Curtis carefully freed the canvas from the mount, swapping it for a forged copy of the painting removed from the seam of his dinner jacket.

*

In the bathroom further down the corridor, the suffering male guest stood to leave the cubicle before thinking twice. He needed a further evacuation. He slammed the cubicle door behind him with such ferocity that the loosely fastened grille fell, landing sharply on his head. Rothstein hadn't affixed it properly. Nursing his head and cursing, the guest peered inside the shaft to see Curtis's scuba gear in a neat pile.

*

A slightly hunched Curtis and Rothstein returned the forged painting to its pride of place on the wall. They stood admiringly.

Curtis smiled with palpable satisfaction. 'You've got to pick a pocket or two.'

'So if you're Oliver Twist,' Rothstein mused, 'does that make me the Artful Dodger?'

Curtis shrugged out the creases in his dinner jacket. 'Nancy.'

Curtis and an aggrieved Rothstein stepped into the hallway, heading back towards the bathroom and their escape route, before being overtaken by a flurry of armed guards in a hurry. They deftly sidestepped them and slowed.

As reinforcements followed on, Rothstein looked visibly panicked. 'Oh dear.'

'About that back-up plan…'

Curtis and Rothstein crept inconspicuously down the grand staircase away from the heavy-handed stewards enquiry. As they did, a hand pulled Curtis from Rothstein's side and onto the dance floor, where the band were crucifying Bobby Darin's *Mack the Knife*.

'James Curtis!' exclaimed Anna.

Curtis feigned surprise. 'Mrs Ivanovich!'

'Anna, please,' she said coyly.

'It's a lovely party.' Curtis made small talk.

'I don't remember seeing your name on Grigor's guest list.'

'I'm a plus one,' Curtis replied convincingly. 'Last minute.'

'Who's the lucky woman?' Anna asked, surveying the competition around her.

'Lucky man actually.' Curtis pointed to Rothstein on the sidelines, his eye gestures to his friend intimating that he needed saving. Perhaps the Artful Dodger would have dived in to the rescue. But given he was Nancy, Rothstein simply toasted them with a champagne flute, pinkie standing to attention.

Anna was taken aback. 'James! I never knew that you ran with the hounds and the hares!'

'Oh it's not like…' Curtis protested, realising the fanciful misinterpretation.

Before he could finish his sentence, Anna stepped closer and grabbed Curtis's crotch. 'Perhaps next time you come here, he can come too?'

Rothstein smiled while keeping a watchful eye on the upper floor. The guards had grown increasingly agitated.

'Ah well,' Rothstein sighed, looking down at his watch. 'All good things come to an end…'

Rothstein pressed the pin on his watch. Upstairs in the bathroom, the sprinkler system activated, drenching the guards, followed by the sprinkler system in the ballroom, drenching all of the guests to match.

Ball gowns became sheer and panic enveloped the room.

Anna broke away from her mating dance with Curtis, looking around to observe the chaotic stampede for the exit. By the time she turned back, he was long gone.

On the lawn outside, the security guards watched as soaking guests filed out into the Russian winter chill. Female guests visibly shivered, cuddling themselves with their own bony arms while their male patriarchs protested angrily.

Among the flood of guests escaping the flood of water inside were Curtis and Rothstein, separated by a sea of bodies quickly nearing the security guards. As they approached them, the guards were anxious to stop them departing, insisting on checking invitations, but the mass of bodies was overwhelming.

It was extraordinary bad luck that the security guard with the shepherd dog stopped Curtis.

'Sir, can I see your invitation?' The guard was most insistent.

Curtis looked around to find Rothstein had disappeared, without trace. He was cross. He returned to face the security guard.

'Of course.'

Curtis reached into his inner jacket pocket before pulling his hand out. The security guard couldn't have seen the sideswipe of Curtis's wrist coming, losing all balance and landing face first in the snow. By the time the other security guards had noticed their man down, Curtis had broken into a sprint across the powdered lawn, his feet sinking deeper and deeper into the snow as he headed for the cover of the tree line.

It was his only hope.

That small private army was now on his tail, accompanied by a family of shepherd dogs salivating at the prospect of a kill.

And Chef's special.

Curtis deftly traversed the side of the sloping bank from the tree line. The adrenalin was by now coursing through his veins, driving him. Dropping over a high wall, sat in front of him was a blood red 2018 Ferrari 488 GTB.

His blood red 2018 Ferrari 488 GTB.

As he ran towards it in his sodden shoes, he pressed a key fob in his hand. The V-8 engine had almost started before he had even closed the door.

He was hell and gone.

Curtis, his face a picture of concentration, felt like a hare after the firing of starting pistol. The head start was important.

It could save his life.

It wasn't long before the hounds were in pursuit. Three motorcyclists and two fast cars were out of Ivanovich's compound gate before Curtis could clear sight.

The Ferrari sped through the nearby village. An articulated lorry pulled out in front of him on a tight junction and was in the middle of reversing to retake the corner.

There was no way around it.

With no time to brake, the Ferrari veered off through a hedge straight into an adjoining field. With no time to make adjustments, the first motorcyclist slid under the lorry, dazed and battered but just about surviving the experience. The second had time to brake but found himself without his own head when one of the fast cars in pursuit slammed into the back of him, shunting both vehicles into a fiery demise beneath the reversing lorry.

While Curtis took no pleasure in the likely death of several of Ivanovich's men, his conscience could learn to live with it.

It was them or him.

The third motorcyclist and second car followed the Ferrari into the field. The level ground beneath the tyres would have been almost traversable were it not for the tall shards of winter crops. The Ferrari acted more like a lawnmower, cutting through the field, no doubt removing Curtis from the farmer's Christmas card list.

The third motorcyclist and second car struggled against the crops and the ground, giving Curtis the advantage. Until a helicopter came into sight, shining a spotlight down on the Ferrari shooting through the field like a red bullet.

Curtis began to target the tall stacks of bundled hay, driving through and obliterating them to obscure the view from behind and above.

The third motorcyclist came alongside Curtis and was about to fire lead liberally into him. But he wasn't expecting Curtis to fell him, opening the driver's door on him unexpectedly. The motorcyclist lost his balance and landed amongst the felled crops. He had no time to avoid the second car driving over him, reuniting him with the earth.

The Ferrari re-joined the road, slamming into the side of another car in pursuit and sending it into a spin. The battered car blocked the road behind for larger traffic as the Ferrari sped away, extending the gap between itself and a solitary headlight behind.

The first motorcyclist.

Curtis heard the rocket before he could see it and the rocket had hit its target before it could know it was its target.

The motorcyclist – or what was left of him – shot into the air as the rocket sought out the motorcycle beneath him.

Curtis was bemused. And then very afraid.

Was the helicopter friend or foe?

No time to find out.

As Curtis continued down the road, another shot came from the helicopter, firing over him at the road ahead. This time it wasn't a rocket but a sprinkling of minute spiked balls littering the asphalt.

Foe.

Curtis realised too late, blowing all four of the Ferrari's tyres as he drove over the spiked metal. The Ferrari careered out of control, spreading fresh snow asunder only to be prevented from landing belly-up in the fast-flowing river by a felled northern pine.

The helicopter circled above, unable to land. Three special op soldiers, wearing brilliant white ski fatigues blending seamlessly with the ground below, descended from a winch rope, weapons in hand. They dropped to the ground nearby, adopting flanking positions as the first of their number arrived at the car. He opened the driver side door to find Curtis unconscious but audibly breathing, head resting against an airbag that, going by the condition of the rest of the Ferrari, had saved his life.

The captain reached for his CB radio. 'Delta One to Alpha Zero. Target acquired.'

# 3
# SUPPING WITH THE DEVIL

The hessian sack reeked of blood and death. Its intermittent removal was always welcome, less so the bucket of icy water that followed.

Arms bound behind his back with blood-soiled worn rope, Curtis felt the water burning his lungs. He was slowly drowning.

His body's reflex action dictated that he should spring up.

His prison guards, holding him down and controlling his every movement, had other ideas.

It was clearly just the start of what they all expected to be a very long, tortuous session with little purpose.

These were old dogs showing off their old tricks.

As the security apparatus of the Soviet Union, the Committee of State Security was better known by its acronym, three letters that struck fear into the hearts of Soviet citizens and foreigners alike.

The KGB.

Given there was nothing else in common between fascism and communism – in theory polar opposites, sworn enemies even – it was remarkable that the one thing that both needed to function was a healthy sense of terror drummed into its enemies as well as its own people.

The Nazis had the Gestapo.

Their successors in the Soviet client state of East Germany had the Stasi.

The Soviets had the KGB.

All dealt with the same problems.

And all peddled the same solutions.

If the walls of this dungeon, deep below ground at the old KGB headquarters in the heart of Moscow's Lubyanka Square could talk, would the cacophony of terrified voices sound so different from those that perished west of the river Vistula?

Of course, it was no longer the KGB. Following the failed coup against the last Soviet Premier Mikhail Gorbachev in the summer of 1991, in which KGB units along with its then boss Vladimir Kryuchkov were instrumental, the KGB was dismantled. Broken up into its component parts before being patched back together under one roof again as the FSB: the Federalnaya Sluzhba Bezopasnosti.

Meet the new boss, same as the old boss.

As a half-drowned Curtis had his head removed from the bucket, a nearby guard chinked two live electricity cables against each other. Old habits die hard, he thought. They sparked and arced as he turned to approach Curtis. Curtis flinched, summoning enough fight and spirit to kick the approaching guard away and to crack another in the ribs before being knocked square in the jaw by a third.

The blow felled him.

His head lay at 90°, his vision blurred almost dreamlike, as the vignette figure of a suited man approached.

His calm manner had an air of creepy familiarity to it.

As did his voice.

'Good morning James.'

In the doorway, puffing away on his pipe as if he was waiting for a table in Mayfair's East India Club, stood Colonel Arnold Crombie. Every inch the former military man, despite being well into his sixties and with lifelong follicle challenges, vanity dictated that he dye his remaining hair jet black. The skin sagging around his neck belying his advancing years, here was a stagnant breath of ill health and long buried military secrets. Crombie managed to pollute even this room.

'Crombie.' Curtis was bemused. But an old urge soon returned. 'I should stab you with that pipe.'

The guards pointed their guns at Curtis as he sat up petulantly.

Crombie smiled. 'Making friends I see.'

Curtis spat the mouthful of congealed blood, decorating Crombie's shoes from Church's of Jermyn Street. 'What do you want?'

Crombie removed a handkerchief from his pocket, wiping down his shoes with a grimace before discarding the rag. 'Just a little chat.'

'I've got absolutely nothing to say,' Curtis replied ferociously, 'to a lying, cheating, two-faced crook like you.'

'You've been a busy boy.' Crombie flung down a file two inches thick, laden with paperwork and photographs. 'An impressive criminal record you've been stacking up for an old Harrovian.' Curtis snarled at the pious and judgmental jibe. Crombie looked around the dank, dark cell, as if he were in a museum. 'This must feel more like home these days. Just in time for Christmas too.'

'Nothing better to do with your Sunday mornings Crombie?'

Crombie laughed heavily. 'Than watch James Curtis beg for his life!?'

'Who's begging?' responded Curtis with dismissive bravura, despite knowing that Crombie had a point.

Crombie flicked open the file with disdain. 'James – you were caught stealing Picasso's *Naked Woman on the Beach* from Grigor Ivanovich after breaking into his house during his Christmas party.'

'That's funny, I thought it belonged to Paul Rosenberg's family.'

'Given his brother-in-law is the Russian Interior Minister,' Crombie continued, 'I'm surprised he hasn't shot you himself!'

Well he did try, Curtis thought.

Crombie left it a beat. 'I work for the British government.'

Curtis shook his head. 'Of course you do.'

'Her Majesty has a proposition for you.'

The guards unexpectedly uncuffed Curtis. He rubbed his red raw wrists, one of many parts of his body in a whole world of pain.

'Dirty bitch.'

Crombie placed a pile of clean clothes down on the near prehistoric metal-framed prison bed nearby.

'Get changed, before I change my mind.'

Curtis seethed as he watched Crombie walk away. Taking another look back at the instruments of torture around him, he reluctantly reached for the clean clothes.

*

The powerful turbo shaft engines drove the Eurocopter Super Puma's four-bladed main rotor and five-bladed tail rotor as they spun through the icy air high above the Swiss Alps, straddling Interlaken to the north and Lauterbrunnen to the south. In its main cabin, a cavernous space even in this short fuselage configuration, sat Curtis and Crombie. Over the din of the engines, the pilot's voice barely crackled on the headset.

'Touchdown Geneva 1600 hours, Colonel Crombie.'

Curtis snarled at the title.

'Very good Major,' Crombie replied aloofly, revelling in his status, knowing how it would rankle with Curtis.

Curtis quickly did the maths.

'I thought the Queen had a proposition for me Crombie?'

Crombie cranked his head in mock disgust as the helicopter crossed the vast Alpine peaks, eclipsing the low setting winter sun on the horizon in the west.

# 4
# THE THEORY OF EVERYTHING

Founded in 1952, the Conseil Européen pour la Recherche Nucléaire – better known by its acronym CERN, for obvious reasons – was established to halt the European brain drain after the Second World War. The victorious Allies had all benefitted from the forced emigration of predominantly German scientists, but coming out of almost six years of total war the focus of scientific research and development had inevitably retained a militaristic bent.

CERN was intended to counter that, with Article 2 of the CERN Convention emphasizing that it "shall have no concern with work for military requirements and the results of its experimental and theoretical work shall be published or otherwise made generally available".

Set in two hundred and fifty acres in Geneva on the Swiss border, by 1965 its sprawling footprint had grown to cover another thousand acres in neighbouring France.

Focused on collaborative research into high-energy particles, its scientific research facilities housed thousands of the leading scientists in their fields, comprising some of the world's largest machines – particle accelerators

– looking at the universe's smallest objects: subatomic particles.

Despite the later substitution of the word Conseil for Organisation in its name, it continued to be known colloquially as CERN after its doors opened in 1954. Three years later the activation of its first particle accelerator – a 600-megaelectron volt synchrocyclotron – enabled CERN scientists to verify the decay of a pi-meson, or pion, into an electron and a neutrino. This discovery was instrumental in the development of the theory of the weak force.

It was the first of many significant discoveries.

CERN scientists were revered and regular recipients of the Nobel Prize for Physics, from Georges Charpak's 1968 invention of the multi wire proportional chamber, a particle detector that revolutionised high-energy physics with applications in medical physics, to Carlo Rubbia and Simon van der Meer's experimental verification of the electroweak theory in the Standard Model of particle physics in 1983.

In 1989, CERN inaugurated its most ambitious machine to date: the Large Electron-Positron Collider (LEP). With a circumference of seventeen miles straddling the Franco-Swiss border at the foot of the Jura Mountains, it was able to accelerate both electrons and positrons, allowing extremely precise measurements of the Z particle, one of the carriers of the weak force.

A decade later the LEP was shut down, to be replaced by the Large Hadron Collider (LHC), whose purpose was nothing less than recreating the conditions in the seconds after the so-called "Big Bang". Despite a blip just days after starting up in 2008 forcing it offline for eighteen months, it restarted in 2010 and on July 4th 2012, it struck gold. Scientists proved the so-called Higgs boson, the last remaining unverified part of the Standard Model of particle physics.

CERN was a place where big discoveries were made. Even Sir Tim Berners-Lee's World Wide Web was created there, as a way of scientists linking electronic documents together and a means of transferring them between their computers.

As he stepped out of the Super Puma onto the icy helipad, Curtis could not think of a single reason why he should be there.

'What are we doing at CERN, Colonel?'

Crombie ignored Curtis's question as he marched towards an unmarked door. Flanked by two heavily armed men in militaristic uniforms without insignia, Crombie approached them. Proffering credentials, the armed men saluted and stepped aside to reveal a retina scanner – the ultimate security device. Crombie placed his protruding chin onto the base plate of the scanner. The machine whirred, accompanying a crimson line scanning his retina from top to bottom then side to side. Crimson gave way to green as the door audibly unlocked. Crombie pushed against the door and they were soon inside the confines of CERN, via the tradesman's entrance.

The clinical white-walled corridors belied the building's scientific purposes. Crombie marched and Curtis followed as they made their way down into a rabbit warren of seemingly identical corridors, accompanied by the two armed men a constant distance to their rear.

From time to time they would pass white-coated scientists, entering or leaving endless faceless doors to starboard and port, alongside armed men on what seemed to them a routine patrol. Like a visiting Royal, Crombie lapped up all of the attention, leaving Curtis ill at ease.

They clearly didn't know Crombie as well as he did.

The white-walled corridors gave way to a stretch of laboratories, with banks of computer hardware and terminals manned by the very same men and women in white coats. Curtis felt their eyes boring into him, standing out like a sore thumb in a world of mad scientists and probably madder soldiers. A world of zeroes and ones, he thought. Perhaps even heroes and zeroes.

The never-ending walk, the lack of any kind of escape plan and Crombie's silence left Curtis feeling restless.

'If we're heading for Narnia, Crombie,' Curtis grumbled as they approached a slightly ajar door, 'I think we took the wrong turning back there.'

Curtis was too busy anticipating Crombie's non-reply to notice the cat until it was upon him, though the jangling of metal pieces bouncing against each other had registered a moment earlier grating on his tortured senses. The cat slowed for a moment, as if sizing up Curtis as an old friend, before scarpering away from them down the corridor.

Crombie passed through the door and the armed escort indicated that Curtis should follow. His eyes did not leave the cat until it was out of sight.

This room stood apart from all that had preceded it, out of kilter with the clean and clinical of the corridors and the laboratories. It was an ornate office, replete with heavy furniture and a magnificent oak boardroom table at its centre. On the desk, a Newton's cradle rocked gently back and forth.

Crombie's office perhaps, Curtis pondered.

At the table, in its high-backed leather chairs, sat two scientists. They could not have been more different from each other. The first, a tanned and balding middle-aged man, exuded more nervous energy than his sedate female elder.

'Curtis, this is Dr Gideon Eli,' Crombie had finally found his tongue as he removed his coat and hat, placing them on a nearby stand before placing himself firmly behind the desk. 'He is one of the most respected nuclear physicists of his generation, and deputy head of Special Projects here at CERN.'

Eli extended his hand to Curtis, accompanied by a warm smile. 'Welcome to CERN, Mr Curtis.'

Bemused, Curtis shook it.

'And this,' Crombie continued, 'is Dr Ida Schildberg, emeritus professor at Harvard and two-time recipient of the Nobel Prize for Physics.'

Schildberg was a slight woman, with shocking white hair draped lifelessly on her shoulders. She stood and approached Curtis, cupping his hand with both of hers as if she was touching someone important or special.

'Hello James,' Schildberg said in clipped English. 'I've so very much been looking forward to meeting you.'

'Really?' Curtis felt like he was a visiting rock star, not a glorified cat burglar.

'You must be tired after your long journey.' Eli gestured for Curtis to take a seat at the boardroom table. 'Can we get you something to drink --- tea? Coffee? Something stronger?'

Curtis smiled. 'Something stronger.'

Eli walked over to a nearby drinks cabinet, removing four crystal tumblers and a bottle of bourbon. He placed them on the boardroom table and began to decant.

'I'm sure you've got lots of questions for us,' Eli said understatedly.

'Just one,' Curtis cut in. 'Why am I here?'

Eli acknowledged the cutting to the chase, as well as the dual meaning of the question. 'A question we ask every day Mr Curtis.' He handed him a liberally filled tumbler, chinking crystal with him. 'Mazeltov!'

The contents of the tumbler drizzled down Curtis's throat like honey. Curtis let his tired eyes close momentarily as he savoured it. They opened to find Eli having taken just a small, polite sip.

Eli smiled. 'You are aware of what we do here, yes?'

'Doctor Eli,' Crombie cut across their conversation, 'Mr Curtis has been somewhat tied up these past few years, so I suspect his subscriptions to the scientific journals have lapsed.' He took his own liberal sip of bourbon. 'Start from the beginning. And best keep it simple.'

'Ok.' Eli rubbed his hands, as if beginning a big lecture. 'Well, CERN was established in 1952 as Europe's answer to the brain drain of our scientists to the United States and Soviet Russia. Over almost seventy years, we have been at the forefront of scientific research into particle physics, proving all of the elements that make up the Standard Model. One by one, the mysteries of high-energy particle physics have unravelled at the hands of the thousands of scientists who have worked here. But until recently, one crucial element remained unsolved.'

Curtis could not have looked more bored. 'You're talking about the Large Hadron Collider and the existence of the Higgs boson, the theoretical particle that gives all subatomic particles mass?'

Schildberg, Eli and Crombie all exchanged surprised glances, taken aback by Curtis's knowledge and interest.

Curtis smiled. 'Must have read about it before my subscription lapsed.'

Eli smiled back. 'Well, in 2012, we did indeed prove the existence of the Higgs particle, boson, an enormous feat in scientific progression. But we also found something else.' There was a twinkle in Eli's eye. 'Something extraordinary.'

It was left to Curtis to puncture the silence. 'Does God exist?' he suggested sarcastically. 'What happened to the dinosaurs? Who's holding Elvis?'

Eli wagged his finger as he laughed nervously. 'Not yet. In our efforts to prove Higgs, we realised that an almost infinite number of particles could occupy the exact same space – just at different times or points in time.'

'Like, in a parallel universe?'

'Yes, something like that.' Eli took a larger sip of his bourbon. 'You're aware of the "accident" at CERN a few weeks after the Collider started, when we had to shut down the Collider for a time?'

Curtis nodded.

'Well, the only accident was our unexpected discovery. We had already discovered Higgs – but we had stumbled upon what we're now calling Trans-Animate Displacement. In essence, particles occupying the same space at different times can be interchanged. Swapped.'

Curtis gave a pregnant, disbelieving pause. 'You're talking about time travel?'

'Yes,' replied Eli matter of factly.

Curtis was faux jolly. 'Well, why didn't you just say so? Send me back to this time yesterday and I'll choose the blue pill.'

Crombie rolled his eyes but Eli had more patience.

'You don't believe me, Mr Curtis?'

'Oh I believe you Dr Eli,' Curtis retorted. 'I just don't know what the fuck it's got to do with me. So if you'll excuse me—.'

As Curtis stood up from his chair, Crombie pulled out a service issue revolver from its shoulder holster and placed it down on his desk.

Schildberg sat up, rising to her feet before gliding almost angelically towards Curtis.

'I would think much less of you if you did believe the words of strangers without proof, James.' She reached out her hand. 'Give me something – anything – from your pockets or on you. Something that only you have. Something unique to you.'

Curtis pondered her sincerity before grudgingly accepting it at face value. He padded himself down, initially drawing a blank. The perils of being in a jail cell. Then he saw, on the little finger of his right hand, his family ring: 18 karat gold with the serif letter 'C' etched elegantly into its surface. It had been given to him on his eighteenth birthday by his late father, posthumously from his grave. It was all he had left of him. Reticently he removed it.

'This is a treasured family heirloom.' Curtis stared coldly back at Crombie who avoided eye contact. He turned back to Schildberg as he handed her the ring. 'I want it back.'

Schildberg smiled before removing her own diamond engagement ring from her wedding finger. It resisted. The ring had possibly never been removed. 'This ring was given to me on bended knee at the foot of the Eiffel Tower by my late husband. It means the world to me too.'

Schildberg put her engagement ring alongside Curtis's family ring on the boardroom table. They rested one atop another, an act of sincerity and faith building between them. Behind her, Eli produced a pet carrier from underneath the boardroom table. Inside: a white cat, not dissimilar to the one Curtis passed in the corridor.

'This is my companion, Rudi.' Schildberg smiled as she removed the cat, stroking him in her arms. 'He is equally dear to me.'

Eli collected the two rings in his hand, slipping them one at a time onto a narrow collar before placing it around Rudi's paunchy neck. He then placed a small metal flight case on top of the boardroom table. The latches were released and the lid opened to reveal a metal bracelet with a small recessed digital display. It looked like an expensive digital watch.

Curtis padded himself down. 'Hang on, is that my phone? I think it's the 1980s – they want their watch back.'

'It's not a watch.' Eli was growing a little tired of Curtis's cynicism. 'Technically it's a Quantum Triangulation Device but we call it a time bracelet. With this device, we can create a small field around the object or being we wish to transport to another time. Everything within the field is transported – air, other objects, even dust, even part of this table. We can program the bracelet to transport the contents of the field to any point in time at these very co-ordinates. We can send Rudi back a minute. An hour. A year. A hundred years, even.'

Schildberg smiled warmly as she stroked Rudi. 'When shall we send him James?'

Curtis pondered, his natural disbelief jarring hard with his innate faith in scientific development.

'Ten minutes. I want to see my ring again before he dies of old age.'

Eli set the time bracelet using small depressions in the surface to change the display. When he was finished, he looked up at Schildberg for her approval before stroking Rudi's head and starting a countdown timer on the time bracelet.

Rudi purred as he dropped all fours gently onto the top of the boardroom table. Schildberg and Eli stepped cautiously back, causing Curtis to instinctively follow. He was reminded of the running man wearing the t-shirt with thirteen fateful words: "I'm a nuclear scientist. If you see me running, try to catch up!"

Before Rudi reached the end of the table, readying himself to jump down and head for the door – his own personal break for freedom – what looked like a blue-hued force field crackled into existence. Its bright light caused Curtis to shy away, though the others appeared to be expecting it, used to it even. Within seconds, the blue hue – and Rudi too – had disappeared into the ether.

Curtis was astonished. 'Where did he go? And what have you done with my family ring?'

Schildberg cupped his hands soothingly. 'But you've already seen him today – haven't you? When you came in, he passed you, no? The metal of our two rings jangling against each other.'

Curtis was not impressed. 'What is this, a magic show?'

'No, Mr Curtis.' Eli was indignant. 'We leave magic to the Scientologists. We don't do science fiction – we do science fact.'

The clash of Curtis's brawn and Eli's brain was interrupted by a purring in the doorway. It was the cat from when Curtis had first arrived at CERN. And from the sentimental necklace of jewellery around its neck, it was also the same cat Eli had just sent back in time: Rudi.

Schildberg picked up Rudi, holding him while Eli removed the narrow collar. He presented it to Curtis, who snatched the family ring back.

'How do I know it's the same cat?' Curtis asked cynically. 'It's not like it can tell me about its trip and show me holiday snaps.'

Schildberg was amused at Curtis clutching at straws to explain rationally what must seem irrational to a suspicious mind.

'Therein lies our problem James.' She kissed Rudi's brow as Eli removed the time bracelet before placing the cat back inside the pet carrier.

Eli carefully placed the time bracelet back in the flight case, depressing the lid shut gently. 'Stage One involved inanimate objects. Simple items like stones and metal ore with specific chemical compositions so that we could monitor any degradation in the quantum transfer. When we were satisfied that the field was transferring all particles within it intact, we moved on to Stage Two, living matter like Dr Schildberg's cat. As you can see with your own eyes, that has been a monumental success. So now it's time for Stage Three.'

'Stage Three?' Curtis asked.

'Human trials.' Eli was sheepish as Curtis soon realised the import of Eli's words.

'No. No way! You can find some other monkey to put on top of the rocket.'

'Perhaps you'd prefer me to take you back to Russia?' Crombie's forefinger travelled the rim of his crystal tumbler.

'Let the FSB have some more fun with you. I hear human testicles are a delicacy in some parts of Siberia.'

Curtis stared angrily at him. 'But why me!?'

Crombie smiled sadistically. 'Why not you?'

Curtis stood up, storming over to the windowsill and thumping it with his clenched fist.

'Let's just say,' Eli interjected, 'that your leap first, ask questions later approach has come highly recommended.'

Schildberg stepped forward. 'We need you James.'

After a pause, Curtis turned to face Crombie. 'I want the slate wiped clean Crombie.'

'Your criminal record will be expunged, though I'd give Grigor Ivanovich a wide berth if I were you.' Crombie took a measured sip from his tumbler. 'If you come back, of course.'

'How do you even know I'll come back?' Curtis rested back against the sill. 'What's stopping me slipping off alone into the night?'

'Me, I guess.'

A new yet familiar voice joined the discussion from the doorway. As Curtis turned to see who it was, everything started to make sense.

'Hello James,' said Luka Rothstein.

# 5
# GUINEA PIGS

Wearing a white coat, Rothstein looked like all of the other scientists at CERN.

It took no time at all for Curtis's blood to boil.

'You son of a bitch.'

Rothstein was taken aback by the venom in Curtis's voice.

'Oh, don't blame him.' Crombie leapt to his defence. 'He was in almost as much trouble as you when I first laid eyes on him.'

Schildberg interjected. 'So James — are you with us?'

Curtis observed the room. How could he have missed this, the set-up of all set-ups? He stepped over to the drinks cabinet, picked up the bottle of bourbon, placing his other hand covetously on an unopened second, and took an unhealthily large swig.

'I wasn't aware I had a choice.'

*

The bedroom was not dissimilar to that of a modest motel or a private hospital room. Banal, with beige painted walls flanking a white rail running power points and interconnectivity around the room, it was clean and uncluttered, albeit a little basic.

A showered Curtis sat at the end of the bed, a bathrobe his only creature comfort, the television volume on low just for company. The first bottle of bourbon was long done, resting on its side next to him as he was hard at work on the second. He stared angrily at the mirror, looking at himself, his face a fit of fury.

The electronic door slid open. He sensed someone joining him in the room before it closed after them but didn't care to see who it was.

He expected it to be Rothstein, begging forgiveness.

He was mistaken.

'Where was my invitation?' Schildberg asked in that soothing Germanic lilt.

Curtis took another healthy swig as he looked over to her. 'You're funny Doctor. But it's a party for one, I'm afraid.'

Schildberg picked up the empty bourbon bottle resting on the bed. 'So it would seem.' She let it sit between them as she perched herself on the end of the bed. 'Do you drink to enjoy – or to forget?'

'A bit of both,' he replied curtly. 'Now if you don't mind?'

Curtis got up and put some distance between Schildberg and himself. She looked up at him with sad eyes. She knew more about him than he thought.

'I lost my father too.'

Curtis was taken aback. 'What's that got to do with anything?'

Schildberg was well briefed. 'I know what happened to your parents James. I know your father got caught up in politics. That it cost him his life. And that bringing you into this world cost your mother hers.'

'You know nothing!' Curtis never did like talking about his family. It brought back suppressed feelings of anger and resentment, which usually led to him doing something stupid.

'I only knew my mother growing up.' Schildberg looked away from Curtis. 'My father was lost in the war, so I never really knew him either.' Her gaze returned to Curtis. 'We're all orphans eventually James. It's what we do as our parents' children that defines us. Not the manner of their passing. There lies a madness.'

Curtis acknowledged her point with a little bob of his head.

'Once this is all over,' Schildberg was reassuring, 'you'll have the opportunity for a fresh start. A new future for us all.'

'And what about Colonel Crombie?' Curtis half-smiled. 'You can't trust him. You may be doing this for the science but he's got other plans. He always does.'

'Don't you worry about Crombie.' Schildberg was nothing if not sincere. 'I've been around long enough to see the Crombies of this world come – and go. Some people like to be around when we make history.' Schildberg looked up. 'James – this is history. You do understand that, yes?'

Curtis finally felt as exhausted as he looked. Schildberg rose and turned off the television.

'Get some rest. Tomorrow's going to be a special day.'

Schildberg turned on her heel and headed for the door. She stopped.

'Please don't be too hard on Luka, James.' Her head was bowed. 'He was only following orders. I'm sure he would have told you, if he could. It was he who recommended you.'

With friends like that, he thought, who needed the Crombies of this world.

Curtis faux smiled without looking at Schildberg.

'Good night, Doctor.'

*

The test facility was an equally clinical room, not dissimilar to an x-ray facility in a hospital. Curtis and Rothstein were both being manhandled by pre-test medics, to the extent Curtis mused that he'd had less attention at an orgy. As they stood on raised circular platforms a metre apart, Curtis felt more like an astronaut preparing to embark on a perilous space flight than the first time traveller. Well, human time traveller anyway, though he doubted either Rudi or himself would make it into any history books. Curtis stared doggedly ahead as his time bracelet was fitted around his right wrist for the first time. Rothstein glanced over, hoping for a flicker, some signal that all could be well between them given time. He had been unsettled by the ferocity of Curtis's reaction to him. He thought this would have been right up his street.

Schildberg and Crombie stood nearby in a control booth behind a thick glass-panelled screen, shielding technicians operating a bank of complex computer systems from exposure to any of the malign effects of Trans-Animate Displacement.

Above and all around them, closed circuit television cameras recorded the test for evidence.

And posterity.

Crombie leant in to Schildberg, already anxious. 'If this goes south, I want each and every one of these cameras wiped.' His tone was cold and ruthless. 'This test never happened.'

Crombie stepped off, his point made. If the guinea pigs didn't return, there were no guinea pigs. She knew the stakes were high, though perhaps not that high.

Schildberg joined Eli as he briefed Curtis and Rothstein.

'For this test, we will send you back in time twenty-four hours. You will transfer separately to the same point in time. Be alert and aware of all of the sensations of your transit. We'll want to know all about them later.'

'Blessed be the lab rats.' Curtis was snarky.

'Under no circumstances,' Eli continued, 'are you to interact with anyone here at CERN, let alone your "other selves", during your trip.'

Rothstein sought to make light of Eli's dour, almost funereal demeanour. 'The consequences would be disastrous.'

Both Curtis and Eli ignored Rothstein's attempt at playfulness. "Doc" Emmett T Brown delivered it better.

'We've hidden money in the lining of your coat in case of emergency.' Eli reached over for Curtis's coat, folding it over to reveal a padded compartment. 'We need you to provide some proof of where you've been. So buy a newspaper, go get some dinner. And get a receipt.'

'Tax deductible?' Rothstein was trying too hard.

'Your time bracelet will be controlled by us on the test. Whatever you do, do not tamper with it or remove it for any reason.' Eli could not have been any more school masterly if he tried. 'I don't care how much it itches or annoys you. It is your new best friend.'

'Well, there is a vacancy.' Curtis could be snide at times. It was not one of his more endearing features but it was better than knocking the teeth out of Rothstein's mouth one at a time, which was probably his first preference at that point.

Eli took a step back, looking at the two men with pride. He beamed at them. 'May our curiosity be blessed with good luck.'

As Eli walked towards the control booth, Curtis called after him. 'You do know what curiosity did to the cat, Doctor?'

Eli smiled back at him. 'Not our cat. And not on my watch.'

Eli walked behind the thick glass screen. Schildberg placed her hands together, almost in prayer, gently nodding at Curtis and Rothstein in turn.

Eli leant in over one of the technicians. 'Rothstein first.'

Schildberg took a deep breath as Eli counted down.

'Three... two... one...'

The now familiar blue-hued force field energised around Rothstein, quickly enveloping him. He looked ahead stoically before the field evaporated, taking him with it.

Curtis stared dispassionately ahead as Eli turned to the technician. 'Now Curtis.'

Curtis caught the eye of Schildberg. 'See you on the other side, Doctor.'

Schildberg smiled. 'Bon chance James.'

'Three... two... one...'

The force field energised around Curtis. As with Rothstein, it enveloped him. Curtis felt like a patient undergoing an operation, being told to count down from ten as the anaesthesia took hold. He had never got past seven, though he was one of the few to enjoy the experience. He glanced down at his family ring, now back with pride of place on his little finger.

And then he too was gone into the unknown.

Into their past.

Into his future.

*

The street scene was one of festive cheer. Shoppers and tourists mingled with merrymakers, supping mulled wine and picking at moorish hot chestnuts from conical paper cups at the Christmas market. But for every happy person at Christmas there was always someone less so. Someone who life had perhaps left behind. A homeless man sat, buttocks inextricably affixed to the stone cold concrete pavement as they passed him by, breath visible in the cold December air, his tin can empty but for a few low-value coins.

Behind the homeless man, in an alley off the beaten track, a blue hue rose ten feet up the mottled brickwork. It reached a crescendo and then it was gone.

Curtis didn't know if the contents of his stomach were brought up by the Trans-Animate Displacement or the almost two bottles of bourbon he had sunk the night before. Either way, it was no way to arrive in yesterday. There was nothing worse than being sick when there's nothing to come up. Curtis wretched again and again until his body finally got the message.

He pulled himself together and looked at his time bracelet. The display, in house colours, read December 17th 2021. 12.01pm.

Yesterday.

Right now, Curtis thought to himself, in a FSB torture chamber half a continent away his "other self" was currently learning to be a fish. Crombie was yet to arrive with his deal-or-no-deal and all of what was now happening was yet to unfold.

Curtis wondered if, while he had been learning to drink water FSB-style, his current self had been a thousand miles away chucking his guts up in a Geneva alleyway.

There was a lot about time travel that could make you go crazy.

He chose not to think about it anymore.

Curtis was hunched, knees bent, ready for any further involuntary expulsion from his stomach when he felt an arm around his shoulders, almost inaudible words being whispered into his ear.

'It doesn't last long. Just breathe. Breathe. Breathe...'

With his soft hands and his soothing voice, Rothstein may have made a reasonable paramedic.

But he was a lousy friend.

Rothstein left Curtis's side and stood face on. The bout of sickness was over. He reached forward for his old friend's shoulders. He was full of boundless energy.

'We just made history!'

Curtis nodded. 'Yeah, we did.'

Rothstein couldn't have seen the first blow coming but he would remember it for days to come. As he sat on the ground, nose broken, blood dripping to the ground, Rothstein came to understand the anger, the frustration, the betrayal felt by Curtis.

'You fucking prick!'

Before Rothstein could even respond, Curtis had dragged him from his pathetic seat on the ground, slamming him so hard against the wall that loose mortar dropped on them from above.

'You set me up!'

'No, I, I didn't...' Rothstein struggled as another punch rained down on him before he finally punched back, catching Curtis's lip. It was a dirty fight worthy of any bar brawl.

After a few moments, both men stood apart, wounded, lame, bedraggled, hot under the collar and panting desperately.

Rothstein grasped for air, throwing his hands into the air with resignation. 'I didn't set you up James, I swear!'

Curtis ran the back of his hand against his bloodied lip, admiring Rothstein's lucky shot.

'The program needed you,' Rothstein pleaded. 'People like us, people like you, who go the extra mile, who leap into the unknown, who somehow always come out on top of situations. It's a big thing.'

Curtis scowled. 'You make it sound like you've found the cure for cancer.'

Rothstein bowed his head. 'But I had no idea they'd do it like this. I was in the dark as much as you.'

Curtis extended his arm, his hand flat and parallel to his body. 'Enough. We're done talking.'

Curtis tucked his shirt back into his trousers, rearranged his coat and ran his hand through his locks to make himself look almost presentable before stepping off.

On the street nearby, a newspaper vendor stood, gnome-like in the winter breeze. Curtis sidled over, slapping a note into his hand before grabbing one of the dailies from him. He didn't stop to read the newspaper, thrusting it into Rothstein's chest as he inevitably followed after him.

Curtis saw the homeless man, ice and snow his companions on the cold ground beneath his feet. Without thinking, he reached into the lining of his coat, removing the €1000 in high denomination notes from his emergency stash. He took €50 from the stack and dropped the rest into the homeless man's tin.

The homeless man's eyes lit up as he handled the notes disbelievingly. 'Merci, monsieur...'

'Joyeux Nöel.' Curtis stepped off.

'Where are you going?' Rothstein called after him.

Curtis didn't stop to reply, as he headed towards a bustling café. Alone. Rothstein looked down at the homeless man before feeling obliged to follow Curtis's lead in his act of charitable generosity.

*

The café was alive with joie de vivre. But Curtis sat alone in a booth. Alone with his thoughts.

He hated this time of year. Christmas was a time for being with family.

He had no family. Not anymore.

Rothstein shuffled awkwardly through the crowded café, arriving at Curtis's booth. Curtis was unmoved as Rothstein sat across from him.

'Look, I'm sorry, alright?' Rothstein was lamely apologetic. 'I never wanted it this way. I really didn't.'

'Well what way did you want it Luke?' Curtis's gaze remained fixed on the menu, without looking up at his old friend.

A waitress approached. She was strikingly beautiful, her white shirt tied in all the right places. Her perfect English tones belied her Swiss heritage. Switzerland was in so many ways the linguistic smorgasbord of Europe. Something for everyone.

'You guys ready to order?'

Rothstein smiled. 'Where've you been all my life?'

The waitress looked him up and down before replying icily. 'Looks like I haven't been alive for most of it.' Checking herself, she defrosted a little, even managing a little smile. 'You're not from around here?' she asked rhetorically.

Rothstein answered instinctively and clumsily. 'We're on, er, a short business trip.' He tried to regain the initiative. 'So --- what's a guy like me got to do to get a date with a girl like you?'

'Change.'

The coup de gras was delivered straight from the freezer, leaving Rothstein flummoxed and flailing, much to the amusement of Curtis. Before he could challenge her, the waitress cut across him. 'Look, your chat may work back home but it ain't cutting it here. Now --- what can I get you?'

Rothstein shrank back into his seat. Curtis smothered a smirk, pretending to be immersed in the menu once more before finally intervening.

'What would you recommend?' Curtis asked. 'Other than a change of friends.'

Rothstein pouted, his arms folded defensively. The waitress smiled at Curtis.

'The club sandwich is popular.'

'Does that have bacon in it?' Rothstein cut in. He looked over at a perplexed Curtis. 'Can't eat bacon.'

'I didn't know you were Jewish.'

'I'm not...' Rothstein shuffled nervously, picking up the menu before making a quick choice. 'I'll just have a burger with fries and a milkshake.' He flung the menu down and gazed out of the window, keen for the encounter to end.

Curtis collected the other menu and handed them both to the waitress. 'Make that two.'

The waitress left the booth, leaving Curtis and Rothstein to sit in tumbleweed silence. At the same time, they both broke ranks.

They both stopped abruptly.

Rothstein tilted his head. 'What?'

Curtis gestured. 'You go first.'

'But you had something to say?'

'I'm sure it can wait.'

Rothstein bowed his head before looking up under his furrowed brow. 'I'm sorry I lied to you.'

Curtis chewed his gum. 'I'm sorry you lied to me too.'

The waitress returned with a basket of cutlery and condiments, placing it between the two men. Curtis reached for his own. 'How did you get mixed up in this?'

Rothstein clasped his hands, leaning forward sheepishly. Here came the confession. 'I used to work at CERN. I was there when they found Higgs. I was there when they discovered Trans-Animate Displacement. And I was there when they ran out of money. Despite all of those massive achievements, they pulled the plug on funding. All of that science, all of that potential. It would all have been for nothing. And then along came this British government type ---'

'Crombie.' Curtis scowled.

'Yeah, Crombie. He offered to take the project over, funding was no object. But the military – NATO – they had first dibs on any serious scientific breakthroughs.'

'Well, when you sup with the Devil...' Curtis was not overly sympathetic.

'You can imagine what he was like when he found out about Trans-Animate Displacement. He was like the cat who found the cream factory. Crombie got more and more involved. And when it came to human trials, he insisted on who would be the guinea pigs.'

Curtis nodded his head gently. 'Me.'

Rothstein spread his hands in a mea culpa. 'I had no choice.'

There felt like there was nothing much left to say.

'You know, even though I felt bad about entrapping you,' Rothstein interjected, attempting to truncate the renewed silent brooding, 'the flipside was that I knew you'd be interested in the gig anyway.'

Curtis's face was thunderous. 'Interested is one thing Luka — but I've lost my freedom, my liberty and now my self-respect, working for a government that betrayed my father and a man I wouldn't piss on if he was on fire.'

Rothstein's eyebrows furrowed once more. 'Your father?'

'My father,' Curtis clenched his fist on the table instinctively, 'was an arms dealer. And a good one. He had clients all over the world. The US and the UK governments were his biggest. He'd ship everything from bullets and microchips to small guns and big guns. In the Eighties, he was approached to supply the Libyans with parts – despite an arms embargo. He didn't want to do it, but he was leant on by an official at the Ministry of Defence who threatened to take his other contracts away if he didn't play ball. After the Lockerbie bombing in 1988, everything changed. He was indicted for breaking the embargo. The MoD official denied all knowledge and threw him under the bus.'

Curtis was clearly getting emotional, making Rothstein squirm in discomfort all the more.

'Facing extradition and hundreds of years in an American prison, one day he blew his brains out.'

Rothstein shook his head. 'I'm sorry James. I knew your father had died. I didn't know how. Or why.'

Curtis looked at Rothstein, his gaze piercing. 'And the official at the MoD? Colonel Arnold Crombie.'

*

By the time they had left the café, the homeless man was long gone. They walked in silence, the sound of their shoes sinking into the freshly minted layer of snow beneath their feet all that was punctuating the vacuum. They headed for the alleyway, out of sight of the more joyful Christmas revellers. They cut sober, somewhat forlorn figures.

Safely out of sight, they stood a metre apart awaiting transfer.

Rothstein turned his head to Curtis, who faced towards the wall, his face inscrutable.

'We're both orphans James.' Curtis twitched at the word. 'I wish we weren't but we are. But it does have its upside. It means we can do things that other people can't, take risks others would avoid. Taking this trip was a risk, a risk worth taking. Imagine the possibilities. Think of the good we could do. The wrongs we could right.'

Curtis turned his whole body to face Rothstein. 'Don't be naïve Luke. Crombie didn't "save" your project – he stole it. Who knows what for but going on form I doubt very much that good comes into it.'

Rothstein's time bracelet came to life. Curtis backed away, turning to face the wall once more, leaving Rothstein deep in thought as the blue hue engulfed him. Rothstein was gone.

Curtis barely had time to reflect on the implications of Rothstein's confession before his time came.

But as the blue hue engulfed him, his old friend's vigilantism was far from the back of his mind.

# 6
# TRUE POTENTIAL

Ida Schildberg's eyes studiously scanned the report in her hand. The first human trial of Trans-Animate Displacement, a day she had been praying for and dreading in almost equal measure, had been remarkable for its unremarkability. The two test subjects had been returned to CERN safely, along with a mountain of data in their Quantum Triangulation Devices that her team would take years to analyse. Biological assessment alone of Curtis and Rothstein would take months.

But the bottom line was now undeniable.

Trans-Animate Displacement worked on humans.

Eli stood in front of her, almost unable to contain his excitement and enthusiasm. 'Neither subject shows any sign of cell degradation or mutation from the Trans-Animate Displacement process. It's a remarkable achievement Dr Schildberg. The scientific community will be astounded to hear about it.'

Once the community knew of their discovery, it would be his name alongside Schildberg's on the Nobel Prize for Physics.

Crombie, stood leaning against the window pillar, his usual inscrutable self as he puffed on his pipe, briefly caught

Schildberg's eyes as she closed the report and removed her reading glasses, leaving them dangling around her neck.

'I would still like to continue testing before we consider publishing our results Gideon. Until then, this...' She placed her hand gently but firmly on top of the now closed report. 'This must remain strictly confidential.'

Eli thought he clocked the gaze of Schildberg towards Crombie. Looking for reassurance and approval, he thought. It didn't stop him feeling deflated as he left her office, a more humble and functional surrounding than Crombie's. The door shut abruptly behind him.

'I know what you're going to say.' Schildberg's voice, so often authoritative and confident, was if anything resigned.

'Congratulations?'

'Apart from that.' Schildberg was almost afraid to ask her next question. 'What happens next?'

Crombie drew hard on his pipe. 'A day is useful. A lifetime? And to another country? Even more so.'

'We've never sent anything back that far.' Schildberg looked anxious as she studiously avoided Crombie's gaze. 'We must walk before we can run. We don't know the effects of longer distance Trans-Animate Displacement.'

Crombie smiled. 'Time to find out. As for the other thing...' Crombie knocked out his pipe against the windowsill, stepping towards her desk. 'There will be no grand announcement. No huge fanfare. No publishing of results. No peer review. No Nobel Prize for Dr Eli. Remember: this is a military programme under my direct command.'

Schildberg sank back into her chair. 'This will hit Gideon hard.'

That was an understatement.

'He'll get over it.' Crombie headed towards the door. 'He'll have to.'

Crombie left Schildberg deep in vexed thought. As the door shut behind him, she leant down to open the bottom drawer of her desk. She removed a small flight case and placed it in front of her. She tapped her fingernails gently against its mottled surface before opening the latches.

Inside was a third time bracelet.

*

Dressed like Fred Astaire and Frank Sinatra in Forties' grey suits, pencil ties and curved collars, Curtis and Rothstein entered the test facility with a sense of trepidation. The facility was a flurry of activity. The small tribe of scientists from the first test seemed to have brought along a cat herd of underlings, now that they knew it worked. Everybody wants to be associated with success, Curtis thought, but he could probably count how many of these lab rats would have turned out for their empty casket funerals had their trip to yesterday gone wrong. Eli scuttled across, bouncing around the facility like a child's pet bunny rabbit.

Curtis looked himself down before turning to Eli. 'So what have we come dressed as?'

'It's so that you fit in,' Crombie barked from behind the control console. 'For once.'

'Fit in where – a museum?'

Crombie puffed on his pipe before taking it into his hand. 'We're sending you back to London.'

Curtis padded himself down. 'But I've mislaid my passport.'

Crombie took another drag. 'You won't need it in 1941.'

'You what?' Curtis spluttered before turning incandescent. 'You send us back one day and already you think you've mastered the technology to not only send us back eighty years but six hundred miles as well?'

'This is all about mastering the technology,' Crombie smiled sadistically. 'We've proven time. Now we must prove space too.'

Eli gingerly stepped in to try to defuse the tension. 'As before, your orders are to observe, not to interfere. To blend in, go unnoticed. You'll spend two hours in wartime London. You're to collect newspapers and any other time-sensitive evidence you see fit and bring them back with you.'

Eli stepped towards the console. His intervention had done little to calm Curtis. 'This is a suicide mission,' he called after him.

'Only if you fuck it up.' Crombie smiled as he took a long toke on his pipe. 'So don't fuck it up.'

Eli returned with two sets of papers. 'In case of emergency, we've prepared identity documents for the time.' He handed one set apiece to Curtis and Rothstein. 'Also your belts probably feel a little heavy. That's because hidden within the lining we've fitted fifty gold sovereigns, currency for the time.'

'Standard SAS issue,' Crombie piped up, omnipresent.

'When Dorothy and Toto left Kansas, maybe.' Curtis was far from impressed.

Eli brushed aside the sarcasm. 'With these you'll be able to pay your way if —' Eli paused and chose his next words carefully. 'If there is any delay with the return journey.'

'A delay...' Curtis sniggered. 'Well, I suppose there's one bonus in 1941.'

'What's that?' Crombie asked.

'No danger of bumping into you.' Curtis was acerbic as he tucked the identity documents safely in his inside jacket pocket, before stepping slowly towards his launch pad.

The white coats all crowded around the control console, keen to avail themselves of the protection of the thick glass screen. Schildberg found herself pushed to the back as underlings crowded in around the main console.

'Good luck gentlemen.' Eli's bland scientist routine was beginning to grate on Curtis.

Crombie leant across one of the technicians, brushing aside Eli. 'Send them both simultaneously,' he whispered out of earshot of Curtis and Rothstein. The technicians looked anxiously back.

Curtis stared down the bridge of his nose at Crombie. 'After this, we're done Crombie.' He placed his hat on his head. 'Remember that.'

Eli counted down as before. 'Three... two... one...'

The blue-hued force fields energised around both of them. Both Curtis and Rothstein had thought they would travel separately. Crombie was clearly testing the technology to its very edge. As before, they were soon enveloped. The fields bumped against each other despite the distance between the two launching pads.

As he counted down in his head, Curtis just hoped he arrived with all of his own body parts.

Rothstein wasn't known for his own boyish good looks.

*

A thin layer of dust nestled atop a dozen barrels of ale. It wasn't for want of cleaning. The landlady was a clean freak above ground but down in the pub's basement, there was only so much that even she could do. The almost constant rattle of mechanised traffic on the roads above ground meant that even the slightest residue descended from the low ceiling.

Though given what was going on in the sky above them, at least they had a ceiling.

The blue-hued force field delivered Curtis and Rothstein simultaneously into the belly of the pub. Time travel remained a sick-inducing experience for both of them, but they were slowly getting used to it.

Rothstein reached his arm across towards Curtis.

He shrugged it off. 'I'm alright.'

Curtis resisted the temptation to punch him again. 'Where are we?'

Rothstein looked across at the kegs. 'Heaven?'

Curtis looked down at his time bracelet. The display read: May 12th 1941. 11.15am.

It was the right time.

Was it the right place?

*

Wide-eyed and ears open, Curtis and Rothstein stood behind narrow wooden doors atop an even narrower and uneven winding staircase. The veneer used on the door certainly smelt familiar but it would be the voices that would offer the final reassurance.

On the other side of those doors stood a microcosm of wartime life.

The lounge of the Marquis of Granby, in London's impoverished East End, was almost deserted, aside from a handful of the more elderly Great War veterans. Those of younger years were all mobilised. Men were either in the forces, counting their lucky stars but nonetheless licking their wounds after the catastrophic retreat of the British Expeditionary Force from Dunkirk the previous summer, or they worked in the supply chain for the war effort. As in the Great War, this meant the unfamiliar sight of women doing everyday roles traditionally associated with men.

Curtis and Rothstein stepped through into the lounge. Not one of the inhabitants batted an eyelid, carrying on in their own little worlds, oblivious to the two intrepid time travellers in their midst.

An old man polished off the final inch of his pint of bitter, drops of it remaining lodged in his furry white beard. He wiped them away with his arm before inching towards the door. Rothstein looked at Curtis before stepping ahead to hold the door open for the old man. Curtis dived into his grave without hesitation before catching the attention of the young barmaid. 'Two pints of whatever's good please.'

'Only got Barclays Pale Ale, love. Draught's off.'

'That'll do fine.' He placed hard currency on the counter as the barmaid began cracking open two bottles before pouring the rustic ale one at a time into old-fashioned handled pint glasses.

The old man had bequeathed Curtis a present: his discarded copy of today's Daily Express. At least this wouldn't cost him fifty gold sovereigns. Curtis picked it up, letting it unfold in his hands. It had a peculiar texture compared to modern newsprint and read like one of the many old newspaper front pages he had seen in museums or as souvenirs on major anniversaries. But this newspaper was just hours old, though as in modern times it was still yesterday's news.

What a day yesterday had been. Every story on the front page was newsworthy but two caught his eye:

RUDOLF HESS CRASHES IN SCOTLAND

Hitler Deputy daring mission for peace with Churchill.
Confusion and denial in Berlin.

HOUSE OF COMMONS IN RUINS AFTER LUFTWAFFE RAID

Since the dying days of the Great War, Hess had been obsessed with aviation. It was an obsession that ran parallel with his political life. During the turbulent aftermath of the war, he joined the right-wing Thule Society, participating in often violent rebellion against the Soviet Republic of Bavaria established by the Spartakusbund, militant communists bent on taking over Germany having been inspired by their kindred Bolshevik spirits in Moscow and St. Petersburg.

Enthralled by the oratory of Adolf Hitler, who he had first heard speak at a packed political meeting at the Sterneckerbräu beer tavern in Munich (on a first date with his future wife, Ilse), Hess joined the Nazi Party in 1920, becoming a member of its Sturmabteilung (the SA, or stormtroopers) two years later.

It would prove to be a fateful decision.

Within months Hess would find himself in a cell alongside Hitler at Landsberg prison outside Munich. Both were serving time for the failed Munich putsch, when Hitler, Hess and the SA had stormed a political rally at the Burgerbräukeller and taken hostages.

In prison, Hess cemented his position at Hitler's side.

It was Hess who Hitler dictated *Mein Kampf* to.

It was Hess who readied the tome for publication.

Hess was there from the beginning.

But unlike Hitler, Hess dreamt of a life outside of politics.

With American aviator Charles Lindbergh making the first solo flight across the Atlantic on May 20th 1927, flying from Long Island to Le Bourget outside Paris in thirty-three hours, Hess sought to ride the wave of wild acclamation that greeted such feats by flying in the opposite direction, against the prevailing winds.

He made extensive preparations while pitching for sponsors from industry. But those preparations came to naught and the spoils of the first non-stop flight back across the Atlantic the following spring – in a Junkers W33L no less, flown from Baldonnel in Ireland to Greenly Island on the Labrador coast – went to two compatriots and an Irishman instead.

The disappointment did little, if anything, to dim his enthusiasm. In 1929 he gained his private pilot's licence and the following year he became the proud owner of a two-seater BFW M23b monoplane, a generous gift from the Nazi Party newspaper Völkischer Beobachter (People's Observer).

When Hitler was appointed Chancellor in January 1933 by the ailing President Paul von Hindenburg, Hess was rewarded for his zealous devotion with his appointment as Hitler's deputy.

Despite the rise of the Nazi Party to government and the organs of the state coming under his control, he continued to build up many flying hours before achieving his first aeronautic triumph in the first National Air Race around the Zugspitze Mountain in March 1934. Hess won the race, becoming the proud owner of the Zugspitze Wanderpokal challenge cup. He came a creditable sixth the following year.

Soon after the German invasion of Poland in August 1939 provoked a resumption of hostilities in abeyance since November 1918, Hess asked Hitler for permission to join the Luftwaffe. His reasoning was that, with the country at war, it needed its best pilots in the air and not behind desks.

And he was undoubtedly one of its best pilots.

But he had another reason.

On the day that Poland was invaded, Hitler had announced in a speech to the Reichstag that Field Marshall Göring, Commander-in-Chief of the Luftwaffe and war hero, would be his successor in the event of his death, side-lining Hess. It was the first of many a snub and hurt Hess deeply, especially given that like Göring he too had been a senior member of the Geheimer Kabinettstrat (Select Cabinet Council), established to advise Hitler on foreign affairs.

Hitler refused Hess's request, forbidding him to fly any aircraft for the duration of the war. But Hess was a veteran of a war that everyone thought would be over by Christmas and lasted four years more than that. Playing on Hitler's over-confidence, he had the ban commuted to just one year.

However Hitler had cause for such confidence.

German victories followed in quick succession, with Poland's conquest followed by the subjugation of Denmark and Norway the following April and France's capitulation by June.

With Göring feted, Hess was desperate for some of his stardust.

And he had a secret plan to achieve that which had eluded Germany's political elite, as well as restore his own flagging prestige.

By September 1940, Hess was plotting peace overtures to Britain, allegedly with Hitler's knowledge. He sought the advice of Albrecht Haushofer, a close friend and confidant since his imprisonment at Landsberg. After considering many potential names, Hess settled on the Duke of Hamilton, an aristocrat and former MP who Haushofer had befriended during the interwar years.

Though Hamilton and Hess both attended a banquet during the Berlin Olympic Games in 1936, they had never actually met. But Hess had convinced himself that in Hamilton, a fellow aviator, was an ally, a man who had opposed the government of Winston Churchill and also had the ear of the new monarch King George VI.

Haushofer wrote to Hamilton on Hess's behalf, sending the letter via neutral Portugal, and suggested an exploratory meeting in its capital Lisbon. The letter would never be answered, having been intercepted by MI5, but Hess continued his preparations to meet Hamilton regardless.

If Hamilton wouldn't go to him, he would go to Hamilton.

In Scotland.

For which he needed a German warplane.

With his one-year flying ban now over, Hess visited Ernst Udet, the Generalluftzeugmeister (Chief of Aircraft Supply). He wanted Udet to supply a Messerschmidt Bf110 twin-engine "destroyer" for some occasional flying practice.

Udet, aware of Hess's pact with Hitler, agreed on the proviso Hitler signed a permit.

Hess didn't want to risk a refusal from above so he abandoned his official enquiries, instead using the clout and prestige he retained in his office to pressurise the factory owners that assembled single-engine Messerschmidt Bf109s for the Luftwaffe.

Though the single-engine variant didn't have the range to reach Scotland, the Germans were aware that the British had reconfigured their Spitfires - devoid of armaments and with additional fuel tanks on-board - for long-range photoreconnaissance.

If the British could do it, so could they.

One by one the factory managers declined his request, worried that the death of the Führer's Stellvertreter (Deputy) in one of their Bf109s could be disastrous for their own prospects too.

Almost out of options and at the end of his tether, Hess visited Willy Messerschmidt at the Augsburg-Haunstetten airfield where Bf110s were being built and tested. To his surprise and relief, his appeal to an old friend to fly the safer Bf110 was met without objection.

So in October 1940 Hess began training in the Bf110 under chief test pilot Willi Stoer.

After nearly a dozen flights, Stoer let Hess fly solo.

The following month, Hess wrote to his beloved Ilse: "I firmly believe that from the flight I am about to make one of these days, I will return and the flight will be crowned with success. However, if not, the goal I have set myself will have been worth the supreme effort."

Hess had finally made up his mind, in the absence of

any response from Hamilton to Haushofer's letter, to fly to the Duke.

He knew that he lived at Dungavel House near Glasgow. This was a long way from Augsburg, so he practiced long-distance flights over the mountainous Thuringer Forest range in Germany – with its peaks of almost a thousand metres similar to those he would meet on arrival in Scotland. He added refinements to his own Bf110E 1/N aircraft, including 900-litre fuel drop tanks and a radio compass that he could use to navigate using the German transmitting station at Kalundborg in Denmark – which just so happened to share its latitude with Dungavel House.

He also received secret daily weather reports from the Zentrale Wetterdienst Gruppe (Central Weather Group), as during the war public weather forecasts were forbidden. Every day, a call was made to the ZWG by Hess's secretary Hildegard Fath asking for the forecasts for locations X, Y and Z.

Unbeknownst to her, X was Oslo, Y was Kiel and Z was Edinburgh.

Hess had kept his mission a secret from everyone bar Haushofer and his senior adjutant, Lieutenant Karlheinz Pintsch. Just before what was clearly an earlier attempt at the flight in January 1941, Pintsch was given two letters, both to be opened only if he didn't return within four hours. The four hours elapsed and with no sign of Hess, Pintsch opened the first of the letters. It was addressed to Pintsch himself and explained that he had flown to Britain to attempt to make peace.

Hess had returned before he could deliver the second letter to its addressee.

Adolf Hitler himself.

Four months later, on May 10th 1941, he would try again.

After a day of uncharacteristically paternalistic affection for his infant son Wolf, Hess lunched with party ideologist Alfred Rosenberg, later to become Reichsminister for the Eastern Occupied Territories after the commencement of Operation Barbarossa – the imminent invasion of Russia. After Rosenberg left, he headed for the Führer's mountain retreat in Berchtesgaden, the Berghof, blissfully unaware of what was about to unfold. Hess dressed elegantly in a blue-grey uniform with the rank insignia of a Hauptmann (Captain of the Luftwaffe), with dark blue tie on a blue shirt and high boots before bidding his wife goodbye.

It was her favourite shirt and tie combination.

It would be the last time they would see each other until Christmas Eve 1969, twenty-eight years later.

After arriving at Haunstetten with Pintsch, Hess changed into a black leather flying suit belonging to Stoer's successor as test pilot, Helmut Kaden, along with fleece-lined flying boots. As he emerged carrying his oxygen mask and dark brown fleece-lined flying helmet, Hess was helped into the cockpit by Pintsch and Kaden, who rapped his knuckles on Hess's helmet before telling him: 'Hals – und Beinbruch!' ('Break your neck and legs!').

At 5.45pm German Summer Time, chocks were away, flaps were set to 20° and fuel was switched to main tanks. Momentarily the Bf110e was no longer on the 1,100 metre runway but was airborne, gaining altitude before making a wide sweep east of the Lech.

Hess climbed in a north-westerly direction, disappearing out of sight.

Never to be seen again by either Pintsch or Kaden.

He set a course of 320°, towards the German city of Bonn. At first the ground looked foreign to him, making him unable to check his position. But soon after Darnstadt loomed on his starboard, followed by the Main meeting the Rhine. A few degrees off track, he made a minor course adjustment. The Rhine disappeared to port, only to reappear along with the Siebengebirge (Seven Mountains) in the distance and later the spa town of Bad Godesberg in Westphalia, just south-east of Bonn.

From Bonn he altered course to 335°, taking him near to the town of Haldern on the German-Dutch border. He continued on the same heading near Arnhem and over the Zuider Zee, passing between the Dutch Frisian Islands of Vlieland and Terschelling.

To avoid detection by the sophisticated British Chain Home radar system, whose twenty-two radar stations dotted around Britain's coast had been used to devastating effect during the Battle of Britain the previous year, Hess turned east for nearly half an hour before returning to course 335° for his long journey across the North Sea. At 8.10pm, he overflew a pair of German U-boats, which began emergency dives until they recognised Hess's low-flying Messerschmidt as a friendly. Thereafter, Hess climbed to the more economical altitude of 5,000 metres, outside of the range of British radar but visible to German radar stations in Denmark.

It was only then that Hess's mission was blown within Nazi circles.

Oberstleutnant (Lieutenant Colonel) Adolf Gallard, a celebrated fighter ace commanding a Fighter Group on the

Channel coast, received an urgent telephone call from his boss, Reichskommissar Göring.

His orders: to take off with his entire group and shoot down Hess in his "rogue" Bf110.

In the twilight it would have been impossible to make out Hess's Bf110 from others airborne. Besides, Gallard believed that even in the unlikely event that Hess made it to the British mainland, their job would be done for them by Fighter Command's Spitfires.

While the Führer slept soundly at the Berghof, Hess checked his latitude by turning a radio compass to a bearing from Kalundborg. He continued until he reached the Nordpunkt just before 9pm and then turned to port on a course of 245° towards the small coastal town of Bamburgh in Northumberland.

Though the summer sun was low in the sky, it was still too light for safety. Having miscalculated sunset at this northerly latitude, Hess turned and flew back and forth between 065° and 245° to kill time while awaiting the protection of darkness.

He was now at his most precarious, dancing on a pin as Fighter Command became aware of their unexpected – and unsuspecting – guest.

The Chain Home station at Ottercops Moss, north-west of Newcastle-upon-Tyne, first reported the intrusion to the Filter Room at RAF Bentley Prior soon after sunset, having established that Hess was a bandit using the RAF's IFF (Identification Friend or Foe) system. Though they mistakenly identified three or more aircraft travelling due west, a single coloured counter was placed by a teller next to Holy Island on the Filter Room's plotting table map, distinguishing it from friendly aircraft.

Designated Raid 42, the tellers "told" Hess all the way to the coast where radar duties were taken over by a network of manned Royal Observer Corps posts.

The ROC's network of small posts had been constructed during the interwar years, covering the whole country and manned by some 10,000 civilian volunteers, many of them a Dads' Army of veterans of the Great War now too old for active service, as well as those too young to enlist.

Hess may have chosen the perfect night weather-wise but his mission also coincided with one of the heaviest raids by the Luftwaffe on London before their withdrawal east to what would soon become the Russian front. Though the worst of the Blitz had passed for Londoners, incendiary bombs had landed on the chamber of the House of Commons, destroying the building's roof and gutting its interior 101 years after it had been rebuilt by Charles Barry and Augustus Pugin.

It bode ill for Hess's message of peace, smacking of negotiation with a tiger while your head was firmly in its mouth.

Orders were issued by 13 Group headquarters to 72 Squadron's two Spitfires, on patrol over the Fame Islands to intercept Raid 42. Due to the lack of notable targets, 13 Group's area in the north of England, Scotland and Northern Ireland was thinly defended.

Approaching the coast just after sunset, Hess spotted the peak of the 2,676-foot high Cheriot. With two British destroyers sailing below him at an oblique angle across his track near Holy Island, he headed towards the Cheriot itself to avoid anti-aircraft fire. He also took advantage of the growing layer of mist lathering the English coast. Though not thick, the light of the moon made visibility from above difficult for any pursuers, so he went into a shallow dive from 5,000 metres, increasing speed.

The ROC post at Embleton on the mainland reported Hess's Messerschmidt by sound and bearing just after 10pm while another at Chatton in Northumberland correctly identified it as a Bf110 from its silhouette in the twilight.

This caused huge confusion, as there was no logical reason for a sole fighter to be flying over the remote countryside. 13 Group reported that the flight group must have split and what was spotted must be a Dornier Do17 bomber, not a Bf110 fighter.

Hess climbed up one side of the Cheriot hills, sliding down the other. He was now in Scotland. He turned to 280°, heading for St. Mary's Loch near Broad Law and passing very close to Dungavel House, flying at treetop level and waving at unsuspecting farmers below.

Alas, while Dungavel had a very small and sloping grass airfield, it had remained unused since the outbreak of war. Even when it had been used, it paid host only to light biplanes and some high-wing monoplanes, leaving it unsuitable for a heavy aircraft like Hess's Bf110.

Hess didn't recognise Dungavel or the airfield as he passed overhead and so continued west towards the coast. Pursued by what he thought was a Hurricane (but was in fact a Boulton Paul Defiant from 141 Squadron that had also joined the hunt) and by then running dangerously low on fuel, Hess climbed to 6,000 feet, switched off the Bf110's engines and feathered the propellers.

He was going to bale out and ditch the plane.

Hess tried to clamber from the cockpit but with the aircraft still travelling fast, its slipstream forced him back in.

Remembering just in time that modern aircraft needed to be put on their back in order to bale out, he attempted a half loop instead of a half roll. The manoeuvre, and the centrifugal forces it unleashed, caused Hess to black out.

He came to as the plane stood on its tail, suspended mid-air, almost stalling. He pushed off with his feet, pulled his D-ring cord on his parachute and both plane and pilot were heading for earth.

Five hours after leaving Haunstetten, they both arrived in Scotland.

Only Hess survived the impact.

Hess landed in a meadow a few metres from the front door of Floors Farm, twelve miles west of Dungavel. Its owner helped him to his feet and Hess introduced himself as Hauptmann Alfred Horn, telling the owner he had an important message for the Duke of Hamilton. After an overnight stay at Maryhill Barracks in Glasgow, the next morning Hess finally got his wish, being granted an audience with the Duke of Hamilton, though under armed guard and with the security services listening intently.

It wasn't the reception he had dreamed of, or anticipated, in the many months of planning for his trip.

He told Hamilton that he had come on a mission of humanity, that Hitler didn't want to fight Britain but instead wanted peace. He urged him to get together with members of his party to discuss making peace proposals. Hamilton gave him short, albeit polite shrift, telling the Deputy Führer that if Britain made peace now, the two nations would find themselves back at war with each other within two years.

That night Hamilton met with Churchill. Ironically Churchill's private secretary Jack Colville had been reading a popular fantasy novel about Hitler parachuting into England to make peace – Peter Fleming's *The Flying Visit* – while rumours abounded in intelligence circles that Hitler might be skyjacked in his personal Focke-Wulf FW200 Kondor and flown to an RAF base Kent by his apparently disaffected pilot Hans Bauer.

But the arrival of Hess as an ambassador for the Nazi regime was stranger than fiction.

His appeals to the British government fell on deaf ears, in part because it was clear from the venom of Goebbels' propagandist response to the flight that Hess represented neither Hitler nor his regime, and in part because peace was no longer a viable option.

And despite atoning for the moral guilt of standing near Hitler with what Churchill later described in his memoir *The Grand Alliance* as "his completely devoted and frantic deed of lunatic benevolence", coming of "his own free will and though without authority (having) something of the quality of an envoy", Hess fell victim to the post-war Cold War machinations between east and west.

Machinations that would see him imprisoned for the next, and final, forty-six years of his life.

'Anything interesting in the news?' Rothstein peered over Curtis's shoulder.

Curtis looked up from the newspaper. 'Yesterday's news. Tomorrow's fish and chip paper.' He slid the first pint across to him.

Rothstein caught it in his hand as he perched next to Curtis. 'Not bitter then?'

Curtis smiled back wryly. He folded the newspaper, dropping it into his pocket. 'No draught. Besides, life's too short.'

They chinked glasses before downing the pale ale.

Almost like old times.

*

The war may have been history for the likes of Curtis and Rothstein but it was very much a reality for those around them. As they stepped out of the Marquis of Granby onto the cobbled streets of New Cross, the toll of the Luftwaffe's relentless bombing of London was everywhere.

Rubble from bombed-out houses, obliterating families and their homes in a split second, was strewn across all of the streets. Though the people of London had a resilience never seen before or since, the pain and anguish of this harsh life was etched in all of their faces.

Curtis and Rothstein sidled along the street, coats over shoulders, with the newspaper folded and resting in Curtis's jacket pocket.

'These people had no idea if they'd survive the war,' Curtis mused, 'let alone win it.'

'They really had a tough time, huh.'

'Just be grateful we didn't have to live through all of this shit.'

The rubble replaced playgrounds for many children. A stone's throw from the local church, a brother and his older sister had rested their tired hand-me-down bicycles against the fallen debris to play on the rubble. They looked like a pair of raggedy street urchins, desperately in need of a bath and a good meal.

Behind them, a Bedford MW truck pulled in. Its driver was clearly lost. Leaving the engine running, the driver stepped down from the cab and ran towards an old lady, shaking the dust out of her rugs nearby. He was after directions.

'Angela!' the little boy cried to his sister. 'I've got my foot stuck!'

The little girl shook her head. 'I told you to be more careful Brian!' She was innocently cross but made little effort to help him. He had to learn not to get himself into these scrapes.

The Bedford's engine continued to turn over as the old lady tried in vain to give the driver directions he could remember. The handbrake rattled, vibrating with the revolutions of the six-cylinder inline engine. One revolution too many and the handbrake snapped down to the floor of the cab. The truck was off, beginning an unstoppable acceleration towards the mound of rubble – with Brian atop it.

Curtis barely noticed the truck careering towards them, nor did he pay attention to the driver running down the street behind it, his face a picture of panic and desperation.

'Stop! That's my truck!' he shouted, mistakenly thinking that it had been stolen.

Only then did Curtis look up at the driver's cab and find it empty. The terrible truth that the 2.1-ton moving brick was unmanned dawned on him. As the truck gathered pace, pedestrians dived for cover. He looked across to find Brian still stuck in the rubble. Curtis dropped his coat and sprinted towards Brian, Rothstein following in his wake.

The truck was catching up with him quickly. It was just inches away from Brian when out of nowhere, Curtis's arm snatched him from the top of the rubble.

Within an instant Brian's bike had succumbed to the will of the truck, crushed under its wide tread wheels as it mounted the rubble. All that could stop it was the nearby church railings.

The truck dropped awkwardly to its side and a deathly, stunned silence descended on the street.

Brian lay in Curtis's lap, struggling to catch his breath. Curtis smiled with relief. 'Are you alright son?'

The little boy was hyperventilating. He couldn't quite get his words out. 'My... my... my... my bike's crushed.'

Curtis smiled. 'Don't worry, we'll get you another one.' He sat Brian up and dusted him down. 'What's your name?'

Before the little boy could answer Curtis, his sister bellowed.

'Brian Bowen!' His older sister muscled in on Curtis, embracing Brian with a smothering big sister cuddle. 'I told you to be more careful!'

Brian tried to shrug his sister off. 'Leave me alone Angela, I'm alright!'

Angela was having none of it, checking over every inch of Brian. But as she came fully into view, Curtis's smile evaporated.

Angela dragged Brian away towards her own undamaged bicycle, pulling him behind in her wake like her own little teddy bear. Brian looked back at Curtis, his face saying a thousand "thank yous" before they were around the corner and gone.

Curtis collected himself from the rubble in a daze, Rothstein helping him up.

The truck driver ran over, profusely apologetic and all over Curtis like a rash. 'I'm so sorry!'

Rothstein clipped the truck driver across the ear, flinging him away from Curtis angrily. 'Not as sorry as you would have been if you'd killed the kid.' He turned to find Curtis heading zombie-like back towards the Marquis of Granby.

'Where are you going?' Rothstein called after him.

'Brian Bowen...' Curtis muttered under his breath.

# 7

# NO GOOD DEED

It was a pensive Curtis that sat in the window booth of the Marquis of Granby, observing the carnage of the street scene outside. Emergency crews were hard at work pulling the truck back onto its belly. Like they didn't have enough work to do already.

Rothstein returned from the bar with two tumblers of sherry. 'Sorry, they still haven't changed the...'

Before Rothstein could finish his sentence, Curtis had necked both.

Rothstein smiled. 'You're thirsty. I'll get us another...'

As he stood, Curtis's hand shot across the tabletop to stop him, grasping at his lapel. 'Do you realise who that boy was?'

Rothstein racked his memory. He hadn't really been paying attention as the truck had careered towards them. 'Brrrrr...'

'Brian Bowen,' Curtis finished Rothstein's sentence.

'Right,' Rothstein pretended to remember. 'That was it.'

'And his sister was Angela Bowen.'

'Right.' Rothstein was perplexed as to where this was all going.

'That was my grandmother.'

Curtis released his grip. Rothstein sat in amazement. 'Your GRANDMOTHER? Then the boy was...'

'Meant to die. Uncle Brian died in a freak accident with a truck when he was just five. In May 1941. Gran lived with that guilt for the rest of her life. Apparently she was never the same again.'

Rothstein was dumbstruck. 'That's — that's amazing!'

'How so?' Curtis asked blithely.

'You not only saved a little boy's life today, you saved your UNCLE's life!'

Curtis banged his clenched fist against the table. The two empty tumblers lifted off it momentarily. 'Don't you get it? He was meant to die!'

'Says who? God?'

'I don't believe in God,' Curtis replied dismissively. 'But neither do I believe anyone else should play God either.'

Rothstein slumped in his chair, somewhat incredulous. 'I don't believe this. You've saved your own flesh and blood and you feel BAD about it?'

'We just changed history. Eli expressly told us not to.'

'Or what? The consequences could be disastrous? We're still here, aren't we? Your hand's not disappeared, has it? You've not bagged a date with your mother tonight, have you?'

Curtis sighed. 'I wish you'd take this more seriously...'

An air raid siren averted Curtis and Rothstein coming to blows again. The people on the street abandoned their efforts with the truck, scuttling towards the nearby Underground station entrance. The predominantly septuagenarian clientele of the pub disembarked somewhat slower. If there was a God, Curtis thought, this would be his waiting room.

As they bounded down the concrete steps into the New Cross Underground station, in the distance flak could be seen exploding indiscriminately across London's skyline high above, the capital city's forlorn attempt to stave off the Luftwaffe.

*

For a then predominantly class-based society, the faces of the Londoners huddled on the cold concrete floor of the westbound platform represented the broadest cross-section. The banker, the baker. The soldier, the sailor. The mother, the minister. The seamstress, the sweeper. All of their faces read the same grim yet stoic determination.

But only the rats seemed happy.

Detonating above them, each falling bomb unsettled the dust and the earthworks over their heads. As he sat at the base of the steps away from the crowd, Curtis wondered openly if the station could take a direct hit. He looked anxiously but discretely at his time bracelet. It wasn't exactly a pocket watch, blending into the era. Something the designers at CERN should really think about when, or if, they got back safely.

Still an hour to go before they could leave.

Rothstein winced with the falling bombs. He looked judgmentally across at Curtis.

'You realise we could end all — ALL of this?'

'What are you talking about?' Curtis responded dismissively.

Rothstein leant in, not wanting to be overheard. 'This war cost over eighty million people their lives. Eighty million people like Brian. Millions of families like yours that had to deal with the pain and heartache of losing loved ones.' He looked around, pointing indiscriminately at the crowd. 'I wonder how many of them will have to die before it's all over.'

Curtis looked at their faces. Rothstein was right. Some of them would die. Probably tonight. He turned back to Rothstein. 'There are no winners in war Luke,' he sighed. 'Just death and misery.'

Now Rothstein really was incensed. 'That's easy for you to say – you just saved one of your family from dying.' He beat his chest with his palm. 'My family lost people too, you know. My great-grandfather was a great pilot. One of the best. He did one of the bravest things. But all his bravery got him was a plane crash that nearly killed him and a prison cell that finished the job. And then the world moves on, forgives the vanquished and forgets about people like him. All of this because of Adolf bloody Hitler!'

Rothstein's raised voice was starting to attract the attention of others cowering for their lives.

Curtis leant in. His tone was deadly serious. 'Beware the law of unintended consequences. We weren't meant to fuck about with history.' He put his hand on his friend's. 'The important thing about power is knowing when not to use it.'

*

The bombing had abated. The Londoners gathered their worldly possessions and began to billow out of the Underground station, a routine by now part of everyday life for them.

Curtis placed his hand on his friend's shoulder. 'Come on. Let's go home.'

Rothstein smiled back weakly.

As Curtis made for the steps, Rothstein dropped to ground level, ostensibly to tie his shoe laces. Curtis looked back. Rothstein hollered over the body of people passing between them. 'I'll be right there.'

Curtis nodded and headed for ground level at the vanguard of the group.

Rothstein's smile had subsided. He looked deadly serious. His shoe laces were tightly knotted already. He raised his left trouser leg to reveal a secondary time bracelet, strapped around his ankle, hidden.

Primed, timed and ready.

*

Nothing could have prepared Curtis for the devastation above ground. The Luftwaffe's volley had set London ablaze, decimating the skyline.

The church. Gone.

The old lady's house. Gone.

The Marquis of Granby. Gone, apart from a swinging door to the basement where they first landed.

The sirens of fire trucks echoed along the streets, the crackle of fires punctuated by the wailing of a mother into a father's shoulder as two fire fighters removed their lifeless child from the rubble.

It made Curtis sick to the pit of his stomach.

'We have the power to stop all of this.' Rothstein's mantra echoed in his head. It took all of Curtis's willpower to shut out the thought.

The basement may have survived the firestorm above ground but it was strewn with detritus. Curtis and Rothstein sidestepped the carnage somewhat forlornly. Curtis thought to himself at least this wasn't the future. Unlike the inhabitants of London, at least he knew that things would be different in the future.

That was some small consolation.

They checked their time bracelets. It was almost time to go home.

'You did good today,' Rothstein effused. 'I know you don't believe that but you will, in time --- some day. And when we get back, you should go and see Brian in his nursing home and get him to tell you again about that time with the truck.'

Curtis smiled. As the time bracelets beeped, Rothstein extended his hand.

'I don't know what the future has in store for us James, but it's been a pleasure making history with you.'

'Likewise,' Curtis said somewhat less emphatically, reluctantly shaking Rothstein's hand.

A force field enveloped Rothstein as Curtis removed his hand just in time. Rothstein smiled. 'Welcome to tomorrow.'

Before Curtis could say anything, Rothstein was gone, evaporating into the spring evening along with the blue force field. Curtis checked himself, panicking as he thought he had lost the newspaper. He felt it in his jacket pocket. He exhaled in relief as the blue force field enveloped him.

A beat later, he too was gone.

Welcome to tomorrow indeed.

# 8
# TICKET FOR ONE

The air was damp with a perspiring mist as Curtis arrived back. For the last time. Not that he would have noticed as he threw up his pint of weak wartime pale ale and the sherry. He could never get used to Trans-Animate Displacement. With every journey he felt like he had left a part of himself behind.

Never again.

'Thank God I don't have to that again, Luke.' Curtis looked up but Rothstein was nowhere to be seen.

Only then did he realise.

Where the hell was he?

He should have been stood in the test facility.

Instead Curtis was stood in an alleyway between what looked like Victorian buildings and warehouses. Sodden wooden pallets straddled the thoroughfare.

'Luke?' he called into the darkness. 'Where are you?'

An eerie silence was all that responded to Curtis's plea. Then, out of the darkness came a "ticker ticker". He knew that sound well.

It was the sound of a worn fan belt.

And it was approaching at speed.

The driver clearly wasn't expecting anyone to be stood in his way. It being dark, by the time his headlights trained on Curtis, it was too late to do anything other than brake hard and swerve to avoid. By chance, Curtis dived the opposite direction to the truck, which slammed hard into the wooden pallets, sending thousands of wooden splinters airborne.

Dazed, Curtis picked himself up from the ground and stumbled over to the truck. Steam billowed from underneath its crumpled bonnet. The fan belt was clearly detached, flapping with regularity as the engine spluttered and hissed.

This truck was going nowhere.

As Curtis got to the driver's side of the cab, it was clear that neither was the driver, his head lodged within the steering wheel in a contorted fashion, his jaw pressed against the horn. Curtis knew from the vacant look on the driver's face as he pulled him out of the steering column that the man was dead, his neck broken for certain as his head flopped back.

But that wasn't what shocked him.

That was the Wehrmacht uniform the man was wearing.

Only then did he realise that the truck was left-hand drive and that the number plates were continental-style.

'Great,' Curtis muttered. 'Not only have you left me in 1941 but you've sent me to the wrong fucking country. Fuck you Crombie.'

Before Curtis could check his time bracelet was working, he heard the rapidly advancing march of troops, getting closer with every passing second. His 1941 British identity papers were going to get him put against a brick wall and shot.

He had to hide.

And fast.

Curtis reached ever more frantically for the handles of a succession of locked doors as the clatter of gun metal bouncing against belt buckles grew louder. Finally one of the doors gave way and he was crouching below a window in a cavernous warehouse.

Just in time.

On the other side of the window, an officious gefreiter (Corporal) came to a halt before barking orders at underlings in German. Curtis instantly regretted moving the driver from the steering wheel.

Had he left him, it was perfectly plausible that the driver had crashed and that no one else was involved.

But he had unwittingly removed any seed of doubt that someone else was involved by moving him.

The driver couldn't have done that to himself.

It was only a matter of time before they combed the area and found him.

He surveyed the warehouse from his crouched position. It was deserted, aside for an unmarked canvas truck parked in the middle of it. As he looked at the truck, he realised he was not alone.

There was someone in the driver's cab.

Swirls of cigarette smoke permeated from the ajar window, with the occasional flick of ash. All Curtis could see was the arm of the driver. He wasn't wearing uniform from what he could tell. He could have easily been a civilian. He clearly hadn't seen him enter.

Further reinforcements were arriving outside. The gefreiter was growing increasingly animated. Curtis had to do something and he had to do it fast. With that perilous thought, the truck engine idled as its driver attempted to start it up.

Looking away to flick the end of his cigarette away, he didn't see Curtis clambering silently into the back of his truck.

The floor in the back was uneven, peppered liberally with sacks covered in what seemed to Curtis like a hessian material. As the truck moved off, the contents of the sacks felt like small stones or rubble, jolting against his back and buttocks.

He'd had more comfortable rides.

The truck's tyres screeched against the polished concrete surface of the warehouse as the driver locked his steering wheel hard left, guiding the truck through a narrow open shutter. The route took the truck out into the alleyway directly abutting the thoroughfare where the unfortunate accident had taken place. Through the canvas, Curtis could hear the gefreiter continuing in his earlier perfunctory vein.

As the truck approached a white-walled underground tunnel, bathed in garish orange strip lighting, its suspension caused Curtis to bob about in the back, bruising further against the contents of the hessian sacks.

Curtis decided to take a look at the root cause of his pain. He was horrified to discover that he wasn't lying on a bed of rubble but in fact highly concentrated explosives.

Though Curtis thought he had suppressed his gasp, the driver thought he heard something in the back of the truck, briefly looking over his shoulder before concentrating on the road ahead.

Curtis braced himself as best he could. He eagerly awaited the driver reaching his destination. Only then could he hope to discover his intentions with the bounty in the back of his truck.

The truck left the claustrophobic nondescript tunnel and banked right. Curtis dared not move but thought he could hear sea birds.

Perhaps he was near a seaport and could make his way out of Germany by stowing away on a shipping vessel. If he was on the German coast to the west of Denmark, perhaps he was in Wilhelmshaven or Hamburg. If he was further east, perhaps the old free city of Danzig (or Gdańsk as it later became known as part of post-war Poland). If he was less lucky, he was looking at Königsberg, later to become the Russian enclave of Kaliningrad.

The wind outside whipped the canvas of the truck but it didn't feel Baltic. He reasonably hoped for Wilhelmshaven, the closest of all the likely ports to friendly but occupied Belgium or Holland.

Though it felt like an eternity, moments passed before the truck reached its destination. Curtis looked up to see the metal roller shutters trundling upwards on a rickety track. The truck ambled across the threshold and down the ramp into the basement of what felt like a deep underground car park.

Even surrounded by the canvas, the swift change in temperature as the truck travelled deeper and deeper underground was palpable. Row after row of strip lighting, coupled with the driver taking the sharp corners of the concrete ramps and little spurts of straight runs made Curtis feel queasy.

It would be six further levels below ground before the truck finally reached a standstill in the very basement of this underground labyrinth.

The driver had brought the truck to a stop in the centre of the level. As in the warehouse, his was the only vehicle, this time in the middle of an area of reserved parking bays.

The driver turned the engine off and, after checking the time on his watch, he made himself comfortable. What he was waiting for, Curtis could only guess. Was this a secret rendezvous, a surreptitious handover of arms, a pit stop on a longer journey or a pick-up? Whichever it was, he had to be ready.

The silence of the wait was punctured by the alarm of what sounded like a digital watch. Curtis didn't think to question what a digital watch was doing in wartime Germany.

The driver woke from what must have been a daydream, removing his overcoat and carefully placing it on the passenger seat nearby. He reached forward and opened the glove compartment, withdrawing what looked like a canister before slamming the compartment shut. He calmly got out of the cab, shutting the door behind him.

Curtis could sense the driver making his way around the truck. If he was to open the back, the only advantage he had was surprise.

If he suspected, he was already a dead man.

But the canopy remained draped.

Instead, a hissing sound crept through the thick material. It sounded like the letting down of a tyre or maybe even the use of a spray can. It was followed by the clip-clop of the driver's shoes, ambling away from the truck.

Clunk, click and the driver was safely making his way up through the different levels in an elevator.

Curtis peered through a crack in the canopy before satisfying himself that he was now alone. He realised he probably didn't have much time.

As he dropped out of the back of the truck, he dusted himself down. Even in this subterranean basement he felt a shiver. He was dressed for May.

This didn't feel like May.

Curtis opened the cab. All that was in it was the abandoned overcoat. Not really the fashion he would have chosen but beggars and all that. He put the overcoat on, closed the door and, seeing the elevator was returning to this level – with whom inside, he wondered – he decided to play safe and leave the way he came in.

As he shifted towards the concrete ramp to the higher levels, he didn't see that the driver had spray-painted a word on the side of the truck.

Freiheit.

The German word for "freedom", for "liberty".

It was a long and dizzying trek back up to ground level. Curtis's heart sank when he saw that the only exit from the car park, other than the elevator, was through the now-closed roller shutter. He looked around for an operating switch but none existed.

He pulled at the shutter. It was very heavy. Even if he had the strength to open it, it wouldn't stay open long. He knew he had the strength to pull it so far up but would have to roll underneath it with haste if he was going to make it to the other side in one piece.

Curtis braced himself before pulling it as hard as he could. The metal rivets clattered as the shutter sprung up a metre. Curtis was on his back, rolling underneath the shutter before it could settle back into the metal groove.

He didn't realise his wallet, including his false identity papers, had dropped out of his pocket, remaining on the other side of the roller shutter.

Nor did he see the small, rudimentary CCTV camera above the roller shutter that had captured every moment of his exertions.

But he had other things to worry about on the other side of the roller shutter, as he stepped ashen-faced and perplexed onto the familiar cobbles of London's Leicester Square.

# 9
# WILLKOMMEN

The sense of disorientation as Curtis stepped along the cobbles was all consuming. With every step, he felt like Alice must have arriving in Wonderland.

Of course Alice was dreaming.

He hoped to God – yes God – that he was too.

Every delirious step took him down Memory Lane. Memories flooded back from his childhood, going to watch the Christmas lights being turned on with his father, warmed only by mulled wine and roasted chestnuts in paper cups. Later memories, like the time he took his first girlfriend to that cinema, making out on the back row, paying no attention to the film, only to have his heart swiftly broken soon after when her father disapproved of him, added a bittersweet twang.

But that was a different life.

A different time.

A different place.

Because why would German soldiers be stationed in London?

Why were all street signposts and shop signage in German?

And how could he be stood in Leicester Square right now?

He didn't know where to look first. He had walked out of the underground car park to find himself stood on the south side of the Square. All of the familiar brands that had featured in the Square that he knew were gone.

The cinemas – including the iconic Odeon Leicester Square, the venue of film premieres for time immemorial, with its gargantuan billboard hanging perilously above a glass balcony for the great and the good – were all unbranded kinoplexes. The films showing were all vintage German films.

The American chain restaurants had given way to fare more traditionally associated with German cuisine, with bierhaus, gaststätten and delicatessen peppering every side street corner.

As Curtis stumbled along the old north side heading in the direction of Covent Garden, he found himself stood at the entrance to the Unterbahnhof, a rebranded London Underground that looked more like the Paris Metro or Berlin U-Bahn than the creaking Victorian relic he had grown up with.

Outside the familiar station steps, a street vendor was handing out free copies of a daily newspaper.

It was in German.

Everything on display in the kiosk behind him was in German, all of it free except for a small, still-bundled and untouched English-language edition growing damp on the ground next to him. It appeared that to read the news in English would cost him 20 Reichsmark.

Curtis took a German edition from the vendor. His German was a little rusty, having spent more time at

Whistler and the après ski bars of Val Thorens than the Swiss Alps, but he doubted the vendor would have taken gold sovereigns in payment.

Besides, his grasp of German was ample to comprehend the enormity of the printed page in his hand.

The newspaper was Der Times, a Germanised rebranding of The Times of London.

He walked and read, paying little heed or care to other pedestrians, frequently bumping into them with little if any apology.

The headline for the main story read:

US TALKS PEACE WITH GERMANIA

Breakthrough ahead of State Visit by
US President Barack Obama to Hessburg

Hessburg.

Where was Hessburg, he thought.

It wasn't a placed he had heard of.

Perhaps it was an obscure alpine retreat tucked away in the dense forests of Bavaria or the snow caps of Austria.

He didn't notice that he was reading the Hessburg edition of Der Times.

Other front page articles mused the potential impact for trade and co-operation as the Cold War thawed between Germania and the United States, after almost eighty years of distrust, juxtaposed with the news of twenty-nine dead commuters following a deadly suicide bombing on the Unterbahnhof. The article laid the blame squarely at the door of the Freiheit Movement, with the bombing having all of the hallmarks of previous atrocities committed by the terrorist group.

Curtis struggled to process the information before stopping dead in his tracks at the date of the newspaper.

December 20th 2021.

Or as he knew it: yesterday.

Curtis stumbled in shock towards the centre of Trafalgar Square, each footstep heavier than the last.

The newspaper slipped from his fingers, percolating down to the ground as a crowd brushed him aside, obscuring his view temporarily of perhaps the most unbelievable sight of them all.

In front of him was a sea of placards, held high aloft a troop of hundreds of marching protestors, all chanting in English. It looked like a Campaign for Nuclear Disarmament rally from the Eighties, with the vocally-animated great unwashed pushing the boundaries of peaceful protest to their limits. The placards featured violent expressions of English in all its glory.

GIVE US THE VOTE
RIGHTS FOR ORIGINALS
NO MORE APARTHEID
ENGLISH VOTES FOR ENGLISH PEOPLE
ICH BIN EIN LONDONER

The crowd almost sang its angry chant. 'Give us the vote! Give us the vote! No more apartheid! Give us the vote!'

Constructed between the 1820s and 1840s on the site of the former King's Mews, Trafalgar Square was one of the most iconic landmarks in London, if not the most. With seven major roads converging to drive vehicular traffic around it, it had long been London's beating heart, even more so than nearby Piccadilly Circus (which was akin to a blocked artery) or Parliament Square (allegedly its brain) to its west down Whitehall.

Flanked to its east by the National Gallery and alongside it the church of St. Martin-in-the-Fields, the railway hub of Charing Cross and Embankment stations intersected to its south underneath The Strand, which ran parallel with the river Thames heading eastwards towards the City, London's financial hub.

Political rallies had been commonplace at the Square from the Suffragettes to the anti-war protestors before the Second Gulf War. At Christmas, it was also the traditional home of 20-metre tall Norwegian spruce tree, donated by the people of Oslo every year since 1947 in appreciation of the British war effort.

This Christmas was clearly no different, its five hundred white lights brightening an otherwise dull winter morning.

The Square had always been a public space without any green space. And at its centre stood the main player of the Napoleonic sea victory it sought to commemorate, Admiral Nelson himself.

With a seventeen-foot statue of the great man at its head, Nelson's Column stood one hundred and eighty-five feet above a series of foundations, erected in honour of the controversial First World War admirals John Jellicoe and Richard Beatty. At its base grazed four bronze lions by Sir Edwin Landseer, cast by Baron Marochetti into all four corners.

As Curtis took in this spectacle of modern political activism, he was brushed to one side by a swarm of heavily armed, SS-badged policemen. They adopted flanking positions, swiftly surrounding the protestors from the elevated steps in front of the National Gallery behind Curtis while he meandered into the heart of the Square.

One of the policemen put a loudhailer to his lips. 'This is an illegal march,' he barked impatiently in almost pigeon English, delivered in a thick German accent. 'This is an illegal march! Return to your homes or we will detain you.'

The crowd brushed aside the policeman's no doubt anticipated threats, continuing their chanting. Sweat dripped nervously down his brow, as he raised his loudhailer for one final attempt at peaceful diplomacy.

'This is your last warning! This is an illegal march and we have orders to disperse you!' His tone had hardened. 'I will NOT ask again. This is your LAST chance…'

Curtis was mesmerised by the spectacle as he found himself at the foot of Nelson's Column itself.

Then he checked himself. Something felt different about it. The column itself was eerily familiar but at its top no longer stood the great man himself but a bronze cast of a very different kind.

He squinted at the cast, trying in vain to make it out.

Was that an Eagle?

As Curtis's gaze rested on the column itself, his eyes settled to find an engraved bilingual sign.

A sign that began to explain everything.

HESS SQUARE

In memory of the war hero Rudolf Hess
first Deputy Führer of Germania
April 26th 1893 – May 28th 1941

Martyred in the Tower of Hessburg before
the Liberation of London (now Hessburg)
Ich hab's gewagt – I have dared

Hessburg…

London was now Hessburg?

Curtis shuddered.

The only explanation: the Nazis won the Second World War.

And London, England, Britain was now occupied by them.

*

Six storeys beneath Curtis, the stationary truck sat in a calm and tranquil peace compared to the thronging rally above ground.

A peace that was shattered as the high explosives Curtis had lay precariously on suddenly detonated in a catastrophic eruption of fire and flame.

*

In his feet, Curtis was convinced he could feel an earthquake heading rapidly for the surface.

He looked all around him, at the shaking buildings flanking the Square, the panicked faces on the protestors, the falling masonry narrowly avoiding the already agitated SS policemen.

The rumbling built to an inevitable and deafening climax. The National Gallery disintegrated in a ball of fire and stone, a million shards of glass in flight hurtling alongside them without discriminating between protestor and policemen.

It was an anarchic bloodbath, the trampled protestors and their placards either ripped apart by a hail of razors or mowed down by angry policemen in vicarious retaliation for the monstrous explosion.

Protestors fell at a rate of knots as a hail of bullets flew from Luger and sedentary machine-gun alike. Curtis braved his own arm, hitherto covering his eyes, to find an SS policeman about to shoot a heavily pregnant protestor at point-blank range. His instinct kicked in.

Curtis's fist connected with the policeman's jaw, hurtling him to the ground and his Luger into the air. As Curtis caught the gun, he looked up at the stunned protestor. Her relieved smile said it all.

It was only a temporary relief for both of them.

The haft of a gun knocked Curtis face first into the water of the nearby fountain.

His eyes slowly closed, his passing out and the water shielding him from the horrors being inflicted upon the remaining protestors just feet away.

# 10
# THE WHITE TOWER

For almost a thousand years the White Tower had cut a foreboding silhouette on the northern bank of the river Thames.

Soon after his conquest of England in 1066, the new Norman King William the Conqueror had begun erecting fortifications within London's old Roman city walls in order to dominate its indigenous merchant community. It allowed the new regime to control access to the Upper Pool of London, the city's main port until the construction of docks further east during the Industrial Revolution seven centuries later.

Visible from across London, it had but one purpose: control through fear.

Ultimately covering seven hectares, at its heart was its central keep – the White Tower – around which pivoted inner and outer concentric defences or curtains.

Started in 1078, the White Tower was cast from the Caen limestone of the invaders' Normandy homeland. The inner curtain consisted of no less than thirteen towers, among the most notable the Bloody Tower, the Beauchamp Tower and the Wakefield Tower.

The outer curtain was surrounded by a moat, making the fortress accessible only by a single entrance at its south-western boundary and the eponymously named Traitors' Gate, a mooring dating back to the 13th Century from which condemned men, women and sometimes children were ceremoniously brought to face their uncertain future.

So was born the Tower of London.

During its thousand year reign over London, it had served as everything from a royal palace and arsenal to a mint, even a menagerie, but it was perhaps most notorious for being a political prison and place of many an execution.

Much blood had been spilt at the Tower over the centuries, with the highest political crimes punished with torture within its walls before an ignominious and often grisly end in front of the baying hordes on nearby Tower Green. It was widely believed to be the last resting place of the teenage King Edward V and his younger brother George, murdered in the turmoil of the Wars of the Roses that precipitated the fall of the House of Lancaster in 1485.

Anne Boleyn, the oft-maligned second wife of Henry VIII, met her maker there along with the so-called "Nine Day Queen", Lady Jane Grey, after Henry met his. Other "guests" had included Gunpowder plot figurehead Guy Fawkes, whose head had joined those of his fellow conspirators on spikes at the perimeter to deter other Catholics from challenging England's fledgling Protestant settlement.

Even Elizabeth I had been imprisoned there briefly by her elder half-sister Mary I (not known as Bloody Mary for nothing) before resting the crown jewels on her own head after her death soon after.

Considering the elaborate tortures conducted at the Tower over the years by successive regimes, there could be no better home in London for the Gestapo.

James Curtis was in illustrious company as the Gestapo officer thrust his head underwater for the seventeenth time. From under the water, his face must have been the picture of numbed relief from the horrors above the surface. For someone in the right frame of mind, it would not be hard to submit to the channels of water coursing into their lungs, to an end to their life almost on their own terms.

But the Gestapo were well-trained and highly experienced torturers. They never let things go that far. That would remove their power over their victim. They would only release them from their agonies once every morsel of useful information had been gleaned. Only then would the broken and humiliated be eliminated.

Curtis had yet to say anything noteworthy.

After all, he probably had more questions than they did.

Which meant this was only the beginning.

Almost drowned, his sodden future carcass was removed from its potential watery grave with exquisite timing, to be met with yet another punch from his jailers. His bound body met the hard floor, his jaw cracking upon impact while he coughed up what was left of his lungs.

A bespectacled man approached. He was not like the others. He was clearly a medical man, an SS-Surgeon, whose curious role was to keep the victim alive as long as possible in order to prolong the torture, maximising the potential for obtaining information.

More hypocritical than Hippocratic Oath.

Curtis was being kept alive to die later, when convenient to his jailers. His experience at the hands of the FSB in Moscow just a few days earlier felt like a weekend mini-break at a country spa in view of what lay ahead.

The SS-Surgeon ran a rudimentary scanning device over Curtis's weakened body. It purred with an electronic heartbeat all of its own, with a display oscillating in anticipation of a signal that never came.

'He has no implant,' the SS-Surgeon announced to the room. 'He must have removed it, Herr Obergruppenführer.'

Over the SS-Surgeon's shoulder stood SS-Obergruppenführer Dietrich Hauser.

Deputy Head of the Gestapo, Hessburg Division.

And a thoroughbred bastard.

Hauser's Aryan credentials were clear even to Curtis's bloodied eyes. In his early thirties, with short-cropped blonde hair and sparkling blue eyes peering out from a chiselled face, his body was clearly a temple filling his immaculate SS uniform.

Originally produced by the Hugo Boss company in the mid-1920s, the uniform had changed remarkably little over the course of a century. Brown shirt with black leather buttons, black tie and black breeches. Black jackboots, polished naturally. Black tunic with four silver buttons, three parallel silvered threads on the shoulder tabs. On his left sleeve rested a red-white-and-black swastika armband while on his right a diamond, enclosing the gothic letter 'H' for Hessburg. On his black belt sat a holstered 9mm Luger, his service pistol. Nearby sat his black cap, with silver death's head and Party eagle, atop his black leather jacket.

For a solid block of a man, Hauser glided towards Curtis more like a ballet dancer than an SS officer.

His voice, when he finally spoke, was flat and functional, betraying no emotion. 'Why would a law-abiding citizen remove their identity implant?'

Curtis said nothing as he slumped back into the chair, hands bounds tightly behind his back with blood-stained rope. He wondered if they had the same supplier as the FSB.

Hauser glared at him with those piercing blue eyes. 'Do you know where you are?'

Almost on cue, Curtis heard a cacophony of screams – male and female – echoing down the corridor from elsewhere in the Tower. Curtis wondered if it might be a recording, designed to intimidate the prey of the SS, but given their predisposition to violence he doubted they would go to the effort or expense with life coming so cheap.

Unaffected and nonplussed, Hauser nonchalantly chewed off the corner of a ratty nail, admiring his otherwise immaculate hands almost like a woman after an expensive manicure.

Curtis spat out the blood that had formed in his mouth, it landing close to Hauser's gleaming polished boots. 'If you're Mickey Mouse, does that mean I'm in Disneyland?' he retorted.

Hauser broke eye contact with Curtis, instead slowly arcing around him like a predator playing with his food. 'You are in the very Tower that your own King Richard is widely believed to have murdered his own nephews so he could steal the English crown.'

Curtis smiled to himself. 'He must be something of a role model for you.'

Hauser stopped. 'Indeed.' He sat on the stool beside Curtis, moving in uncomfortably close to his ear. 'You and

I are not related.' Hauser's bland tone all of sudden became menacing. 'So imagine what I am going to do to you before your next witticism.'

He had a point.

'Who are you?' Hauser barked, slipping effortlessly into bad cop mode. 'Who are you working for? What have you done with your identity implant? And what were you doing in Hess Square today?'

It didn't matter what Curtis said. There was no way that this fully-fledged organ of the Nazi state was going to believe him. 'I'm not saying anything until I get my lawyer and my phone call.'

Hauser leant in. 'How are you expecting to talk to someone when I've broken your jaw?'

Curtis didn't doubt that he meant it. It wasn't far off already.

'You are a suspected terrorist, clearly a member of the Freiheit Movement who was seen walking away from the Reichsgalleria in Hess Square just moments before it was destroyed in a bomb attack this morning. You're lucky to still be alive. By rights, you should have been shot on the spot.'

Curtis turned to Hauser, looking him directly in the eye. He could almost taste what the man had for breakfast. The corners of his lips upturned. 'Well why don't you do us all a big fucking favour and give the people what they want?'

Hauser smiled and nodded to himself as he stepped away. The two Gestapo officers went to town on Curtis again.

It was going to be a long night.

*

Behind the one-way glass watching the ensuing panel-beating was Nikolas Hiltz.

As Gauleiter of Hessburg, Hiltz governed all of the territory formerly known as London as well as the Home Counties.

Cutting a dash, Hiltz had clearly been a handsome man in his youth, though by now in his fifties his face was weatherworn. Scars on his temple and cheek were distinguishing features, standing testament to battles won – and lost.

As the punches rained down on Curtis, Hiltz recoiled. He did not approve of the brutal methods of the Gestapo nor the SS, of which like all senior administration officials he was nominally a member. But his was a lone voice within the administration. Yet for all of his reticence and distaste for such violence, he could not fault the effectiveness of it in keeping a fractious society in check. The fear of even a short stay at the Tower had prevailed over the residents of the city since Norman times for a reason. That fear remained to this day.

Yet this man, this Curtis, had no fear. Something about him felt very alien and unnerving for Hiltz. He studied Curtis's effects, laid out neatly on a nearby table. His overcoat was of little note, but the other items were as fascinating as they were disturbing. The bracelet was technology he had never seen before. Hiltz wondered if it was American perhaps. It certainly wasn't from the Reich. The ancient newspaper from the long-outlawed Daily Express looked like it was bought just yesterday, even though it was dated eighty years ago. And the gold sovereigns, dating back to an interwar mint, were equally puzzling.

These were museum pieces surely, from an American museum perhaps.

But why would a man in Hessburg, without an implant, be holding them in his possession?

He picked up the newspaper, feeling the unique texture of the printed paper between his thumb and fingers.

The door flung open, followed shortly by the arrival of a gefreiter entering a few feet into the room before immediately turning ninety degrees on his heel.

An adjutant ready to salute his approaching liege.

With red rosy cheeks, stained from his love of French wine, adorning a white portly face, Reichskommissar Erich von Braun was the poster-boy for fine living. His excess midriff baggage, accumulated over all of his sixty-five years, almost entered the room before he did. His ornate cane, ostensibly a walking aid following repeated bouts of gout, rested under his right arm in true Nazi fashion.

Hiltz saluted. 'Herr Reichskommissar. I wasn't expecting you. An unexpected pleasure.' A lie.

The Reichskommissar shuffled in past his sycophantic adjutant, the door closing with him on the other side of it. Von Braun waved Hiltz at ease before pointing at the mirrored glass with his cane. 'What is going on here?'

'We are interrogating a suspect we captured at the Hess Square demonstration,' Hiltz explained.

'I gave explicit instructions,' Von Braun fumed, 'that all those in custody after the rally were to be executed immediately for their part in this despicable act of terrorism, inflicted on the innocent German settlers of Hessburg, as a deterrent to any others foolish enough to want to follow in their footsteps.'

'Those executions have been carried out, Herr Reichskommissar,' Hiltz defended himself, 'as all of the other suspects were easily identifiable. However, this man's identity implant was missing. Possibly not even there in the first place. And his effects were, well, unusual to say the very least.'

Von Braun brushed his cane over Curtis's effects, half-interested at best.

'We felt they merited further examination.' Hiltz should have kept silent.

'We?' von Braun barked. Even though Hiltz was the second most powerful person in the Reichskommissariat Groβbritannien, von Braun was the first. The only thing worse that taking sole ownership of a controversial decision was lying to him.

'I felt they merited further examination.'

Von Braun remained put out. He swung his cane underneath his arm as he prepared to leave. He turned back to Hiltz. 'Fine. But if he is still breathing at dawn, Hessburg will be looking for a new Gauleiter and you'll either be in a KZ or digging an extra hole in the woods for yourself.'

Von Braun stormed out, followed dutifully by his adjutant down the corridor.

Hiltz had no desire to find himself in one of the KZ – konzentrationslager, the camps – or in the woods on this miserable island far from home.

But Curtis's effects made no sense.

*

Round three was over. Hauser and the two Gestapo officers stepped out of the room for a well-earned rest. Curtis didn't know how many rounds lay ahead with these aggression monkeys but he knew they would get their money's worth from him.

So much for German efficiency.

He slumped in the chair, an oasis of tranquillity in the heart of the room.

The SS-Surgeon approached him with a medical kit. It wasn't for a tetanus shot. Any hope of it being something for the pain was short-lived as the SS-Surgeon rolled out the kit to reveal vials of serum, accompanied by an old-fashioned metal syringe and needle. Through his remaining good eye, Curtis saw him douse the needle with alcohol before drawing fluid into the syringe from one of the vials. The SS-Surgeon flicked the needle with his finger, drawing a sprinkle of the fluid, before plunging the needle into Curtis's left arm. Curtis barely flinched as it was being administered. What was one prick in the arm compared to the rain of fists and jackboots inflicted on him just moments earlier.

A strange sensation enveloped him. Curtis had taken his fair share of recreational drugs in his time but this was a new one even for him. As Hiltz stepped into the room, he realised the changing of the guard signified a change of tack. At least for the time being.

Hiltz smiled at him disarmingly. Good cop, Curtis thought.

'Good evening.' Hiltz spoke English perfectly, better even than his guest.

Curtis looked up at Hiltz with his better eye. 'Let me guess – a truth serum?' he croaked, his mouth parched dry.

'Soap, yes. Quite effective.' Hiltz nodded to SS-Surgeon who placed a straw into Curtis's mouth from which he supped from a bottle of lukewarm water. It could have been urine for all Curtis cared. It probably was. But the bottle was empty in seconds.

'And better for the conscience than the rack or the thumbscrews.' Curtis knew his man. 'Pity it doesn't numb the pain.'

'Well, before I can do anything about that, you need to give me something.'

The SS-Surgeon looked at his watch before nodding to Hiltz. It was time for test questions to confirm that the soap – sodium pentothal – was working.

'I am Gauleiter Hiltz,' he volunteered. 'What is your name?'

Curtis was getting drowsier. 'James Aaron Curtis.'

'When were you born?'

'October 7th 1984.'

Even though the session was being recorded on the other side of the mirrored glass, the SS-Surgeon took contemporaneous notes.

'Where were you born?' Hiltz continued.

'Here – London. Beckenham.'

Curtis's answers were direct and delivered matter-of-factly, as they would have expected. Nonetheless, Hiltz and the nearby SS-Surgeon exchanged curious glances.

'What did you do today?' Hiltz continued with his open questioning.

'I travelled from Geneva to London.'

'Was that by aeroplane?'

'Trans-Animate Displacement.'

The SS-Surgeon looked up from his notebook.

'By what?' Hiltz asked, not having understood him.

'Trans-Animate Displacement. I travelled through time from Geneva in the year 2021 to London in May 1941 before coming back to London in the year 2021.'

Hiltz and the SS-Surgeon looked at each other with inscrutably serious faces before erupting into fits of laughter.

'Are you sure you've given him sodium pentothal, Doctor?' Hiltz asked jokingly. The SS-Surgeon nodded reassuringly while Curtis stared blankly into space, unaffected by their mockery. Hiltz turned back to Curtis. 'What was the purpose of your visit? A little bit of Christmas shopping?'

Curtis's lucid answers continued. 'No, I was part of a time travel experiment run out of CERN in Geneva, Switzerland by Dr Ida Schildberg, Dr Gideon Eli and Colonel Arnold Crombie of NATO. It was the first human trial of their Trans-Animate Displacement process.'

Hiltz beamed, suppressing further laughter as he reminded himself that the session was being recorded. 'I would say it was a success. This NATO --- does it have anything to do with the Freiheit Movement?'

'I do not know what that is.'

Hiltz was concerned. Everyone knew about the Freiheit Movement, whether they were a member of it or not.

'What is this NATO?' he continued.

'North Atlantic Treaty Organisation.' Curtis sounded increasingly like an automaton, as the soap laid siege. 'Set up in 1948 by the US, Great Britain and others after the Second World War to keep the peace during the Cold War.'

'You mean the Cold War with the Americans?'

Curtis nodded.

'So you work for the Americans?'

'No, I work for Colonel Arnold Crombie of British Intelligence. Britain is part of NATO.'

By now, Hiltz was convinced that Curtis was certifiable. But for the benefit of the tape, and his own amusement, he continued the interrogation. He pulled the time bracelet from his pocket, gently manhandling it.

'And this --- what is this, a watch of some kind?

Curtis looked at it. 'That is my time bracelet.'

'And you used it to travel through time?' Hiltz's eyebrow rose involuntarily. 'How does it work?'

Curtis's eyes remained transfixed on the centre of the mirror. 'I don't fully understand. You'd have to ask Dr Schildberg about that.'

'Oh I will, I will,' Hiltz pondered. 'Where do you think you are?'

'I'm in the Tower of London.'

The SS-Surgeon screwed the top back on his fountain pen, placing the pen atop the notepad. His notes were done.

'The Tower hasn't been called that for nearly eighty years, Mr Curtis,' Hiltz frowned. 'It was renamed the Tower of Hessburg after the Deputy Führer Rudolf Hess, who sadly died here in the final days of the war. London was renamed Hessburg too, in his honour.' Hiltz left it a moment. 'But you know all of that really, don't you?'

The effectiveness of the soap was beginning to wane. Curtis wondered if his tolerance of drugs was higher as a result of his misspent youth. His strident, diffident streak was returning.

'That's incorrect, Herr Hiltz. Rudolf Hess was tried at the International War Crimes Tribunal in Nürnberg in 1946 along with Göring, Rosenberg, Speer and many others.

By then, Hitler, Goebbels, Himmler, Bormann – all had committed suicide. Due to his limited role, the court let Hess live but sentenced almost everyone else to death.'

'That's a fascinating story.' Hiltz was being characteristically understated. 'Tell me Mr Curtis, is Dr Schildberg the name of your psychiatrist?'

'I don't have a psychiatrist.'

Hiltz smiled. 'Well, perhaps Dr Hock here can recommend one. There we all were, thinking you were a terrorist or an American spy but it's quite clear that you're neither. You're merely a lunatic and we need to find out which asylum you've escaped from. Perhaps this Dr Schildberg can help.'

Hiltz turned to leave.

'If you don't believe me,' Curtis called after him, 'just Google it.'

Hiltz turned back. 'Googlewhat?'

'Google it.'

'What is this Google-it?'

Curtis looked at him quizzically. 'You have the internet here, right?'

'No, what is that – a secret network?'

Curtis's mind was reasserting its authority. 'Get with the times Herr...'

'Hiltz.'

'Hiltz', Curtis repeated.

Hiltz interest was piqued once more. 'You mentioned some names just then. All of them were famous patriots from the war, but one of them I didn't recognise. Was it — Hiller?'

'Hiller? You mean Hitler!' It was Curtis's time to laugh. 'I've never met a German who hadn't heard of Hitler before, Herr Hiltz!'

'Who is this Hitler?' Hiltz asked.

It was Curtis's time to smile. 'I think it's you who needs the psychiatrist, Herr Hiltz!'

Before Hiltz could counter him, Hauser re-entered the room with more Gestapo officers than he had left with. In his hands: a document and a see-through exhibit bag. He quickly dispensed with the salute that Hiltz's rank warranted, thrusting the document into his hand.

'Herr Gauleiter, I have an execution warrant for the prisoner from the Reichskommissar to be carried out immediately.'

Hiltz laughed as he got up. 'No no,' he waved his hand, 'this prisoner isn't who we think he is.'

Hauser handed him the exhibit bag. Inside it: Curtis's wallet and driving licence given to him by Dr Eli at CERN. It had fallen out of his pocket as he had left the car park at the Reichsgalleria. Hiltz scanned the items. The photograph was clearly of Curtis but the name on the driving licence read John Walker.

Hiltz looked up at Curtis. 'You told me your name was James Curtis – you lied to me.'

Curtis looked up at Hiltz. 'No, I told you the truth. You gave me a truth drug, remember?'

Hiltz thrust the exhibit bag into Curtis's lap. 'Well who is this John Walker then?'

Curtis looked down at the bag and then back at Hiltz. 'It's a false identity given to me by Dr Eli. for time travel purposes.'

Hauser clicked his fingers to the other Gestapo officers who stepped forward to scoop Curtis from the chair and drag him down the corridor. Curtis was still delirious from his dalliance with soap, remaining calm and blissfully unfazed despite their clearly malign intentions towards him.

'No,' Hiltz lunged forward, protesting. 'This man is required for further questioning.'

Hauser stepped between Hiltz and the quickly departing Curtis. 'I have my orders.'

*

It was dusk by the time Curtis emerged blindfolded from the White Tower into the centre of the inner ward. Filing past the remains of Coldharbour Gate, six Gestapo officers escorted him down the five long steps towards the Bloody Tower and beyond it St. Thomas's Tower and Traitor's Gate. Many a condemned man and woman had passed the other way through Traitor's Gate but Curtis's destiny lay many miles upstream to the west, away from prying eyes.

From a window high above in the nearby Wakefield Tower, Hiltz watched with a sense of resignation.

He knew the inevitability of Curtis's death, the unmarked grave, the unanswered questions, as he was manhandled into one of two unmarked military boats.

Or was it John Walker?

Hiltz thought he would never know.

# 11
# ROAD TO NOWHERE

The boat buffeted as the strong Thames current ran against it.

With his eyes blindfolded and his arms tightly bound, Curtis felt helpless as he did all he could to brace himself through his rigid legs.

He needn't have worried.

Sandwiched between Gestapo officers, he wasn't going anywhere.

With his vision obscured and his body still coming down from the SS-Surgeon's dose of soap, Curtis could not overly rely on his senses. But the agrarian-infused air implied that the boat had headed west and inland rather than east towards the Thames Estuary or the northern Kent marshlands.

Other quiet places to die.

He had no way of knowing for sure as the boat finally docked and he was manhandled like a lamb to the slaughter along the jetty, his dragged feet catching each of the uneven wooden boards.

He wondered how many had suffered this ignominious fate before him.

And how many would follow in his wake.

It has often been said that the dead are the lucky ones.

In this world, that was an inescapable truth.

But as he rode alongside his own firing squad, in the back of a drafty canvas-backed truck along an ill-kept single track road, it was the thought of meeting his maker without knowing how any of this had happened that terrified him the most.

It was obviously a result of the time travel experiment. He had warned them that history was tampered with at all of their peril.

He hated being right.

Perhaps Luka and he were not the only guinea pigs in Dr Schildberg's experiment.

Perhaps something went wrong on their return journey from 1941 and they sent others in their place.

Perhaps Crombie gave them orders to meddle, setting off a ripple effect through the history that they all knew.

The law of unintended consequences reigned supreme in this world as much as his own.

Two outriders led the canvas truck through the dense forest toward a remote killing field far away from Hessburg.

Dimly lit by the moonlight, an eerie calm descended, punctuated only by the occasional cricket.

*

High above, obscured by the trees, a camouflaged hand raised a set of night-vision binoculars to unknown eyes, watching the convoy closely. Another hand reached for a CB radio.

*

Hauser sat opposite Curtis, both men with a side to the back of the cab. The SS-Obergruppenführer, flanked by Gestapo officers, snarled at his prey.

'Rebel scum,' Hauser barked. 'The Gauleiter may have swallowed your lies but I know you were a Freiheiter.'

'A what?'

Hauser spat at Curtis a full throat of phlegm. Curtis instinctively recoiled.

'I've told you, I know nothing about these Freiheiters. You're just making this all up!'

'Tell that to your St. Peter.' Hauser smacked Curtis across the face with the butt of his Luger. Coupled with the potholes on the dust track, Curtis lost his footing, crashing with indignity to the floor.

Hauser smiled sadistically.

This kill was his.

'By the time I'm finished, you'll be begging me to shoot you.'

Hauser unsheathed a knife embossed with the iconic SS logo, clearly a prized gift from a loved one or colleague. Curtis heard the blade travel along the leather pocket. He wasn't going to make it to the woods. This German had a bloodlust that could only be satisfied with his personal responsibility for this execution.

Before Hauser could slit Curtis's throat, a flurry of bullets penetrated the canvas and engulfed the truck, ripping Hauser and the other Gestapo officers apart. They almost danced their own death ritual, limbs and torso gyrating to the pierce of each bullet not unlike an accelerated epileptic fit, landing one by one on top of Curtis and each other.

Curtis knew from the screams followed by the silence that something unexpectedly terrible had happened just in time.

Hauser was dead, his stunned face landing millimetres from Curtis on the floor, his piercing stare no more.

All of the occupants of the truck were already dead by the time it swerved off the single-track road, crashing into a tree.

*

The assailants, dressed in black from head to toe with only their eyes visible underneath balaclavas, stepped gingerly over the felled corpses of the outriders, contorted astride their mounts. They were unquestionably dead but they took no chances.

The squelch of blade puncturing flesh had an air of finality about it.

They approached the crashed truck with caution. Steam buzzed from its cracked radiator. For safety, one of the assailants rained a further shower of bullets from his sub-automatic.

The canopy of the truck was peeled back to reveal the contorted death pose of the Gestapo officers, piled atop each other.

One by one they were pulled from the truck, their corpses scavenged for jewellery and other valuables as much as for weaponry and ammunition.

Hauser's face – or what is left of it – looked like it had been mauled by rats.

As the SS-Obergruppenführer's corpse was dragged ignominiously from the truck by a foot, Curtis's body – lying face down abutting the floor – was finally revealed.

'Quiet!' The assailant threw his free hand up.

The assailants came to an abrupt, deathly silent halt. Very faintly, but audibly, Curtis could be heard breathing shallowly. The eyes of the assailants converged as they manhandled his binds.

# 12
# THE FREIHEIT MOVEMENT

Sweat beads rolled down Curtis's face. His skin glistened, golden with the noxious combination of bruising, blood, grime and perspiration. His breathing oscillated between calm and bursts of heavy panicked breathing bordering on hyperventilation.

He was coming down from the soap.

It had always been a crude way of extracting information from suspects, but with life-changing side effects. Victims often suffered bouts of paranoia and delusion – those that survived, of course.

Curtis woke in a state of delirium. He was still blindfolded, still restrained though no longer bound. To his mind, the world beyond was ablaze, white light achingly desperate to creep into the dark edges of his blindfold.

His body involuntarily tried to sit bolt upright, the shackles holding him down restraining him as he pulled at them, flailing in failure.

And then came the soothing voice.

Another doctor.

Another syringe.

Another injection.

'Rest my son,' the voice reassured as the syringe was depressed. 'Rest... rest... res...'

*

By the time Curtis woke again he had expelled the soap from his system. His delirious dreaming, nightmaring even, was over. Though the blindfold was gone, he was still restrained. His eyes adjusted to the lack of natural light slowly. He found himself in what he assumed to be a prison cell, with its arched ceiling, metal door with observation flap and removable fire hole, and hastily painted brick wall surfaces. The bed, a metal-framed bunk, had seen better days, creaking with his every move.

Curtis stopped dead still when he saw the man slumped in the corner, clearly in a moment of snatched slumber. Armed with a sub-automatic in his lap, this well built man was distinctive if for no other reason than he was black. He was the first black person to have crossed Curtis's path since his arrival in this curious world.

Curtis tried to get his attention. 'Hey fella, does the room come with breakfast?'

There was no reply from the man.

Thinking for a moment, Curtis asked the question again in German.

Still there was no reply.

Instead a voice came from the now open doorway. 'He's not being rude.'

Curtis looked up to see two men stood, motionless, observing: a tall, groomed Caucasian man and an even taller, balding black man carrying a doctor's case.

The soothing voice, he thought.

The white man stepped into the room, placing his hand on the sleeping black guard's shoulder. He didn't flinch.

'When the Germans cut out his tongue,' the white man continued, 'they deprived him of the power of speech.'

Curtis frowned. 'You're not Germans?'

The white man and the black doctor looked at each other before laughing raucously. The white man waved his hand across the eye line of the black guard. Far from being asleep, he was just resting. The black guard stood up, revealing an artificial right arm. Without warning, a blade – mildly stained in a misty blood red – protruded from the artificial limb. Curtis's heart skipped a beat and continued to flutter as the black guard edged towards him, gun in one hand, knife being the other.

Before Curtis could protest, the black guard had used the knife to cut him loose from his restraints. His wrists had chafed from the thrashing during his comedown. As he gently rubbed them, he was visibly relieved. 'Thanks.'

The black guard looked at him and nodded ambivalently before sitting back down in the corner and dozing off, his blade safely retracted. The doctor sat on the bed next to Curtis, placing his medical bag alongside him. He opened the bag to remove a small rectangular metal container. As he popped open the lid, Curtis peered over to see a syringe, a needle, alcohol swabs and a number of vials.

The doctor decanted one of the vials into the syringe. Curtis looked on with further trepidation. 'I've had enough pricks for one day, thanks very much.'

The doctor smiled, carrying on preparing the dose regardless. 'You came to us with plenty of open wounds and old bindings. Lots of diseases uptown.'

Curtis reluctantly acquiesced. The doctor made quick work of injecting him with an unknown serum, swabbing the entry point before packing his case and stepping away.

Curtis licked his thumb before running the mildly antiseptic saliva across the entry point. He looked at the white man, the black guard and the doctor.

There was only one plausible conclusion.

'The Freiheit Movement?'

The white man smiled. 'What about them?'

'I'm guessing you are them or I'd be dead already.'

The white man pulled up a stool, sitting on it with poise.

'I'm Rufus,' he volunteered, ignoring Curtis's previous rhetorical question. 'Your doctor today was Kennedy. And this is Skunk, my right-hand man,' indicating the dozing black guard sat over his shoulder.

Curtis smiled. 'No pun intended I'm sure.' Nobody else got the joke.

Rufus had one of those inscrutable, unreadable faces. Despite his soft voice and charming manner, Curtis knew a ruthless man when he met him.

'Who are you?' Rufus asked flatly. 'I would have scanned your identity implant – but we both know you haven't got one.' His gaze sharpened. 'Which is curious in itself. But even more importantly, we need to know where you're from and what exactly you did to warrant the wrath of the Gestapo.'

Curtis was almost embarrassed to respond. 'I'm not sure you'd believe me even if I tried to explain.'

'Try,' Rufus replied coldly.

Curtis took a deep breath, letting his next four crucial words pass his lips as he exhaled.

'I'm a time traveller.'

Rufus clearly hadn't expected that one, bursting into laughter. Even Skunk, in his own world in the corner, managed an upturned corner of his lip.

'Original response,' Curtis groaned.

Rufus tried to suppress his amusement, pinching the bridge of his eyes to dissipate the welling of tears. 'If you're a time traveller, why on earth of all of the possible times and places in history open to you did you pick this God-forsaken time and place?'

'It picked me,' Curtis replied. 'This is the time and the place that I'm from.'

His new friends clearly didn't understand.

'I was part of a military experiment,' he continued as the others listened in silence. 'I was sent back in time to May 1941 to collect proof that the technology worked. But instead of bringing me back to my time, something went wrong – seriously fucking wrong – and I've ended up in the right time but in a London full of fucking Nazis.'

Rufus gave little away as he absorbed Curtis's story. 'Are you saying there are no Germans in Britain in your time?' he asked. The inquisitive tone was that of an incredulous, disbelieving police officer trying to sound fair and open-minded for the benefit of the tape, despite having already made up his mind.

'Yeah as tourists, sunbed hoggers, Premiership footballers even. But not in battle fatigues gunning down protestors in Trafalgar fucking Square!' Even Curtis struggled to believe what was going on around him. 'We didn't win the war for nothing, you know!'

'Win the war?' Rufus's eyes darted between the others before returning to Curtis. 'You call Hessburg by its pre-war name – London. Why is that?'

Curtis was frustrated. 'Because that's what it's called. London! LONDON! The greatest city in the world!'

Rufus looked at Curtis. His face, so serious and impassive hitherto, had the same air of disbelief as the current occupants of the White Tower.

'Kennedy, what have you shot this guy up with? He thinks we won the war.'

Curtis was frustrated but not surprised. He did say they wouldn't believe him.

A messenger, Goth-like and eager with nose piercings, facial hair and body paint galore, arrived at the doorway. He coughed.

Rufus stood. 'Come. It's time to meet Billie.'

Curtis wondered whether he had any mates already but, given the humourless exchanges already, thought better of vocalising. With even Skunk rising to his feet, he realised he wasn't an optional extra.

He was going to meet this Billie, whoever he was.

*

Every joint, every muscle of his body ached as he dragged his battered frame from the indented gym mat of a mattress, the full weight of his body resting on his feet for the first time in what felt like days.

As he ducked under the low rectangular doorframe emerging into a long, somewhat claustrophobic corridor, his nostrils filled with the familiar mustiness of damp. By the lack of windows, the low ceilings and the economic use of space, he was confident that the building was at least partially underground.

There was something peculiar about the feel of this building. Though he had travelled between 1941 and 2021 in the past few days, the décor and ambience smacked of the former. At first, he thought that his senses were displaced, unsettled by his fourth dimensional journey and his involuntary drug use. Then he thought that perhaps the retro décor was deliberate and stylistic.

But the deeper into the rabbit warren he ventured, the more it felt like he was walking through a museum, a place of historical significance.

As he stepped past the guards into the control room, he realised how close to the truth that was.

The control room was a hubbub of peripheral activity, though it was not immediately clear what was being controlled. Low-tech computer systems, primitive yet incongruous in the most part with their surroundings, were manned by an array of youthful computer operators. Among them were black people, Asian people, ginger people. The contrast between the cosmopolitan make-up of these people – whoever they were – and the Aryan residents of modern-day Hessburg could not have been starker.

A radio operator, wearing rudimentary headphones, monitored the frequencies, scanning the airwaves on an equally old-fashioned radio while making periodic contemporaneous notes.

At the heart of the room, spotters flanked an enormous horizontal map of the south-eastern British Isles, a strategic battleground with friend and foe icons lying above it.

As he looked on at the map and the wall clocks of different time zones behind it, Curtis realised where he was.

'This is Bomber Command,' he stuttered unimpressively, overawed by the spectacle. 'This is the bunker from where they fought the Battle of Britain.'

'Well, at least we share some of our history.' Rufus looked on unfazed before calling over to one of the spotters. 'Billie, this is Curtis, the Gestapo prisoner we recovered from the convoy.'

The reply was brusque. 'You're assuming he's a Gestapo prisoner and not a spy working for them.'

Curtis didn't know why he was surprised to hear the voice of a woman. He had presumed, wrongly, that the leader of this spirited band of freedom fighters was a man, an assumption he immediately felt ashamed of.

With olive skin belying her mixed racial heritage, black dreadlocks and striking Amazonian curves visible even under her combat dress, Billie was no man.

She was also no walkover, removing her gun from its holster, cocking it and placing it on the edge of the map, ready for use.

'Whoa there sister,' Curtis protested, raising his hands in mock surrender. 'I'm on your side. Trust me.'

Billie and Rufus were clearly cut from the same cloth. She was equally cool. And equally unreadable.

'Mr Curtis, I believe in trust as much as I believe in ghosts.' Her expression was as humourless as it was menacing.

Rufus beamed. 'Well, you're going to LOVE his story…'

# 13
# SMOKE AND MIRRORS

Hiltz's office was stooped in history in a building that was history.

For a millennium, the Tower had been the prison of choice for political and high society prisoners. In that very room had resided Sir Thomas More, Lord Chancellor early in the bloody reign of Henry VIII, his closest confidante until he refused to accept the break with the Catholic Church in Rome, a refusal that cost him his head.

For fifteen months, Henry had locked More in the Tower, desperate for his old friend and ally to see sense. From where Hiltz's own desk sat, More had written by candlelight and quill about the split in his loyalties between his temporary master on earth and his eternal master in the heavens.

More knew which trumped which in the end.

Hiltz often pondered this quandary with some of the more brutal decisions required of a man in his position. He justified them, on a daily basis, as evils necessary for the greater, common good. Society had proven itself ungovernable by democratic means throughout the wars of the 20th Century, while Bolshevism had proven an inept, and often counterproductive, force for change.

For all of its rhetoric, in practice communism had all of the individual sacrifice of fascism but with none of the results.

Fascism's dominance of the latter half of the 20th Century wasn't because it was loved.

It was because it delivered.

Under Hiltz's leadership, Hessburg had grown into the global epicentre of trade, despite – or even because of – the Cold War with America. With Britain's forced accession to the Greater Reich had followed most of its significant overseas possessions: India, Hong Kong, its assets in the Middle East. Australia, New Zealand and Canada had all resisted but with limited strategic importance given the vastness of the territories against their trifling populations, they were left to their own devices.

It had never been the stated aim of the Reich to subjugate the entire world to its will.

Eurasia was more than sufficient lebensraum for its industrial and military needs.

But such a sprawling Empire required good governance on the ground. Beyond Germany itself were an array of Reichskommisariat, administrative regions made up of clusters of countries which it made sense to govern collectively.

Following General Franco's death in 1975, Spain acceded to the Reich, becoming one with Portugal and the French Basque borderlands to make up the Reichskommisariat Iberische.

The French-speaking lands of France, Belgium and Switzerland were brought under one roof as the Reichskommisariat Westlich Zentral.

The horseshoe of Italy through the Balkans into Greece became one under the Spezialkommisariat Italien, notionally headed by Mussolini until angry partisans strung him up in 1945. A communist uprising in northern Italy was swiftly put to bed later that year and German troops had been forced to be permanently stationed in both the Trentino in the north and Sicily in the south as a rapid reaction force.

Ukraine, Bulgaria, Romania, Hungary and Turkey as far east as the Bosporus strait had proven the military breadbasket of the Reich. Hungarian agriculture had complemented the subterranean oil supplies elsewhere in the Reichskommisariat Ostbalkan.

Western Poland was fully absorbed into Germany proper, as was Denmark to its north, while the other Scandinavian countries came under Reichkommisariat Nord.

This left Britain and Ireland as the north-western territories, governed from Hessburg as the Reichskommisariat Groβbritannien since the liberation of London in May 1941.

It had never been the intention of the German government to invade Britain. Its westward territorial ambitions ended at the lapping waters of Calais. But the persistence of the wartime Churchill government to wage war against Germany, to restrain its resurgence under the Nazi Party and limit its trade with the rest of the world, persuaded Berlin that rather than turning east to tackle the sleeping supplicant Bolsheviks – an enormous undertaking, even for the mighty Wehrmacht – the defeat of Britain was an overriding prerequisite for peace in Europe.

It was a peace bought at a high price.

The Battle for Britain, fought in the skies above London in the summer of 1940, had cost many brave Luftwaffe pilots their lives. It would be the following summer before the Blitz of London, preceding the invasion of southern England, would finally tame the British lion.

Its highest profile casualty was Rudolf Hess.

Held captive by Churchill in the Tower of London after his brave trip to make peace, he died from British bullets just as German paratroopers landed on the grassy knoll outside the White Tower. When London fell, it was a fitting tribute to Hess's widow and his young children – legitimate or otherwise – that the Tower, and ultimately the city, be renamed Hessburg in his honour.

It was from here that Hessburg was run.

Hiltz walked through the solid oak door into his office. He removed his hat and coat, placing both neatly on a coat stand. Then he stopped dead. From the breathing alone, he could tell that he wasn't alone. His hand hovered over his Luger. He looked across at his desk. His chair was turned facing away, looking out through armour-plated glass overlooking Tower Bridge. 'Who's there?' Hiltz asked as fiercely as he could muster.

The chair spun around to reveal Von Braun.

Hiltz was relieved as he saluted his boss. 'Reichskommissar. An unexpected pleasure.'

'Hauser is dead.' Von Braun spoke deadpan.

Hiltz dropped the salute and reclipped his gun holster. He did his best to show sorrow at the news but deep down he knew the man would not be missed. Sadists always thrived in such jobs. Alas some other thug would be waiting in the wings, a protégé to carry on his grisly work.

'How?'

'The execution convoy was ambushed by Freiheit. A Luftwaffe squadron landing at Hesston Flughafen spotted their corpses from the sky. They had laid their bullet-riddled bodies on the ground in the shape of a Union Jack and burned them beyond recognition. Savages.'

'Good God.' Hiltz thought it was rather inventive of Freiheit but dare not say so. He feigned disgust. 'And the Englander?'

'Missing, presumably back with his friends.' Von Braun sighed. 'Coupled with the attack on the Reichsgalleria, I am drawn to the conclusion that they wish to disrupt our negotiations with the Americans. It is only through strength that we brought them to the negotiating table. If we can't control our own back yard, why should they fear us elsewhere?'

'I will order an immediate search of the surrounding area of the attack for any Freiheit bases.' Hiltz offered assertively with no intention of doing anything of the sort.

'It's too late for that,' Von Braun waved dismissively. 'After this latest provocation, and with the President's negotiating team due here imminently, I have invoked Martial Law. Border checks have been stepped up and no Originals are allowed into Hessburg Zentrum until further notice. I will not have the lives of any more Colonials endangered by these English outlaws.'

'Very well, Herr Reichskommissar.' Hiltz proffered an inner sigh. This meant a lot more work.

Von Braun sat back in Hiltz's chair, clasping his intertwined fingers together. 'You were very hesitant to hand over the Englander to Hauser, Hiltz. I presume you have an explanation?'

Hiltz knew that Von Braun was exceptionally fond of Hauser. He was like a son to him. He had to tread carefully. 'I was trying to ascertain whether his story had any basis in fact, Herr Reichskommissar.'

'He is a terrorist, a professional liar Hiltz. Don't be too hard on yourself.'

'It was more than that, Herr Reichskommissar. It was the newspaper in his pocket, dated eighty years ago but which looked like it was printed yesterday. Why would he have something like that? And then there was the bracelet…'

Von Braun leant forward and opened Hiltz's desk drawer. 'You mean this?' reaching in and retrieving the time bracelet.

Hiltz felt uneasy. He didn't like being played. He pointed to the time bracelet. 'That alone warrants further investigation.'

Von Braun pondered, rolling the time bracelet in his hand between his stubby fingers. 'Very well.' He dropped it into his pocket. 'I will keep hold of it until the relevant time.'

'And the rebels?'

Von Braun rose to leave. He pressed his knuckles into Hiltz's oak desk, the colour draining from them. 'After Hauser's demise, Berlin insisted on a robust response.' He looked up at the door beyond Hiltz. 'Come in!' he bellowed.

The door promptly opened and the soft leather boots of SS-Obergruppenführer Reinhard Schultz clipped into the office. He was the overall Head of the SS, just arrived from Berlin. An authentic Aryan, his pumped body filled every inch of his black SS uniform. As with all true believers, his face belied any emotion, compassionate or otherwise. He saluted with vigour.

'Sieg heil!'

Over Schultz's shoulder, Hiltz could see a phalanx of crack SS stormtroopers – the fearless stoßtruppen – lining both sides of the corridor, joining him in the salute with zealous fervour.

Hiltz feared they would make Hauser and his Gestapo bruisers look like Cub Scouts.

# 14
# DEAD MAN'S SHOES

The television crackled with the interference from all of the communications equipment in the bunker.

The Freiheit Movement clearly couldn't afford cable.

As channel gave way to channel, mostly in German but one in English, there was only one story on the news agenda: the bombing in Hess Square. Nothing was spared by the news editors, with the retrieval of corpses from the fountains presented in graphic detail, even down to the pregnant woman that Curtis had tried to save from summary execution.

Being organs of the Nazi state, all of the channels were clearly censored. They all overlooked the reason for the protest and the fact that the protestors were mown down after the bombing. And they all pointed the finger of blame directly at one person.

Curtis.

A black-and-white capture from the CCTV camera of Curtis, approaching then rolling under the shutter of the car park underneath the Reichsgalleria, ran under much of the commentary, giving way only to Reichskommissar Erich von Braun on the lawn outside the White Tower, delivering a solemn address.

Through the television camera, he looked the audience straight in the eye as he held an enlarged photograph of Curtis up to the lens.

'This man,' he spoke in German, 'is an enemy of every peace-loving resident of these islands. He is a danger to you and your families. He – and those who harbour him – will be brought to swift and punitive justice for the atrocity in Hessburg Zentrum yesterday. The Reichslaw will be defended at all costs.'

Billie turned the television off. She had seen enough.

'Quite the celebrity,' she remarked drily, arms folded matronly with her back to Curtis. This left him unnerved.

'You think I had something do with this?'

'Did you?' Billie barked dispassionately.

'Did I what?' Curtis's eyes narrowed.

She turned to face him. 'Did you do this?'

Curtis felt his blood boiling. 'No! Why would I?'

'You tell me.'

Curtis pointed to the television screen. 'They thought I was one of you. That I was responsible for the attack. That's why they brought me out here – to kill me.'

'Why would they think you did it?'

Curtis hoped deep down that she was merely playing devil's advocate. Otherwise he really was in trouble. 'Isn't that what Nazis do?' he asked. 'Make things up and present it as fact to cover their own tracks?'

'Well, I suppose that's something your world and mine have in common,' she grudgingly acknowledged. 'It's a very interesting story you tell Curtis, one we'd like to believe even, but you offer no proof. Our people are dying as the SS punish Originals for what they say you did.' Billie toyed with her gun. It was a clear extension of her authority. 'And saying all that, for all we know you could be just another Colonial spy.' She rolled the gun against her thigh. 'And I do hate Colonial spies...'

Curtis was running out of time. 'Some senior guy in the Tower interrogated me. Said he was the Gauleiter of Hessburg, whatever that is. I missed his name.'

Billie looked up. 'Hiltz. Nikolas Hiltz.'

'That might be it. He took the newspaper and the time bracelet. He has the proof.'

'Good luck getting those back,' Rufus jibed.

Curtis was exasperated. How could he prove who he was? Why should they believe him? He put his hands on his hips in frustration and then realised the proof had been there all along. He pulled his belt off. Billie backed away, not entirely sure of his intentions. He flipped the belt onto its back, pressing out two gold sovereigns from its lining.

'Here.' He placed them into her other hand. 'I was given these by Colonel Crombie as currency to use in an emergency if I got stuck in 1941.' He smiled wryly. 'I don't suppose it occurred to him that I might need Marks as well.'

Billie rolled the sovereigns between her fingers, observing closely every millimetre of their contours. The coins bore the imprint of King George VI. She sighed at her imminent capitulation.

'If we were to help you, what would you want?'

Curtis shrugged as if his needs were modest. 'All I needed is a computer with an internet connection.'

'An inter-what connection?' Billie replied. He could have been talking double Dutch.

'You don't have the internet, do you?' Curtis sighed in realisation. 'So much for the Master Race.' He collected the gold sovereigns from Billie's hand and replaced them in his belt. 'I need to find the truth. We clearly share the same history – up to a point. I need to find out what that point is, when everything changed. And why.'

'Der Reich Historisches Museum,' Rufus interjected. 'The Reich History Museum has the only public computer in Hessburg. It's not exactly unbiased, but it's factual to a point.'

Billie shook her head. 'Hessburg Zentrum is crawling with SS agents looking for him. If he goes there, it'll be like shooting fish in a barrel.'

Rufus pondered, rolling his thumb against his well-groomed goatie beard. Then it hit him.

'What if he wasn't him?' He turned to Curtis, sizing him up with a scheming smile. 'How are you with accents?'

*

Curtis sat in what once upon a time must have been the base dentist's chair. His head rested over a basin, his hair – what was left of it – basted with bleaching strips. His long blonde locks had been trimmed violently. The floor looked like it had witnessed the shearing of a lion. It was all part of the makeover. Gone was the surfing playboy image cultivated over decades of decadence. In its place the clean-cut, virile, Aryan-friendly male.

Rufus was right. If he was to return to Hessburg, he couldn't be him.

Covering up his cuts and bruises with concealer was but the start of his transformation.

Rufus thrust a dossier into his hand. He opened the quilted cardboard cover to reveal a photograph of a handsome American, short-cropped blonde hair and blue eyes. At least he brought the blue eyes to the party. He flicked through the pages of the dossier of the man's life as Rufus ran commentary.

'Harry Holder. 35. You're from Spokane, Washington State. You're a freelance American journalist in Britain to cover the President's trip.'

Curtis looked up momentarily. 'The President's trip?'

'The American President is coming to Britain to sign a treaty of friendship with Germania. Relations soured in the Sixties when the outgoing US President Joseph P. Kennedy Jnr. was nearly assassinated on a state visit to Berlin by Czech resistance fighters.'

Curtis sighed. 'Why does everybody have it in for the Kennedys?'

Rufus continued, oblivious. 'Germania and America nearly went to war over it. But when China and Russia went to war instead in March 1968, annihilating each other with their nukes, North America washed its hands of Europe and Asia, concentrating on trade links with Central and South America and leaving Germania pretty much to its own devices. A Cold War has nonetheless existed between the two world powers for more than fifty years, so this is a big thaw.'

'Run out of oil, have they?' Curtis smiled wryly while continuing to read the dossier.

'Hessburg is currently under curfew,' Rufus continued, ignoring Curtis. He was reminded of university lectures delivered by exasperatingly clever men with exasperatingly little self-awareness. 'Martial law was imposed after the

Reichsgalleria bombing. No Originals are allowed in. But the city is already awash with Americans, so you've got a good chance of blending in.'

Curtis returned to the front page of the dossier. The photograph. With short blonde locks, he wasn't quite a dead ringer but he could pass a minimal inspection. He handled the photograph.

'This Holder,' Curtis asked. 'Is he a real person?'

'He was.' Rufus's forehead creased. 'Sadly no longer with us. But he lives on – in you.'

Kennedy wiped Curtis's lower arm with an alcohol-soaked cloth. He reached for an injection gun, which looked more like a tool of torture than of medicine.

'We're implanting Holder's identity implant. The Germans will use it to identify you at checkpoints or if they stop you to check your papers.'

Kennedy placed the injection gun against Curtis's arm. He looked up at Curtis with the puppy dog eyes and easy smile of a doctor.

'Just a little scratch,' he smiled.

The injection gun fired into Curtis's arm like a red-hot poker doused in chilli oil.

'You call that a scratch!?'

# 15
# SOUNDS OF THE FREE WORLD

Curtis lay restless on the metal-framed bunk. Why was it that beds in prison cells and military complexes were so bloody uncomfortable? Was a bad night's sleep part of the punishment for both?

But it wasn't the bed that was keeping him awake.

Nor was it the little scratch.

Since he first arrived in this alternative world, he had been fighting for his life almost from the get-go. His body had been flooded with adrenalin ever since the truck driver had nearly run him over while he stood, paralysed with travel sickness, in that alley.

For every moment since, his wits were all that had kept him alive.

Now that he was with the opposition, the Freiheit Movement – albeit on a short leash – his body dared to relax. But he couldn't let his guard down. Their leader Billie didn't look like she had lost an argument – or a fight – recently, nor that she planned to start anytime soon. As for Rufus and his loyal band of not-so-merry men, they would throw him to the wolves without a moment's hesitation.

No wonder he couldn't sleep.

It sounded like he wasn't the only one. Curtis got out of bed, slowly walking to the doorway. He thought he could hear singing.

*

The control room was like the deck of the abandoned American merchant brigantine Mary Celeste. It wasn't fulfilling the traditional Command-and-Control functions it had been constructed with in mind. The men and women that now operated from here had no Luftwaffe aircraft raining down on them, no counter assault to facilitate in the skies above.

But while their struggle for survival was no less perilous, by the very nature of guerrilla warfare these were fallow times. And in the aftermath of the Trafalgar Square bombing, that would continue for some time.

So night-watch duties rotated amongst radio operators in turn. Their job: to scan the airwaves for threats as well as opportunities.

And to let the others rest.

Tonight's operator was the messenger Stoltz, one of the many scrawny, geeky misfits that seemed to populate the Movement. He could see why he didn't fit in with the Nazi regime, his curly ginger swirls and fair complexion at odds with the almost inevitable Nordic Aryan ideals of beauty and racial purity. In the absence of Comic-Con, Warhammer 40,000 or a tattoo parlour, someone with his skills and interests in this world was always going to end up here.

Stoltz's eyes were closed as Curtis approached, his head bobbing to the beats pushing the headphones to their operational limits. For Stoltz wasn't listening to German transmissions – no one, not even Erich von Braun himself, could get this excited about those.

Stoltz had tapped into a whiney, whistling, distorted long-wave radio station beaming radio waves across the Atlantic between estranged cousins.

A cultural smorgasbord from the Americas, the land of the remaining free.

The American obsession with country music had clearly survived, much to Curtis's dismay, as Stoltz sat engrossed in Tammy Wynette's *Stand By Your Man.*

Stoltz softly hummed along, clearly not knowing the lyrics properly. If this was his only way of appreciating the music of Nashville Tennessee, crackling across the airwaves barely audibly, Curtis wasn't surprised. But he seemed to know the chorus, limply muttering.

'Stand by yer maaaaannn…'

Curtis couldn't resist. As Tammy reached her crescendo, so did he, bellowing out the final line of the chorus at full pelt.

Stoltz's eyes darted open and he jumped from the chair, almost out of his skin, ripping the headphone cord out with him. He didn't know where to put himself.

'Shit, I'm sorry,' he blurted while frantically scrambling the radio frequency.

'Don't be.' Curtis smiled, a little embarrassed for Stoltz. He even felt a tinge of guilt. 'May not be everyone's cup of tea but it's strangely soothing to hear it.'

'Why?' Stoltz asked awkwardly.

'Because maybe it's proof that we're both from the same universe after all.'

Stoltz's eyes avoided contact with Curtis. He remained mortified. Love him, if he wasn't careful he might faint.

'What station is that?' Curtis knew the way to handle socially awkward people was to ask them about something they were experts on or obsessed about.

'It's called Sounds of the Free World,' Stoltz began, retaking his seat. 'It's a pirate radio station. Rumour has it that it's broadcast from a ship in the middle of the Atlantic Ocean, full of songs from America that you just can't get here. German U-boats have hunted high and low for them but can't seem to find them.'

'Long may that continue,' Curtis smiled at the unapologetic geek. 'Are there no radio stations here?'

Stoltz scoffed. 'Only if you like Wagner, or Bach. The authorities are very strict about culture. Electric guitars and synthesizers are strictly prohibited. Only folksy music is allowed in the bierhaus and dance halls or on the radio.'

'So there's no British music?'

'None.'

Curtis was crestfallen. 'Not even an underground scene?'

'Manchester and Liverpool rebelled against the music laws.' Stoltz was a walking, talking edition of the *New Musical Express*. 'There was a miserabilist band there that did a great track called *Panic on the Streets of Hessburg*. Went down a bomb.'

Curtis laughed. 'The Smiths?'

Stoltz's eyes lit up. 'The Schmidts – you know of them?'

'Know of them? I grew up to them! They were huge in my time, proper anti-establishment voice of the people. *How Soon Is Now, This Charming Man, Girlfriend In A Coma*.' It was a pleasant change for Curtis to be talking about popular culture rather than Nazis, even just for a moment.

'Really?' Stoltz was surprised at their joint cultural heritage. 'Well, they kinda shot them for inciting sedition in the Second Uprising.'

'Christ.' Curtis was stunned. 'They executed Morrissey…'

'Yeah. After that, no one was really up for challenging the state so openly.'

'So I'm guessing you've never heard of The Stones? The Beatles? Oasis?'

Stoltz shook his head. 'Afraid not. Are they American bands?'

Curtis smiled at his innocence. 'No mate, they were British icons. We may not have done many things well but we were market leaders in music.'

Stoltz sighed wistfully. 'I'd have loved to have heard it.'

'It wasn't all good. We used to have this stupid annual competition called the Eurovision Song Contest. To win it didn't require any talent at all. Countries would vote for their neighbours whether their entries were any good or not. Talent was usually a drawback. One year, an Austrian drag queen won...'

Stoltz was incredulous. 'There's no way the authorities here would ever let that happen.'

'This world isn't all bad then!'

The two men laughed, only to be interrupted by a stern cough a few metres away. Their music love-in had awoken Billie, stood in the doorway, stern and matronly. She was clearly unimpressed.

'You've both got an early start. I'd get some sleep if I were you.' She turned on her heel and marched away. At least she didn't bring her gun, Curtis thought. He nodded to Stoltz, stepping off to follow Billie's bedbound example. Stoltz shot a finger to his mouth. Curtis frowned before looking down at Stoltz's other hand.

A gift.

A wireless radio and a set of headphones.

Curtis took the gift in his hand and smiled.

'Try long wave 252,' Stoltz whispered.

*

Curtis never thought he would have been lost in the sounds of American classics.

But as he lay back on the gym mat for a mattress, Sounds of the Free World was literally music to his ears.

The headphones hummed as a southern American DJ drawled.

'You're listening to Classic Hour on Sounds of the Free World.' And to all of our listeners in Great Britain, take care of our President when he lands on your side of the pond this week. No nasty ticking presents for Yuletide please.'

Curtis drifted off to sleep, with a little help from Elvis Presley, Frank Sinatra, Ella Fitzgerald and Billie Holliday.

Classic hour indeed.

# 16
# THE ORIGINALS

Curtis had never fully appreciated the labyrinthine extent of underground London. One of the most densely developed cities in the world, below ground a rabbit warren of tunnels acted as the core infrastructure to keep above ground moving, from sewerage and utilities through to the mass movement of people via the underground network.

One could not exist without the other.

So it felt more than peculiar to be running the gamut of the deserted and abandoned service tunnels of the old London Underground, now the Hessburg Unterbahn or U-Bahn.

While the honour of the world's first passenger railway went to Swansea's Mumbles, its subterranean equivalent was born in the deep London clay two hundred miles east.

The Metropolitan Railway, as it was then catchily known, became the world's first underground railway when it opened in 1863. Built underneath existing road networks using the cut-and-cover method to avoid compensating property owners, the railway – which would eventually become the Circle, Hammersmith & City and Metropolitan lines –

saw gas-lit wooden carriages hauled by broad gauge steam locomotives, as with the rest of the British train network.

It was a huge success, carrying 38,000 passengers on its first day. With the sister Metropolitan District Railway (commonly known as The District) expanding the network out west to Ealing, Hounslow and Uxbridge as well as Richmond and Wimbledon further south, it reached as far as Verney Junction in Buckinghamshire, some fifty miles from central London.

But not all of London could be covered by the cut-and-cover network. With engineering developments, the first deep-level tube line – the City and South London Railway – saw two circular tunnels three metres in diameter dug beneath King William Street in the City (what was today Monument Station) carry electric locomotives hauling so-called padded cells south under the river Thames to Stockwell.

Starting in the early 1900s, the electrification of the underground saw the standardisation of the network, with the merger of the different lines to become London Underground in 1933 inevitable. By the time of the Second World War, there would be over a hundred miles of subterranean track beneath London.

Though the First World War had delayed extensions, with tube stations used as air raid shelters, the interwar period had seen the Central Line west to Ealing completed while the Piccadilly Line took over District Line branches to Uxbridge and Hounslow.

The lines ran above ground until trains reached White City before heading deep for their journey into the centre of the capital. After the Nazi invasion, the early days of the occupation saw the largely intact Underground temporarily closed to civilians, its vast network of track essential to the safe and swift transit of Wehrmacht assets across the otherwise battered metropolis. As one of a number of soothing measures by the new regime as it sought to win the peace, the core nine-line underground network (neither the Victoria or Jubilee lines came to be built) was restored to normal service by 1946, though Germans were forbidden to use it.

Londoners had been stoic and pragmatic throughout the war, which stood them in good stead for the occupation.

But London, at the outer edge of Germania, was the first to suffer and the last to benefit from the inevitable austerity that hit the Reich cyclically, once the total war economy ceased. The first such major downturn came in 1971, with the Middle East oil shocks acting as the blue touch paper for what became known as the First Uprising.

It was swiftly – and mercilessly – suppressed.

As part of the reforms to the Reichslaw, London became a fortress city. The movements of the indigenous population of England – the Originals – were heavily curtailed. Only outsiders with special permission could reside within the city boundaries, broadly following the route of the north and south circular ring road.

These became known as the Colonials.

The Colonials – individuals and families of pure Aryan descent from across the Reich – were granted special rights in London, renamed Hessburg on the thirtieth anniversary of Hess's death in the Tower of London in May 1941. All public sector jobs were reserved for them. Education and healthcare provision was restricted to them. Carnal relations between Originals and Colonials were out of the question, forbidden, punishable by death.

Originals were granted guest worker status in those areas of industry with skill shortages, affording them the privileges not only of hard currency but permitting travel from the suburbs and commuter belt into Hessburg Zentrum.

By the late Eighties, memories of the brutal putdown of the First Uprising had faded, leading inevitably to the Second. The cycle of violence had been overwhelming, leading to mass executions and a guerrilla war insurrection that had agitated ever since.

But it was a guerrilla war that could not be sustained indefinitely. Spurts of violence would be followed by months – sometimes years – with nothing, often lulling the Nazi authorities into a false sense of security.

One such campaign had clearly just begun.

Rufus and Skunk stepped out of the service hatch into what should have been the busy Central Line, with one train every four minutes bringing guest worker Originals from Ealing in the west and Stratford in the east into Hessburg Zentrum.

But not today.

Not with Martial Law in effect.

Curtis and another acolyte, Sumner, followed after them.

'Welcome to rush hour,' Curtis noted wryly.

Rufus carried on walking. 'These tracks would normally be ferrying hundreds of thousands of wage slaves into and out of the capital.'

Curtis smiled. 'Some things never change.'

'But since the bombing of the U-Bahn last week, the whole network has ground to a halt.'

'Your handiwork?' Curtis asked.

Rufus blanched. 'We only target military assets. But whoever did bomb the U-Bahn wanted it to look like we did it.' He came to an abrupt halt. 'We're within the perimeter now. At the top of this ladder is a derelict warehouse off Autobahn 40, which leads directly into King's Cross and the Reich History Museum.'

Sumner began climbing the ladder.

Rufus stood firmly at the bottom. 'This is as far as I can go,' he shrugged sheepishly.

'Let me guess – you've got a price on your head too?'

Rufus ignored Curtis's question. 'Sumner will take you in. He has guest worker status so he won't raise any eyebrows. He'll take you to your contact. They know nothing of you or your mission. Keep it that way, for all our sakes.' Rufus extended his hand. 'I hope you find what you're looking for.'

Curtis shook it firmly. He didn't trust Rufus but he was grateful for his help.

Rufus backed away. As he was almost out of sight, Curtis called after him. 'My contact – how will I recognise him?'

Rufus slowed, grinning as he looked back. 'It's a her actually. You can't miss her. She's a cunning linguist.'

Before Curtis could reply, Rufus was lost into the darkness. Curtis looked up. Sumner was already almost at the top of the ladder. He looked around wistfully before reaching for the first set of rungs.

'Like a monkey up a fucking tree.'

*

By the time Curtis reached the hundredth step, he could just make out the rim of neutral light around the seal of the manhole cover. It was to be the first time he had seen natural light or breathed fresh air in days. He intended to savour the experience.

Given his wanted man status, he had no way of knowing when, if ever, he would experience it again.

Sumner popped the seal, moving the cover up and across with caution.

The warehouse should have been empty, abandoned, deserted.

Other than the sniffing nose of a ravenous rat, it was.

The cover slid across the cracked linoleum floor of a storeroom and Sumner was up and out. Curtis followed, pivoting on his backside while blinded by dawn sunlight. It stung his eyes like a wasp. As he gradually adjusted to the natural light, Sumner was in the nearby hallway, covertly checking that they were alone.

'What is this place?' Curtis asked.

'It's a secure drop. It's one of the ways we have of getting into and out of Hessburg without coming into contact with any border guards.'

Curtis looked around the tired building, an art deco construct that would have been a block of ridiculously expensive apartments in his time, now abandoned and desolate. He stepped towards a window, wiping away grimy condensation with the back of his hand. He was taken aback to see the A40 into London outside. In his world, the road would have been gridlocked, snaking along as those who should have known better insisted on getting behind the wheel of a gas-guzzling 4x4. Instead, the road was relatively quiet, with the calm transit of a procession of German-marque cars – BMWs, Mercedes, Audis, Volkswagens, peppered with the occasional Skoda – all driving on the wrong side of the road.

Beyond it, London's skyline stood alien as it now belonged to new masters.

Sumner placed his hand on his shoulder, pulling him firmly away from the window. 'Best keep a low profile.'

'Right,' Curtis replied, self-checking.

*

A few moments later, a vintage Mercedes was ambling along the A40, towards the spaghetti junctions west of White City and Shepherds Bush.

At its wheel, Sumner – day-jobbing as a taxi driver.

Behind him, Harry Holder, the innocent-looking American journalist in his care.

The radio hummed low as company for the nervous drive into Hessburg Zentrum. Sumner flicked through the FM channels, only to find a sprinkling of chat shows in German amongst a sea of dour music stations playing dry folk and classical music.

Being a German car, it was pre-programmed to ignore any unsanctioned radio stations.

No Sounds of the Free World today.

Frustrated, Sumner turned the radio off. He looked at Curtis, reflective as he watched this imposter city pass by his window.

'So…' Sumner endeavoured to make light conversation. 'What did you do in your other life? For a living I mean.'

'I worked in the steal industry.'

'Really?' Sumner was interested. 'Military or commercial?'

Curtis was embarrassed. 'Different kind of steal,' he beamed.

'Ah.' Sumner realised. 'Old ladies and handbags?'

'No, middle-aged men and stolen Nazi treasure on the whole. I would rob from the thieving rich and return it to its rightful owners, who used to be the filthy rich.'

'What – for a fee?'

'No, for free,' Curtis replied matter-of-factly.

'For free?!' Sumner didn't believe him at first.

'I didn't need to work. My father died when I was young and left me plenty to live off in a trust fund.'

Sumner still struggled to comprehend. 'So you risked everything for nothing?'

'Nothing but a great deal of satisfaction,' Curtis smiled smugly. 'And it kept me busy.'

'My family are dead too.'

Curtis immediately felt guilty for equating his father's suicide – his choice at the end of the day – with the genocide of the Nazis in this world. 'Sorry to hear that.'

'Happened when I was very young. I would have died with them if it wasn't for my mother. With no time to spare, she hid me in a coal bunker on our farm. We were just farmers, going about our business, keeping our noses clean, but they accused us of sedition against the Reich. Burned the farm to the ground. The maize over their bodies smouldered for three days. They then demolished the ruins and built a new airport runway on it. It was cheaper to steal it from us than to pay us the peppercorn it was worth, even as Originals.'

It was a harrowing story. Curtis didn't really know what to say. But given Sumner had confided in him, he felt obliged to aid him to get it out of his system.

'Where did you go?'

'I wasn't sixteen yet, so I hadn't had my identity chip implanted yet. I was a homeless orphan. And an Original. I was pretty fucked.'

Curtis sighed, his eyes deflated.

'Mr Curtis.' Sumner's voice was soft. 'I hope you find what you're looking for and get back to your own time. Because this one, this one is shite.'

As if Curtis didn't feel enough pressure already.

The traffic had been slow but steady approaching the end of the final flyover, a few hundred metres shy of Great Portland Street.

And then they saw it.

'Shit.' Sumner began to sweat. It was a heavily fortified roadblock, stretching across the eastbound side of the A40. There shouldn't have been any this far in, as they had travelled underground beneath the standard entry-exit points back in Acton.

Curtis tried to remain calm. 'Do you think they suspect something?'

'God no. How could they?' Sumner radiated positivity, wiping the sweat from his brow and composing himself. 'This is the SS. Sledgehammer to crack a nut. Just keep calm and remember who you are – Harry Holder.'

Curtis hoped his American accent would pass muster as the Mercedes inched towards the checkpoint. A barrier – and half a dozen heavily armed SS stoßtruppen – stood between them and success.

Failure meant certain, and likely immediate, death.

One of the towering officers angled over and into the driver's side window, from which Sumner beamed confidently, while his colleagues patrolled the perimeter of the car with a Doberman and a stick mirror to check its underside for explosive devices.

'Identity check,' the officer commanded officiously, running a scanning device along Sumner's arm first. The device, little more than a Nintendo Gameboy in design, buzzed until it recognised Sumner's implant. The screen turned green, indicating that George Sumner was an Original with a guest worker visa to enter Hessburg Zentrum.

Curtis readied his own arm for scanning, perhaps too willingly, like a child enjoying the novelty of something new. As the scanner found his implant, the screen turned blue, revealing him to be Harry Holder, an American citizen on a short stay visa.

'Herr Holder?' the officer asked without looking at him.

'Yep, that's me,' Curtis replied in a tepid west coast American accent.

'I know it's you,' the officer replied humourlessly in clipped English. 'You are American, yes?'

'How can you tell?' Curtis replied without a hint of sarcasm in the thickest American drawl he could manage.

'What is the purpose of your visit to Hessburg?'

'I'm visiting your renowned Reich History Museum as research for a story on the President's visit.'

'I see.' The officer's eyes bore into Curtis suspiciously. Perhaps it was the idea of a journalist writing a story. 'Enjoy your stay.' He couldn't have meant it. His demeanour changed sharply, his pearly white teeth almost blinding as they reflected the crisp winter sun. 'You're safe now – beyond this point is only for Colonials and guest workers.'

The officer tapped the steel roof of the car and indicated for the barrier to let them through.

The Mercedes travelled through the roadblock, down the overpass and on towards Regent's Park. Its passengers couldn't have seen the security man in the kiosk, behind the one-way glass, reaching for a red telephone.

Inside the car, the palpable tension evaporated.

'Very good, Herr Holder.'

Curtis exhaled. 'Fifty pence, five pence.' The allusion was lost on Sumner. 'What do they mean by Originals?' he asked as he loosened his collar a little.

'The English, the Celts, immigrants from across the former Empire. Basically all non-Aryans who live in Britain now.'

Curtis was curious. 'Why the distinction?'

'Originals are not permitted to live in Hessburg Zentrum or to hold government jobs. In areas where there are a shortage of workers or the work is menial, guest worker visas for Originals can be issued but they can be withdrawn at any time, without explanation or reason. The rest of us are forced to scramble together a living outside Zentrum.'

'Hardly convivial for integration,' Curtis barbed.

'Integration?' Sumner laughed out loud. 'Colonials and Originals are forbidden to mate. The sentence of the Peoples' Court would be summary execution if you're lucky, a death camp if you're not.'

Curtis sighed. In this world, death was probably a mercy to many.

*

The Mercedes passed the Euston U-Bahn station heading east. A few hundred metres further along, Sumner flashed his indicator left for the turning circle outside the old St. Pancras Hotel, a towering gothic-era building that by some miracle had survived the Blitz. The hotel, which acted as a gateway to Reichstar cross-channel tunnel rail services to the Reich mainland, was heavily patrolled by armed Orpol – members of the Ordnungspolizei.

There was no room for error.

The Mercedes came to a halt in a drop-off zone outside the hotel. A porter approached them, opening the rear passenger door. Curtis sidled across the back seat.

'I'm only allowed to drop you off. The Museum is around the corner but this is where you'll meet your contact. She'll take you in.'

'How will I know who she is?' Curtis had to ask, even though he expected no more illumination than he had already got from Rufus.

'Don't worry,' Sumner smiled. 'She'll make an impression.'

Curtis rolled his eyes. 'Thanks. For nothing.'

'Don't mention it,' he smiled. 'I'll loop around every thirty minutes, so keep an eye out for me. And remember the night-time curfew. I'm still an Original. I've got to be out of Zentrum by sunset otherwise the Gestapo will have me doing deep-breathing exercises in the Thames.'

Curtis shook his head at the gallows humour as he got out of the car.

It drove off.

Once again he was alone in a foreign land.

*

As the big hand of the clock tower above the station marched past nine o'clock, then ten, a pacing Curtis had the distinct impression that he had been found out.

Or worse still, stood up.

In his time, right now he would be texting his date to let her know she should make other plans for the future. In fact, in his time, no such thing had ever happened as he had never been stood up. He was the one to do the standing up, relationships being necessarily brief and all too often with attached women.

Curtis surveyed the quiet streets. There were more people in uniform than not, the plodding Orpol Unterwachtmeister (policeman) bearing the brunt of the enforcement of Martial Law across the capital. He had seen one particular officer three times in his loop. Curtis already felt his suspicious stare boring into him, despite his efforts to appear unmemorable and inconspicuous. Despite his new hair do and his implant saying otherwise, he was all too aware that under the make-up he was a wanted man and desperately wanted to avoid any unnecessary conversations with an overzealous Unterwachtmeister.

The Unterwachtmeister was about to approach Curtis. He knew it.

He was braced for confrontation and a pacy retreat.

When the tap on his shoulder came, he was ready.

He was not ready for the soft, tender lips that locked with his own as he swung around.

# 17
# ELSA

The mouth that pressed against his own was moist and small. While the passionate embrace of a stranger was probably grounds for sexual assault in some cultures, in cruel Hessburg in 2021 Curtis wasn't complaining. His eyes had dared to close instinctively, but not before he caught her crystal blue eyes and spirally blonde hair almost suspended in mid-air above her slender shoulders. He felt mildly inappropriate as his hands inevitably held her body close, her slight frame and soft body parts in danger of causing a more overt physical response.

The Unterwachtmeister was no voyeur. He left them to it.

Aware that his footsteps had grown more distant as the seconds ticked by, Curtis opened his eyes and gently disengaged. As the woman opened her own eyes, he sensed her savouring the lingering taste of him on her too.

If this wasn't his contact, damn he wished it was.

The woman, in her mid-twenties he thought, pivoted on her heel, placing her arm inside his while gently pulling him along the walkway. Underneath her chic overcoat with its sash belt he sensed a business suit, atop legs that went on for miles. Her heels, six inch he suspected, put her just above the five foot ten mark.

In a word, perfect.

'Sorry I'm late.' The woman spoke English with a mild continental accent. Swiss private schooling he thought. He knew them well.

'For a while I thought you were standing me up,' Curtis protested, almost forgetting that he was impersonating an American.

She smiled. 'You have much experience of that?'

'No!'

'Well, we're all learning something new today.' She casually observed their surroundings, confirming that no one was in earshot before introducing herself. 'I'm Elsa. Dr Elsa Brühl.'

'Harry Holder,' Curtis cautiously replied. 'But you can call me Harry.'

'Harry eh...' She smiled. 'Is this your first time in Hessburg, Harry?'

'Since its makeover, yes.' It paid for him to remain cautious.

'So you are a journalist, yes?'

Curtis replied smugly. 'I have a way with words.'

'A cunning linguist too?'

You could have warned me Rufus, he thought as they crossed the road towards the Reich History Museum.

First opened in 1759 as the British Museum, housing the collections of the physician and naturalist Sir Hans Sloane bequeathed to the British nation on his death, its original home at Montagu House in Bloomsbury had soon become outgrown.

On his death, Sloane's 70,000-strong collection included 40,000 printed books, 7,000 manuscripts, extensive natural history specimens, prints, drawings and antiquities from Egypt and the Sudan, Rome and Greece, the Ancient Near and Far East as well as the Americas. It was now home to over thirteen million objects.

In the earlier part of a quarter of a millennium of archaeological exploration and wartime plunder, the Museum added the Rosetta Stone – key to deciphering Egyptian hieroglyphics – along with the Colossal bust of Ramasses II and most controversially the Elgin Marbles, the sculptures removed from the Parthenon on the Acropolis in Athens.

Under the neoclassical architect Sir Robert Smirke, Montagu House would later be demolished, making way for the Greek temple-style new entrance made up of forty-four columns in the Ionic Order towering forty-five feet high. Closely based on those of the temple of Athena Polias at Priene in Asia Minor, the pediment over the main entrance was decorated by sculptures of fifteen allegorical figures by Sir Richard Westmacott, depicting the progress of civilisation.

But Sir Robert was not the only architect in the family.

His brother Sydney took his place in 1846, making his mark with what was perhaps its most striking feature: the Round Reading Room. Opened in 1857, with space for over a million books and a dome a hundred and forty feet in diameter, for a time it was second only to the slightly wider Pantheon in Rome as the world's widest dome.

Despite the Luftwaffe's best efforts, the Museum and its collections survived the war largely unscathed, with the exception of the Duveen Gallery – originally designed by American Beaux-Arts architect John Russell Pope to house the Elgin Marbles – which succumbed along with 150,000 books in the courtyard and galleries around the top of the Great Staircase.

The pilots were never going to cry about the books.

The dark Victorian reds that predated Russell Pope's tenure as architect found more in common with Nazi colour schemes than his modern pastel shades. With London's occupation and transformation into Hessburg, the British Museum had been rebranded the Reich Historisches Museum der Groβbritannien to honour the past achievements of this latest addition to the Reich, with extensive remodelling of Sir Robert's Great Court to become the largest covered square in Europe, protected from the elements by 1,656 uniquely shaped panes of glass from the finest engineers in Austria.

As they tiptoed up the pristine steps into the foyer, they passed under the enormous Reich flag, extending halfway out into the road, flapping gently in the wintry wind.

The foyer was no less unashamedly nationalistic, decked out in the strident black and red colours of the Reich and peppered with Nazi iconography. It was garish and strident, brash and confident, ill judged and jingoistic, all at once.

'I'll be back in a moment,' Elsa whispered, unlocking her arm and marching towards a receptionist. Curtis saw ahead of him a gift shop. He dared himself to delve into its hidden treasures.

He made his way along the aisles of Nazi paraphernalia, from swastika key rings and snow globes of the regional capitals of the Reich – Paris, Rome, Madrid, Budapest, Stockholm and, of course, Hessburg – to Strength through Honour wall posters and t-shirts and a German language book section.

Curtis recoiled at that which had been much mocked during his lifetime being paraded so openly.

At the periphery of the extensive book section sat a lonely basket of unloved books. On closer inspection, these clearance books all shared one thing in common: they were all in English.

It was clearly not the policy of the state to actively eradicate English, more to let it fizzle and die out of its own accord. Something similar had happened to the Welsh language after the armies of Edward Longshanks conquered the Celtic enclave in the 13th Century. While Welsh remained in use by the native Brythoniaid, the incoming Norman nobles conducted the business of government, commerce and – most importantly – justice in Anglo-Norman French, later to morph into English. All laws were drafted and court proceedings conducted in English, forcing the conquered to, at the very least, become bilingual if they were to be able to properly defend their rights. By the time of the full assimilation of Wales into England over two centuries later through the 1536 Act of Union, the indigenous language was a minority pastime, only in regular use in the very western fringes of the British Isles. It took until the Thatcher governments of the 1980s for Welsh to become protected as an official language, legally equal if not culturally superior to English in the Principality, just in time to prevent it joining Latin in the garden of oldest dead languages.

Curtis mused that it would take more than a Thatcher to save English from a similar fate.

He picked up one of the books: *A History of the 20th Century.*

Translated from the original German.

Interesting bedtime reading.

Curtis approached the counter, book in hand. The mild disgust of the shopkeeper caused him to instantly regret drawing attention to himself, but inside the book could be some vital clue as to where it had all gone awry.

After paying for the book – an extortionate 20 Deutschmarks, compared to the 5 Deutschmarks for its German language original – Curtis flicked through the opening pages as he stepped out of the gift shop.

He nearly jumped out of his skin as he came face to face with Hermann Göring.

# 18
# HISTORY 101

It was a sea of history, a history familiar yet so different from the world Curtis had grown up in. The faces of the antagonists, the villains of the piece, were all household names. But instead of perishing in the Reich Chancellery bunker in April 1945 or at the end of a long rope after the Nürnberg trials, to go down in history as butchers and brigands, here they were, lionised as towering bronze busts in a pantheon, having prevailed.

And turned history on its head.

The vast exhibition hall adjacent to the gift shop commemorated the hundredth anniversary of the Nazi Party, a party that had begun in the bierhaus of Bavaria and had spread its tentacles across land and sea to dominate the world, bending it to its will for a century.

As painful as it was for Curtis to step through the exhibition hall, with the vanquished lauded as victors, he knew that within it – somewhere – lay the answer to the question dominating his thoughts.

How?

The history of the 20th Century was a bloody tapestry of turmoil and terror, nowhere more so than in Germany.

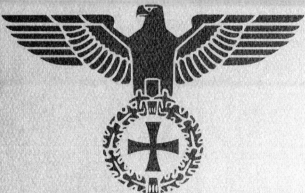

# GROßDEUTSCHES REICH

## Greater German Reich

Oberkommando der Wehrmacht

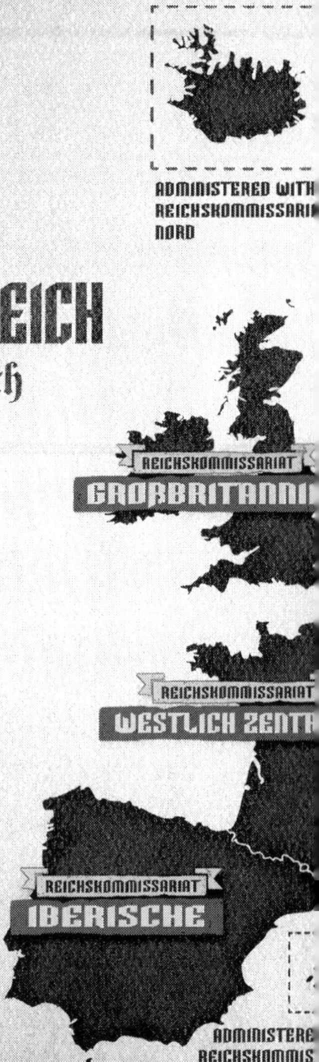

REICHSKOMMISSARIAT
NORD
GERMANIA
REICHSKOMMISSARIAT
OSTBALKAN
SPEZIALKOMMISSARIAT
ITALIEN
STERED WITH
LKOMMISSARIAT

The Great War, the First World War, the war to end all wars, had been inevitable. Germany was the engine of Europe, unified under Bismarck in 1870 and by 1914 an unstoppable economic force if left unchecked. By the early 1900s it had supplanted France, Russia and, taken without its Empire, Britain too.

But the one thing it so desperately craved, money just couldn't buy.

Land.

Sandwiched in the busy heart of mainland Europe, with the decadent Austro-Hungarian and Ottoman Empires to its south, the diminished France to its west (having ceded Alsace and Lorraine to Germany following its defeat by Bismarck) and the creaking Russian Empire to its east, Germany felt that its right to expand – as had all of its neighbours – was hampered by the niceties of modern diplomacy.

Curtailed overseas by the British Empire, limiting its foreign conquests to Togoland, German East Africa, German South West Africa, Western Samoa and the Chinese enclave of Tsingtao, its only hope of expansion was from conquest.

The supremacy of the British navy – so amply displayed by the launch in 1906 of the first modern destroyer, the 18,000 tonne HMS Dreadnought, at a stroke rendering the rest of the continental navies obsolete and sparking an arms race to catch up – meant that inevitably such conquest could only take place in the familiar territory of central Europe.

The treaty quagmire of the turn of the century was but a prelude to the opportunistic exploitation by all sides of the assassination of Archduke Frank Ferdinand, the unloved heir to the Austro-Hungarian Emperor Frank Josef, in June 1914.

What should have led to little more than yet another local Balkan war, to follow two conflicts in the two years preceding the Great War, instead provoked a catastrophic scramble for territory. All of the great powers were guilty of such opportunism in the heady summer of 1914, seeking to settle scores or to put would-be challengers back in their box.

More was achieved in the first four weeks of August 1914 than in the four years of broad stalemate that followed. Russian humiliation at Tannenberg – where 125,000 of the Tsar's soldiers were taken prisoner in a single day – set in train the slow realisation that the venture that Europe's elites had embarked on lightly would be costly and not without a high degree of risk.

None of the participants could afford to lose.

Despite a stalemate from the settling of the western and eastern fronts in late 1914 through to Russia's ignominious withdrawal in December 1917 after the Tsar's overthrow, the advantage lay with the Germans. Well-supplied, well-organised and set in highly defensive positions, they managed their war effort better than the remaining Entente powers and their Alliance partners. Much of their war effort was curtailed by the need to prop up their increasingly junior allies in Vienna and Anatolia. Had the Schlieffen Plan, which called for a blitzkrieg suppression of northern France through neutral Belgium in order to return to the eastern front by the time the Russians had mobilised, been followed without the distractions of propping up the archaic Austro-Hungarian army's pitiful efforts in Serbia and elsewhere in the Balkans, Germany's war machine may have been unstoppable.

Instead a long war ensued, fought remotely from smoke-filled rooms in London, Paris, Berlin and St. Petersburg. It eventually became clear that victory could only be achieved by maximising supply lines while limiting supplies to others.

And this was Germany's downfall.

Britain, and as a result France, were kept in the war only by extensive trade convoys from the United States of America. The United States remained neutral in the European war but continued to trade with the jilted motherland. It was a support mechanism the Germans were determined to smash.

The German fleet of U-boat submarines terrorised transatlantic shipping routes during bouts of unrestricted submarine warfare, determined to strangle allied shipping and force Britain out of the war.

As American civilian casualties grew, the entry of the United States into the war soon became inevitable.

A lull in unrestricted submarine warfare in the Atlantic extended well into 1916 but with stalemate in northern France as well as eastern Prussia, a risky gambit was played to force the British out and settle the war with France before American forces could land in any meaningful numbers on the continent.

It was a gambit that, with Russia's humiliating withdrawal and the punitive peace treaty forced on them at Brest-Litovsk, very nearly paid off for the Kaiser.

But an inability to capitalise on the advantage, coupled with an exhaustion of the supply of cannon fodder from the Fatherland, doomed the Germans.

By the autumn, they had snatched defeat from what, just a few months earlier, were the jaws of potential victory.

While the defeat proved existentially fatal to Austria-Hungary and the Ottoman Empire, disintegrating into a plethora of ethnically complicated new nation states as encouraged by US President Woodrow Wilson's policy of self determination, the Germans instead had the ignominy to live through the peace.

The loss of the Great War led to massive unrest in Germany, with millions of veterans – the so-called frontschwein – returning from the front to a society afflicted by hyperinflation, food shortages and an overwhelming depression in all senses.

These frontschwein, who had sacrificed so much for so little, felt abandoned, betrayed even, by a decadent and out of touch political class. The militarisation of the lower classes was a genie that would not easily be put back in the bottle, as those veterans and their families shunned the traditional political parties for a new one: the Deutsche Arbeiterpartei or German Workers Party.

During the turbulent 1920s, the party's popularity soared, eclipsing the established Christian Democrats, Catholic Centre and Social Democrats as they struggled to make the fledgling Weimar Republic work.

The DAP – by then rebranded the Nazionalsocialiste Deutsche Arbeiterpartei (the NSDAP or Nazi Party for short) – had returned its first MPs in the 1928 General Election, among them the war hero Hermann Göring.

But in a break from Curtis's history, it was Göring – not Adolf Hitler – who led the Nazis into government in March 1933, taking the reins of power from the terminally ill Weimar President Paul von Hindenburg.

It was Göring – not Hitler – who became Chancellor under Hindenburg.

It was Göring – not Hitler – who became Führer after Hindenburg passed away the following year.

But Göring's leadership of the resurgent German nation, bolstered by a secret rearmament programme providing much needed employment and economic stimulus, would be cruelly short-lived.

Having grappled with an addiction to morphine since an injury at the failed Munich bierhaus putsch in 1923, fourteen years later Göring overdosed.

While the nation and the Nazi Party were left dumbstruck by his early grave, Göring was – at best – first among equals.

The Nazi Party was more than one man.

It was an idea.

With Josef Goebbels as his propaganda minister, Martin Bormann his chief of staff and Rudolf Hess as party leader, former SS chief Heinrich Himmler seamlessly stepped into Göring's vacated shoes, consolidating the grip of the Nazi Party on Germany.

The aims of the German leadership had changed very little between 1914 and 1937.

They wanted living space in 1914, room to expand.

Lebensraum.

But the punitive Treaty of Versailles had shrunk German territory even further, creating a demilitarised buffer zone in the Rhineland, repatriating Alsace and Lorraine to France, ceding the German-speaking Sudetenland to the newly sovereign Czechoslovakia and paving the way for the creation of a new Polish state carved arbitrarily out of its Prussian heartlands. With the Polish land corridor to the so-called free city of Danzig guaranteed and administered by the fledgling League of Nations, the shrunken German state was split in two, with a rump around the historic Königsberg rounding off her humiliation.

One by one Himmler would restore Germany to her former glory – and beyond.

He annexed the Sudetenland, incorporating the ethnically German region back into Germany. After reoccupying the Rhineland, forcing through the Anschluss with Austria and annexing the rest of Czechoslovakia by force, Himmler had reunited the German-speaking populace within one state for the first time since Bismarck.

All without firing a shot.

Yet.

Himmler's immediate aspirations lay in achieving a peaceful realisation of the war aims of Kaiser Wilhelm. With fascist regimes in Madrid and Rome, sensing weakness in Britain and France following their abandonment of Czechoslovakia and disengagement from the distant United States, all that now stood in Himmler's way was the nascent Soviet Union.

While assuring the British and French that his invasion of Czechoslovakia and the forced union with Austria represented the end of Germany's territorial ambitions, he secretly dispatched his foreign minister Joachim von Ribbentrop to sign a Non-Aggression Pact with Stalin's regime, within which lay a secret protocol to carve up Poland between them if war ever broke out.

Poland would cease to exist, an outcome that suited both Germany and the Soviet Union.

Nine days later, on September 1st 1939, Polish separatists took over the Gleiwitz radio station in Danzig, declaring war on Germany and its significant diaspora in the region.

The timing was miraculous.

Himmler had no choice but to send the German Army into western Poland to protect its citizens. Stalin's forces entered eastern Poland, absorbing everything east of the Narew, Vistula and San rivers into the Soviet Union.

Poland was no more.

And Europe was once more at war over German territorial ambitions, with Germany, Austria and Italy staring down the barrel of British and French aggression in the west.

The first few months saw little action, other than the ill-fated Norway campaign by the allies of Britain and France. Neither side was truly ready for war, not even the Germans, using the winter months of 1939 and early 1940 to steel themselves for the main event to come.

But the phoney war forced neutral states like Norway, Denmark, Belgium and the Netherlands to pick a side.

In reality, it made no difference whether they sided with Nazi Germany or not.

If they did, they became a client state with German troops on their soil and a puppet fascist government.

If they didn't, they were occupied with German troops on their soil.

The difference between the two was practically non-existent.

By the spring of 1940, the British Expeditionary Force was in northern France, traversing the same blood-soaked terrain as a quarter of a century earlier. But nothing could stop the German Panzers and Stukas as the blitzkrieg invasion of northern France began that May.

Within a fortnight, Himmler's forces were in Paris as an occupying power and the British had been routed, pushed back into the English Channel.

The disastrous Norway campaign and the evacuation of the remnants of the BEF from Dunkirk toppled the

Chamberlain government in Westminster. The incoming national government, led by the cigar-chomping Winston Churchill, faced the immediate task of preparing for the imminent and the inevitable: the German invasion of Britain.

So long an island fortress, the summer of 1940 saw the British Isles pounded from the sky by the Luftwaffe.

It was the opening salvo of Unternehmen Seelöwe.

Operation Sea Lion.

With northern France directly occupied by the Wehrmacht and a client government in situ in Vichy controlling the south, the airfields of the Normandy coast played host to daring raids on London and the south of England. Many brave Luftwaffe pilots perished as they sought to liberate Britain, as they had France and the Low Countries.

But with the Royal Air Force offering ferocious resistance and the campaign at a stalemate as the weather turned, Sea Lion was paused while the Germans consolidated their hold on Western Europe and dug in for winter.

Experimental long distance artillery was embedded in fortified installations like those at Mimoyeques, including the V1 pilotless bomber, the V2 long-range rocket and the V3 supergun.

The V stood for vengeance.

And vengeance was had.

In May 1941, a year after putting the British to flight in France, the head of the Luftwaffe and by then Deputy Führer Rudolf Hess flew a daring mission to Scotland to make a final offer of peace in person to Churchill.

Instead of being treated as a diplomat on a diplomatic mission, Hess was imprisoned in the Tower of London, where he was tortured by the British intelligence service SIS.

The news of Hess's execution made Himmler's mind up and Operation Sea Lion was recommenced with immediate effect.

London was bombarded, with its Houses of Parliament almost destroyed. All that remained standing was St. Stephen's Tower, housing the Big Ben clock.

The bombardment overwhelmed the RAF who, faced with insurmountable numbers, were forced to concentrate their efforts on London at the expense of the English Channel.

The first German infantry arrived by landing craft on beaches stretching from Southampton to Skegness on June 21st 1941. With air superiority over the British capital assured, the first German paratroopers landed in the grounds of the Tower of London two days later.

Invading forces overwhelmed the rattled British military, whose final act was to evacuate their warmongering leader Churchill, his feeble cabinet, King George VI and senior members of the Royal Family by escorted naval transport headed for exile in Canada.

Some never arrived.

The rest were never to return.

The Duke of Windsor – the former King Edward VIII who had been forced by the British establishment to abdicate the throne in 1936 because of his National Socialist convictions – was reinstalled as monarch with his beloved bride becoming the much-loved Queen Wallis I.

The country remained a constitutional monarchy, with a new technocratic client government established. Led by the former Labour MP Oswald Mosley (following his release from Holloway prison, where he had been incarcerated by Churchill along with his wife Diana Mitford) and his new party the British Union of Fascists, the new government negotiated the Treaty of Berlin, paving the way for the British Empire's accession to the Reich.

Britain's colonial assets baulked at the accession, leading to declarations of independence from India, Canada, Australia and New Zealand. With Hong Kong firmly under German control, the newly independent states were of little practical use to the Germans, so far from Europe and such vast, sparsely populated landmasses.

The United States, under its isolationist President Joseph P. Kennedy Snr., refused the bended knee pleas of Churchill to invade Britain and France to reclaim them from the Reich, dying in heartbroken exile in British Columbia in 1951. He was 77.

Significant tolerance and self-autonomy was granted to Britain along with the recently established Irish Republic which, despite its neutrality and equal disdain for the British, was annexed in the spring of 1942 to ironically be governed from London once more.

German was taught as the official language of the Reich in all British schools, with English demoted to secondary status along with Welsh, Gaelic, Cornish and Latin.

An era of unchallenged peace befell Western Europe, protected from the twin evils of communism and capitalism by the Reich.

But that era came to an abrupt end with Himmler's death in 1967, after three decades as Führer. He was succeeded by Reinhard Heydrich, his loyal lieutenant and former head of the SS.

The new leader of the Reich was soon tested by the First Uprising, a terrorist campaign by communist revolutionaries on mainland Britain and Ireland. What started as a campaign for greater workers rights in the dockyards of Belfast soon became a bloody terror that threatened to engulf the whole Reichskommissariat Groβbritannien.

US President Richard M. Nixon, the first British sympathiser in the White House since the interwar years, broke off all diplomatic relations with the Reich in a fit of pique, relations which had improved dramatically in the years of détente under his predecessor Joseph P. Kennedy Jnr.

With Mexico's fascist regime pledging solidarity with the Reich, a military exchange looked on the cards until events in the Far East changed the map of the world for a generation.

While the European war had ended in June 1941 with the British Armistice, the Sino-Japanese conflict was then entering its sixth year. Japan – an imperialist, militarist state – had dominated south-east Asia ever since its unlikely victory against the Russians in the Russo-Japanese War of 1906. It controlled vast tranches of Manchuria, the heartland of mainland China, along with the Korean peninsula and much of the Philippines.

But the Chinese communists were intent on reclaiming their homeland, establishing the second communist state of the 20th Century. Ultimately the Chinese were victorious, regaining control of the mainland and Korea. The Peoples' Republic of China was declared in 1949 and it vied with the Union of Soviet Socialist Republics for communist supremacy.

Despite a thaw in relations by the Sixties, when the Chinese began to purchase second-hand Soviet military hardware to address the re-emergence of the Japanese threat, in March 1968 a nuclear missile was fired from the South

China Sea. It obliterated the Pacific Soviet city of Vladivostok. A hundred thousand Russians perished instantly.

The launch was an unprovoked attack on the Soviet Union by the Chinese. Rumours of unusual German U-boat activity in the port of Hong Kong at the time proved unfounded.

The Soviets retaliated with total nuclear commitment, its ballistic missiles delivering nuclear warheads across the Jundu Mountains into the Chinese capital Beijing and sparking an unexpected, inexplicable and mutually devastating nuclear exchange.

Within hours, hundreds of millions of Soviet and Chinese citizens were dead or dying, with many millions more to follow from famine as fallout decimated a fifth of the world's inhabited landmass stretching from St. Petersburg to Shanghai.

The communist dream lay in radioactive ruin.

Germania closed its eastern borders as millions of communist refugees sought sanctuary in the comfort of the Reich. The United States, in the face of the complete devastation of Eurasia, retreated within its own borders, solidifying an isolationism that would last well into the 21st Century.

The Heydrich era saw Germania and the United States share the spoils of dual hegemony, leaders in their own spheres of influence in a reimagining of the 19th Century Monroe Doctrine.

From the 180th parallel – the old International Date Line – to the Mid-Atlantic Ridge was Pax Americana.

To the east of the Ridge and beyond the river Vistula was Pax Germania.

With the brutal suppression of the First Uprising complete by 1971, the passing of a childless Edward VIII the following year left the British monarchy with a succession crisis. This presented an opportunity for Heydrich to consolidate the Reich's hold on Britain.

Despite Princess Elizabeth and her four heirs thriving in Canada, the British monarchy was abolished by wide public acclamation, along with the by now widely discredited and corrupt government of Mosley, and direct rule was imposed from Berlin. Regional governors – Reichskommissars – had direct control over their Reichskommissariat, answerable only to the Führer himself.

London was renamed Hessburg in honour of the murdered Deputy Führer, with the seat of government in the Weiss Tower at the similarly renamed Tower of Hessburg.

British autonomy was over.

A significant ex-pat community of British and Irish émigrés laid their roots in North America. By the early 21st Century they held significant electoral sway.

In 2020 they elected the first black US President, Barack Obama, on a peacenik platform to end isolationism and reengage with the world. Nowhere more important to this policy agenda was restoration of diplomatic relations between Atlantic and Pacific, Germania and America.

The result: a treaty of friendship – the Treaty of Hessburg – due to be signed on December 26th 2021 by President Obama and the Führer of the Third Reich Jörg Haider, the first Austrian-born citizen to assume the role.

As Curtis eyeballed a life-size bust of Haider, Führer since 1999 in this universe but a dead man in his, Elsa rejoined him.

'There you are,' she said, her hand reaching out to him.

'This...' He was dumbstruck, overwhelmed with information. 'This — is unbelievable.'

Elsa's eyes conveyed concern. Harry was behaving erratically. And gone was the American accent. If she wasn't careful, he would draw unwelcome attention to them. 'Did you find what you were looking for?'

'Who.'

'Sorry?' She didn't understand.

'Who I was looking for. No, I didn't.'

'Perhaps I can help. What's his name?'

'Hitler,' he replied. 'Adolf Hitler.'

# 19
# THE AUSTRIAN

'Adolf Hitler,' Elsa replied. 'Not a name I'm familiar with. Who is he?'

The very premise of the conversation was ridiculous, yet to Elsa – and everyone else in this world – what she had just said made perfect sense.

To Curtis and the eight billion people living on Earth in his time, it was utter madness.

Curtis got comfortable. 'Adolf Hitler led the Nazi Party. Not Göring, not Himmler, not Heydrich. Hitler. It was Hitler who started the Second World War, resulting in the deaths of more than eighty million people. Gypsies. Dissidents. The disabled. Homosexuals. Jews. All died in concentration camps. This —' He pointed to the pantheon of bronze busts of the Nazi hierarchy. 'This was our future until Hitler pushed his luck too far by invading Russia in 1941.'

'We've not invaded Russia,' Elsa interjected. 'They've been our allies for over a hundred years, since the end of the Great War. The 1939 Non-Aggression Pact...'

Curtis put a single finger to Elsa's lip, wagging the other in a tick-tock motion while smiling. To an outsider, he looked ever so slightly crazed. 'The pact was a ruse by Hitler to buy time. He had always anticipated war. Christ, he wanted war. He wanted to avenge the loss of pride caused by Pétain and Haig in that railway carriage in 1918. But he wanted war in 1942 or '43, not '39. The pact was merely taking advantage of the situation in the west. It wasn't worth the paper it was written on.'

Listening to Curtis politely, Elsa must have thought that his were the rantings of a madman. She remained vigilant to prying eyes and snooping ears while she heard him out. They were hardly amongst friends.

'Hitler got to the gates of Moscow,' Curtis continued, 'in the winter of 1941 before the extreme weather halted his armies. The Soviets were just days from being completely overrun. It bought them time to regroup. They sacrificed tens of millions of soldiers and civilians in a war of attrition with the Germans, eventually pushing them out of Russia and Ukraine. Three years later, the British and the Americans landed in Normandy, opening up a new western front, and between the two converging sides they drove him back to Berlin in April 1945. With the war lost, his dream of a National Socialist Europe with its heart in Germania gone, he killed himself. Stalin secretly kept his skull in a jar in the Kremlin.'

Elsa was repulsed, disbelieving and mesmerised all at once.

'Everyone here died.' Curtis worked his way along the pantheon. 'Goebbels, Bormann, Himmler – all killed themselves. Göring was captured and condemned to hang but the night before his execution he took cyanide.' He arrived at Rudolf Hess. 'Apart from Hess. He lived into his nineties.

Churchill and the British didn't kill him – he killed himself in Spandau prison in Soviet-controlled East Berlin in 1987. The German paratroopers that landed at the Tower of London —.' He corrected himself. 'The Tower of Hessburg. They had orders to kill Hess, not rescue him. Hitler thought he'd gone mad and planned to defect, the price of his amnesty being the German plans to invade Russia.' He saw Elsa chewing her lip anxiously. 'You think I'm crazy, don't you Dr Brühl?'

'I think you need help, yes,' she smiled weakly.

Curtis looked directly into the eyes of Göring's bust. 'I have to find Hitler.' His voice smacked of urgency. 'He is the key to all of this, this mess.'

'Did he fight in the Great War?'

'Yes – why?'

She extended her hand nervously. 'Then maybe I can help you, Harry.'

*

Sumner bore left off the Euston Road. With Martial Law in force, the road was eerily quiet. There was still no sign of Curtis. This was his third loop down Euston Road, picking up the Islington and Hackney back roads before coming at the Reich History Museum from the west. It was a journey he had already made twice that morning.

It was the plan.

Until Sumner saw the elite SS stoßtruppen filing out of the troop carriers at either end of the road.

The troop carriers reversed slowly in front of him, acting as roadblocks. His foot hit the pedal. As he passed through the rapidly closing gap – his only hope of safety – he saw the chiselled face of Schultz, resplendent in his immaculate black SS uniform. Schultz's eyes caught his, boring into his skull as he passed him.

Curtis was on his own.

*

The Reich History Museum's records office was the epitome of German efficiency. It was less an office, more an enormous archive set within Sydney Smirk's dome-roofed Round Reading Room. It was the last resting place of documentation and artefacts of historical importance and value. Having taken over from the British Library, within these walls sat the hidden gems of a millennium of British history, let alone Reich history, from the Domesday book and the last remaining copies of the Magna Carta through to the execution warrant for the tyrannical Charles I signed by regicides led by Oliver Cromwell.

What Cromwell would make of what had become of London, of England, God only knew, though Curtis suspected he would have been ambivalent at best about the fate of Ireland, a land that despised him with considerable cause.

Curtis stood in awe at the splendour of this almost barren room which, aside from the two bookworm researchers and a clerk that they shared the air with, was theirs.

Elsa marched purposefully towards a computer terminal, which looked like it was straight out of the 1970s. The curious mismatch of technologies that pervaded this world added to its unreality.

With the earlier end to the Second World War and the obliteration of Soviet Russia, China and Japan in the Six Hour War of March 1968, the driving forces of technological advancement so omnipresent in his time just hadn't existed here.

Elsa placed her hand on the terminal's monitor. 'This is the first public access computer in Hessburg.'

'The only one,' Curtis looked up, 'so I hear.'

'From here,' she continued, 'we have access to the Roll of the Fallen – an exhaustive project recording the details of every soldier to have paid the ultimate prize for the peace which we now enjoy.' She was being mildly sarcastic. Curtis did like that in a woman. She tapped the monitor. 'We can search for your Adolf Hitler, yes?'

Curtis cracked his knuckles as he gently brushed her aside to sit at the terminal. Behind him, Elsa suppressed a giggle as Curtis looked down at the keyboard's alien Azerty layout – common on the continent but not the English-speaking world in his time – and then up at the monitor's prompts in German.

He got up sheepishly. 'Maybe you should.'

'Maybe I should.' Elsa took his place, grinning widely. She logged in, bringing up the Roll of the Fallen database. 'So the name we're looking for is...' she queried as she typed.

'Hitler. H-I-T-L-E-R.'

Elsa typed the surname into the database's search field and pressed the enter key with a dainty index finger. Curtis's German may have been rusty but he knew what the response said from the unaccommodating sound the computer made.

'No records match.' Elsa sat back in the chair, fingers intertwined. 'No German soldier by that name.'

*

Just a matter of metres away as the crow flew, the SS stoßtruppen that had filed past Sumner began to circle like vultures into the foyer of the Museum. As they dispersed in silence among its rabbit warren of corridors, Curtis – and Elsa – were rapidly running out of time.

*

No German soldier by that name. Curtis pondered momentarily.

And then he remembered.

'Were you looking for "German" German soldiers by that name?' he asked.

Elsa nodded at the peculiarity of English. She knew what he meant.

Curtis punched his palm over-excitedly. 'Hitler served in the German Army but he wasn't German. He was Austrian by birth.'

Elsa was perplexed. 'Why would an Austrian serve in the German Army when his own country was fighting on the same side in the same war?'

'The Austrian Army wouldn't have him. Thought he was a bit of a weed.' It felt good to say that, given everything around him. Oh, the little victories he thought. 'When the war dragged on into 1915 then 1916, he volunteered for the German Army. Given the rate of losses on both sides, no one could afford to be that picky anymore.'

Elsa returned to the search field and amended Hitler's nationality to Austrian. Curtis looked at the imposing vintage clock above them: 11.30am. He wondered how many passes Sumner had made by now. He needed to wrap this all up. But he was still at first base.

Behind him the computer beeped.

A different beep this time.

Curtis knew the significance.

'One entry found.' The surprise resonated in Elsa's voice. 'Adolf Hitler,' she read aloud with impunity. 'Served in the 16th Bavarian Reserve. Born April 20th 1889 Braunau-am-inn, Austria. Died January 30th 1918 Cambrai, France.'

Curtis walked back to the computer to see it for himself. 'Cambrai,' he pondered aloud. He didn't understand. Cambrai was the field headquarters for the sector for much of the war, only coming into play when the tide turned against Germany later in the conflict. In January 1918, the Germans were still preparing for the first of their offensives of that final decisive year. They wouldn't start until that spring.

'He didn't die in battle.' Elsa's words cut through him like a blowtorch through butter.

'How did he die?'

Elsa read from the screen. 'It says he shot himself.'

Curtis slumped in a nearby chair. Hitler killed himself in 1918. That's why he wasn't around for the formation of the DAP, the takeover of the party from Gregor and Otto Strasser, the Munich bierhaus putsch and everything that followed.

But why on earth would he kill himself in 1918? 1945 he understood, he had no alternative as the Soviets would have made what the Italian partisans did to Mussolini look like a children's birthday party. It was gruesome enough what Stalin secretly did with his charred remains, let alone if he'd been captured alive.

While Curtis absorbed the first clue, Elsa realised that they were now alone in the Round Reading Room. Yet over his shoulder, she thought she saw moving shadows.

Shadows of men running, then crouching.

Men with guns.

She quickly pressed the print button. 'Time to go, Harry.'

A nearby dot matrix printer clambered into action, spitting out the letters onto woven paper marching through its roller like a ticker tape.

The instant it finished printing, she tore it away with haste, grabbing Curtis's hand and dragging him to a nearby service staircase.

Curtis and Elsa crept along the corridor, crouching along below eye level, taking baby steps back down towards the exhibition hall. It was immediately clear to both of them that the building was now overrun with SS Stoßtruppen.

There was only one explanation.

Someone had tipped them off about Harry Holder's day trip to Hessburg.

No wonder Curtis had trust issues.

Elsa was outwardly calm but her palms, damp with nervous sweat, told a different story. Curtis felt guilty for getting her embroiled in his mess. She didn't even know his real name.

'You go,' he whispered. 'Tell them what you need to tell them.' As sincere as his words were, they both knew that it was too late for that.

The only way Elsa was leaving the building alive was with him. She knew too much.

She reached for her skirt, rippling it up her slender thigh, to reveal lace stockings and suspenders that, in other circumstances, would have warranted microscopic closer inspection with Cristal champagne, caviar and candles. On her left inner thigh, on a garter belt, hid a small pocket pistol.

She pulled it from the garter and cocked it. 'I didn't care for the job much anyway.' He admired her bravery, even if it was for his benefit alone.

At least they had something to fight with. But going out the front door armed with just the pistol would have been just like Butch Cassidy and the Sundance Kid versus the Bolivian Army.

With the same outcome.

He was anxious that neither of them became a human tea bag. 'Is there a back door to this place?'

'There is,' she began optimistically, 'but it's a reinforced metal door and I don't have the key. Sorry.'

Not as much as he was.

'But there's the next best thing.' She pointed at the ventilation shaft running along the exhibition hall. 'If we can get inside it without them realising, it runs all the way out of the back of the building, to the railway sidings behind the Museum.'

This was turning into a busman's holiday.

'Ok,' he said assertively. 'Keep low and nimble. If you have to shoot, aim for the head.' He smiled. He sounded like he was coaching her on improving her golf swing.

'Ok Harry,' she smiled back.

'And just in case I don't get to tell you later, my name isn't Harry. It's James.' He got the feeling that he hadn't told Elsa anything she didn't already know. But at least now he hoped she saw he had faith in her. That they were in this together.

They shuffled along behind the pantheon and into the reenactment of the front line trenches that German soldiers occupied for four and a half lonely, frightening years.

And then he saw it.

By the time Elsa realised that he had stopped and crept back to him, Curtis's complexion had turned pallid, as if he had come face to face with a ghost. She pulled at him but he remained frozen still. She looked up at the innocuous photograph of The List Regiment in January 1918, shortly before they arrived at the Western Front.

At the flank of the group was Leutnant der Reserve Rudolf Hess, shortly after his convalescence from a gunshot wound received while fighting in Bucharest.

And alongside him Luka Rothstein, wearing a German army uniform.

# 20
# THE FACE IN THE FRAME

The English Franciscan friar and theologian William of Ockham was an influential philosopher and logician in early medieval times, but his main contribution to western civilisation was perhaps his simplest.

Ockham's razor.

Put simply, that the simplest explanation is usually the right one.

The nightmarish dystopia that had replaced Curtis's world, all because Adolf Hitler had died at the end of the First World War rather than the Second, was no accident of fate.

It was all very much planned.

But by one man or by many?

Whether he was a lone wolf or merely one head of a hydra, it was now clear to him that this was all Luka Rothstein's handiwork.

In that split second, everything became crystal clear.

How could he have been so blind? All of that talk of a higher purpose to the project, about why it was so important to keep it alive by selling its soul to Crombie, about how "we" could stop all of this, when all "we" had done was help it along.

Curtis wondered where in time Rothstein was hiding.

Because if he ever caught up with him, he would make their scrap in the Geneva alleyway look like a back massage.

The photograph was the first conclusive proof that he wasn't insane.

At least, not yet.

Now, he just had to live long enough to do something about it.

He heard her voice echo in his ear. 'James… James…' She clicked her fingers in front of his eyes, snapping him out of the daze he had fallen into. This was no time to be daydreaming. 'We really have to go.'

Curtis grabbed the photograph from the display. As he went to place it safely in his pocket, two smoke canisters scraped across the polished tile floor of the exhibition hall.

They weren't evading the SS.

They were being hunted.

The air was soon swirling with mist. Elsa tried to remove the ventilation grille but struggled as the smoke began to overwhelm the room. Her throat burned. Her chest felt heavy. Her vision was becoming impaired. She was succumbing.

Curtis rushed to her aid, tearing out a trouser pocket lining and getting her to breathe through the material. It was a crude method but one that would buy them some badly needed time. He kicked at the ventilation grille, eventually driving the screws out of their wall plugs. The battered grille hung off a final remaining screw. Curtis clambered towards it, reaching for Elsa to join him.

Only then did he see that he had dropped the photograph of Rothstein on the floor while coming to her aid.

Elsa looked back through the swirling mist, seeing the photograph lying on the floor. Still breathing through the material, she lunged forward to grab it. Fumbling around, her other hand landed on it.

With it safely in hand, she instinctively stood up. She was no more than five paces from the safety of the air vent when the sharp, single shot reverberated. Her porcelain cheeks quickly drained of their blood, a contorted expression on her face preceding the rolling of her once-vivid blue eyes as she dropped first to her knees before falling forwards with the photograph in her outstretched hand.

Curtis was heartbroken and distraught. In the mist, he could see the black-suited shadow coming ever closer. He reached forward and snatched the photograph from Elsa's hand.

As he dived into the air vent, an array of bullets flew over Elsa's dead body, lining the wall surrounding the vent.

The mist cleared to reveal her assassin.

Schultz. Stood with still smoking Luger in his hand.

Behind him, the small army of SS Stoßtruppen, rifles trained on the same spot.

But Curtis was nowhere to be seen.

'Scheiße!' he bellowed.

The head of the SS had been robbed of his prey.

*

The birds broke for safety as a Reichstar train destined for Berlin shattered the peace and relative tranquillity of the railway siding at the rear of the Reich History Museum. The razor wire fence, securing the tracks from unauthorised invasion, rattled and jarred as the train built up towards its maximum speed. These bullet trains could deliver a passenger from Hessburg Zentrum to the heart of Berlin in less than four hours, reaching speeds well in excess of 250 kilometres per hour once on the other side of the English Channel.

It had been the French engineer Albert Mathieu that first proposed building a tunnel connecting Britain to the continent back in 1802. Horse-drawn coaches, illuminated by oil lamps, would traverse the undersea construct, with an artificial island mid-channel for changing horses.

Thirty years later, his compatriot Aimé Thomé de Gamond performed the first geological and hydrographical survey of the Channel between Dover and Calais, later proposing to Napoleon III an underground railway running from Eastwater Point to Cap Griz-Nez with a port-cum-airshaft on the Varne Sandbank, all for a measly £7 million at 1856 prices.

By 1876, governments on both sides seemed to be singing from the same hymn sheet. Within five years, pilot tunnels had been dug on both sides, with seven-foot diameter holes bored 1.9 kilometres from Sangatte in the Nord-Pas-de-Calais departmenté.

But intense political pressure saw the plans shelved, amidst fears that a tunnel would compromise the island nation's natural defences.

After the success of the Nazi invasion, a logistical nightmare that the Wehrmacht and the Kreigsmarine never wanted to repeat, plans were already afoot to connect the new Reichskommissariat Groβbritannien to the continental Reich.

Der Kanallink, an ambitious Channel Tunnel project spearheaded by Organisation Todt, became an early priority for the new regime, with the interned local workforce of able-bodied men aged seventeen to forty-five put to perilous work off the Dover coast as well as a disastrous attempt to connect Fishguard in south-west Wales to Dublin.

Of those that left for the Irish Sea, less than half would return, while the Reichskommissariat quietly abandoned its plans.

Finally opened in 1952, der Kanallink was a feat of engineering genius, for which the workforce was rewarded with the trip of a lifetime east to live out the rest of their ever-shortening lives as industrial slave labour in the mines of the Ruhr as well as Upper Silesia.

It was a deportation that sowed the seeds for the First Uprising, as the abandoned children of the deportees grew into young men and women.

Angry young men and women.

With the train's passage came tranquillity restored. All that could punctuate the uneasy calm was the soft clambering sound coming from within the air ventilation shaft. The clambering gave way to a whoosh as Curtis freefell at speed out of the shaft, landing on freshly excavated earthworks from the railway siding. His passing through of the covering grille had left it, along with his shins, in tatters.

As Curtis emerged from the debris, the plume of dust had left its mark indelibly on him. Panicking and anxious after watching Elsa fall to her death in front of him, he made his way towards the Euston Road, trying to look as inconspicuous as possible.

But deep down, he was angry.

Somebody had used him as bait.

Brave Elsa may be the first to die today but he vowed to himself that she would by no means be the last.

*

From an elevated vantage point atop the railway arch enclosing the Reichstar train line, Gauleiter Hiltz watched Curtis walking alongside the embankment back towards the Euston Road. Much to his own surprise, Hiltz left his CB radio in its holster, instead lighting up as the intrepid time traveller made his escape.

There was no sense in doing the SS's job for them, he thought.

Besides, the time traveller was dead anyway.

Why not give him a head start?

# 21
# TOURIST HOTSPOT

The only obstacle to Curtis's cunning plan to blend in was that there was no crowd to blend in to. Perhaps if he had dressed as one of the SS stoßtruppen he would have fitted in. But given the street had been cleared of civilians for the operation on the Reich History Museum, his clever disguise wasn't going to last for long.

He did what he could to obscure his face as he passed the Museum. After all, that was what had adorned newsstands and television bulletins in days gone past. If he could get back to the steps of the St. Pancras Hotel, hopefully Sumner would be waiting and they could get out of Dodge City alive and in one piece.

Of course, it could have been Sumner that shopped him to the SS. He knew the torture that could be exacted by these evil bastards upon better men – and women – than he.

Perhaps he was walking into a trap.

He didn't have long to agonise over it. As he purposefully bounded onto the hotel steps, he passed the very same Unterwachtmeister from earlier, when Elsa's kiss had probably saved his mission, possibly even his life.

It wasn't exactly a favour he returned to her.

All he had given her back was the kiss of death.

The Unterwachtmeister eyed him suspiciously. He looked down at a security bulletin on his handheld identity scanner. There was Harry Holder. He quickly recognised Curtis but played the game, passing by in order to gain the advantage of surprise.

The Unterwachtmeister reached for his gun, swinging around. 'Halt! Stay where you are.'

Why was it that these vassals of the state always sounded the same?

Curtis raised his hands slowly. If he was alone, he could probably overpower him – if he got close enough. But if the Unterwachtmeister had been trained properly, he would know to keep well back.

Distance was his friend.

The Unterwachtmeister reached for his CB radio. 'Den Engländer. Ich habe den Engländer!'

Before the Unterwachtmeister could report his location, a BMW combination mounted the kerb behind Curtis, sending the fervent Unterwachtmeister flying.

Curtis swung around to find the Unterwachtmeister disorientated on the ground.

And Sumner atop the motorcycle.

'Taxi for one?'

Curtis's eyes darted between Sumner and the dazed Orpol, now coming to.

He had no alternative but to trust him.

For now.

Curtis kicked the Unterwachtmeister straight in the jaw, breaking it and knocking the man out cold. He reached for his gun and his radio as the porter ran behind him into the hotel, no doubt to call it in. He dropped into the combination sidecar, filling it with his frame, as Sumner dropped off the kerb and down the steps out onto St. Pancras Road, past King's Cross U-Bahn station.

'What happened to the Merc?' Curtis shouted over the howling wind as the combination flew down the road in the direction of Farringdon.

'I thought I was rumbled,' Sumner shouted, 'so I junked it and hotwired this instead.' The engine clattered over their voices. 'Did you find what you were looking for?'

'Yes,' Curtis replied. 'But Elsa... She's dead.'

'Shit,' Sumner grimaced. 'Billie's going to be pissed.'

That was putting it mildly, Curtis feared. 'It was like they knew we were going to be there.'

'How could they?' Sumner asked, disbelieving.

How could they indeed.

Before Curtis could interrogate Sumner further, he realised they had company in hot pursuit. Curtis looked around to find two high-performance BMWs closing fast – no doubt the Gestapo – flanked by three bikers.

Sumner indicated the gun that Curtis had relieved the Unterwachtmeister of. 'You know how to use that thing?'

'Yes. And I have Elsa's pistol.' He pulled out the pistol she had hidden in her garter, for all the good it did her.

'Good. Make sure you keep two in reserve,' he said matter-of-factly. 'Just in case.'

Curtis had to admire his pragmatism.

The convoy of foxes and hounds bounded along Farringdon Road, running parallel with the overground railway tracks. Ahead they would intersect with the U-Bahn at Farringdon station.

If they could circumvent the rapidly approaching roadblock ahead of them.

An eager SS patrolman stood in the middle of the road, arm outstretched. 'Halt!' he hollered into the wind.

Curtis fired a warning volley, forcing the patrolman to duck while the combination mounted the kerb again, travelling down past the roadblock without tackling it head-on.

Despite his earlier reservations, Curtis was glad that Sumner had traded in the Mercedes for this outdated but nimble contraption.

The patrolman gathered himself and opened fire from behind.

Curtis had shot to distract, not maim or kill. But this time he had no choice. He fired twice. The second bullet sent the poor patrolman off to join Elsa.

The pursuit cars broke away from the pack, leaving the three bikers to fire past the fallen patrolman, sending a plume of dust airborne as they continued into the old Smithfields market.

The combination weaved in and out through the market as stallholders sold their wares, soon followed by the bikers. As Sumner led them around the houses, intermittent, ill-aimed gunfire crackled in the air behind them, causing a panicked dispersal.

'You have a plan, right?' shouted Curtis.

'Yeah,' Sumner shouted back. 'Just have to live that long!'

The first biker, finally having a clear line of sight, opened fire from his front-mounted machine gun. His bullets rippled the sidecar, coming way too close for Curtis's comfort. Curtis replied in kind back at the biker. Though none of them struck the assailant, the counter fire caused him to lose his footing.

The first biker slid with his bike along the gravel, cutting his right leg to ribbons. The second biker could do little to avoid coming into contact, coming a cropper on top of him.

Curtis smiled to himself, a little inner fist pump.

Alas a third biker avoided the pile-up and remained in pursuit.

The combination sped east through Barbican towards the river. They were moving deeper and deeper into the urban, residential east of the capital when the combination all of sudden began to lose power.

Curtis looked across to find the earlier spray of bullets had hit the fuel tank, which had been leaking since Smithfields.

'Time for that plan!' he screamed.

With their sudden lack of speed, the third biker had managed to quickly make up the distance, while to either side of them the two Gestapo pursuit vehicles joined the convoy as it powered along.

The biker pulled ahead of the pursuit vehicles, coming alongside the sidecar. The biker reached for his handgun – his front-mounted machine gun was not of much use when running parallel with its target. With bullets precious, Curtis sat up in the sidecar and punched the unprepared biker in the face. The biker lost his footing, his bike skidding in front of the Gestapo pursuit vehicle to starboard.

The two collided and the Gestapo car careered into a line of parked cars, igniting its own fuel tank and setting several of them alight.

The last Gestapo car remained in touch.

'Get ready to jump!' Sumner shouted.

'Jump where?'

Curtis and Sumner threw themselves in opposite directions out of the combination, which lost all remaining speed as soon as Sumner's foot left the pedal. The pursuing Gestapo car, unable to slow itself in time, crashed into the back of it. The conjoined, mangled metal of the two skidded into a fenced off park, erupting into a fireball upon impact with its final destination.

Curtis and Sumner had landed perilously on the well-worn asphalt. They looked up at the carnage they had caused.

'I'd stick to cars if I was you…' Curtis laid his hand on Sumner's shoulder. Though the finger of suspicion still lay upon him, without his Herculean efforts they would both now be dead.

Sumner returned the smile. 'Let's get back.'

Curtis and Sumner scuttled towards a lane straddling the backs of outward-facing terraced housing. In the distance they heard the chilling roar of mechanised troop carriers heading in their direction.

Reinforcements.

Sumner urged Curtis along towards a manhole cover looming ahead of them. He opened the cover, leading back down into the subterranean world from which they had earlier crawled. Curtis clambered in, followed by his slightly hobbling compatriot.

As he replaced the manhole cover, the SS Stoßtruppen filed out into the street, steeled for an act of vengeance on the unsuspecting local populace that only the security branch of this fascist state was capable of exacting.

Yet more unwitting and innocent victims of Luka Rothstein.

*

Schultz stood under the domed ceiling of the Round Reading Room. It reminded him of Speer's Great Hall in Berlin, completed in 1946 as a celebration of the birth of modern Germania from Europe's ashes, though it wasn't quite as grand.

Only the British, he thought, would waste such a monumental engineering feat on a room full of books for square-eyed academics.

The computer technician coughed to grab his attention. Schultz stopped musing. On the monitor in front of him, he saw the same entry that Curtis and Elsa had seen.

About an obscure dead Austrian soldier called Adolf Hitler.

Schultz pressed print.

# 22
# LOYALTIES LIE

Hiltz walked sombrely amongst the detritus.

What a waste.

The exhibition hall was like a war zone, with rare exhibits strewn and unique memorabilia destroyed forever.

Let alone the human cost.

But the bronze busts in the pantheon stood steadfast and firm, glaring down from upon high like decadent Roman emperors of old.

They should all have been flattered by the comparison.

The hall was cordoned off, out of sight from prying eyes. Not that anybody would dare.

Hiltz saw a wisp of Elsa's hair protruding from a body bag before officials from the Reich Coroner's office zipped her up. That would be the last we saw of her in this world, he thought, as the body bag would go directly to the konzentrazionkamp at Sheppey for immediate disposal. The bill for her cremation would be an unwelcome Yuletide gift for her next of kin.

But as a terrorist, or at the very least an accomplice to one, this was all that she could expect.

She would have known that.

Hiltz was tired of death. He was just two years from retirement. He had given so much of his adult life to service in a foreign land. He wasn't going to live out his own final act in Hessburg of all places, that was for sure. He would head home, head east, perhaps to enjoy the baking Mediterranean sun further south.

One of the benefits of the Reich, particularly for someone like him, was that ability to settle anywhere.

Unlike Elsa, he would die somewhere warm.

The last thing he needed was to preside over a Third Uprising in Hessburg.

Not on his watch.

None of this was helpful.

He surveyed the wall of the Western Front reenactment, which had survived the fire fight remarkably unscathed.

Except it hadn't.

One of the exhibits – a photograph – was missing from its frame.

Hiltz knelt down to read the German inscription etched on a plaque underneath the missing photograph.

THE BRAVE AND GALLANT FUTURE DEPUTY
FÜHRER RUDOLF HESS DELIVERING THE LIST
REGIMENT TO THE WESTERN FRONT
JANUARY 1918

*

As Hiltz stepped out of the Museum between Smirke's columns, the SS stoßtruppen filed in and saluted. At first he thought it was for him, until he saw the Reichskommissar's motorcade pulling up outside the nearby gates. The flag of the Reich flapped wildly on the outstretched bonnet of his limousine.

The loyal adjutant, as eager as ever, jumped out of the front of the limousine and opened the back passenger door.

The Reichskommissar was not getting out.

Hiltz was getting in.

As he approached the car, even from a distance Hiltz could see von Braun's rotund figure bulging out of his overly extravagant uniform.

The instant he was in the limousine, the passenger door was closed, the adjutant back in his front seat and the motorcade back on the road.

Von Braun certainly did enjoy the trappings of the finer life, reclining in his leather-lined, spacious official car supping copious quantities of Schnapps from his well-stocked drinks cabinet, set into the soundproof dividing wall between front and back compartment.

'Herr Reichskommissar,' Hiltz shuffled nervously. 'The spy eluded us once again.'

'No matter.' Von Braun finished off his Schnapps while gazing ahead at everything yet at nothing. 'Herr Schultz is on the trail. He always gets his man.' He smiled mendaciously even when he didn't mean to. 'Did you find anything missing in the Museum?'

'Like what?' Hiltz replied socratically. He knew von Braun too well.

'Like a photograph of Hess.'

'I noticed that.' He was disappointed yet not surprised that von Braun knew already.

Von Braun turned to the Gauleiter. 'Hiltz, do you believe this man Curtis is a time traveller?'

'I thought you were convinced he was a spy?' he replied wryly.

Von Braun placed two small liqueur shot glasses in an armrest holder. 'Oh, I am.' He began to pour. 'The only question is – for whom?'

'The Freiheit Movement,' Hiltz proffered unconvincingly.

Von Braun tutted. 'What interest would that band of half-breeds, gypsies, vagabonds and Negroes have in an obscure Austrian soldier called Adolf Hitler?' He handed Hiltz the second printout that Schultz had given him, from the Roll of the Fallen. 'I have taken the liberty of informing Berlin of our Herr Curtis. The Führer is most intrigued. We are to capture him alive and get him on the next transport out of Hesston Flughafen.'

Hiltz looked at the printout with a degree of resignation. 'Yes, Herr Reichskommissar.' He knocked back the Schnapps.

'You were quite right to want to spare him.' Von Braun put his arm around Hiltz in a paternalistic fashion. They were both old men and such paternalism ill-suited the Reichskommissar. 'This is a great moment. A moment of opportunity – for both of us.' He reclined again, self-satisfied. 'I understand that talks with the Americans are not going so well. This Obama wants to do a deal, to go down in history as the President who ended the Cold War, but the rest of their political elite are suspicious about our trade deals with Cuba, Nicaragua and of course Mexico. They are threatening a blockade if we don't reach terms.' Von Braun sipped his Schnapps. 'We need all hands to the mast if we are to break the stalemate. Peace if we're successful. Victory if we're not.'

Hiltz shifted uneasily at von Braun's warmongering.

'I need to know if where your loyalties lie, Hiltz.'

'How do you mean?' Hiltz responded quizzically.

'To Hessburg – or to me and the Reich?'

'To you Herr Reichskommissar,' replied von Braun's insincere servant. 'Always.'

Von Braun smiled ebulliently as he poured yet more Schnapps.

'By the way,' Hiltz asked, 'I did not see Schultz in the Museum. Where is he now?'

Von Braun supped his Schnapps. 'Doing what he does best. Hunting down rats.'

*

Rufus and Skunk skulked around in the shadows. The Central Line may have been red, white and garish lights when the trains ran but when they didn't it was all about black, brown and grey.

Spending so much of their lives underground and in artificial light had taken its toll on their eyesight. Their eyes could easily play tricks on them, seeing things that weren't there, not seeing things that were. Deciding what was real and what wasn't. If the worst were ever to happen, those decisions could mean life – or death.

Amongst the peculiar sounds of the underground, the dripping of water, the scurrying of rats, the creaking of girders, the thud of falling brickwork – it was difficult to distinguish whether anything else could be causing the noise.

That meant they were always on maximum alert.

In the darkness, Rufus convinced himself that he could see movement in the shadows. He retreated into a darkened corner himself, gun cocked with a bullet loaded in its chamber, while Skunk blended in too. Footsteps became discernible, growing closer and closer. Rufus was ready to end it all for their guests as they passed them.

Rufus and Skunk emerged behind them.

'Halt!' Rufus barked ironically.

As Curtis and Sumner raised their hands and pivoted around to see them, they lowered their weapons. Rufus almost looked pleased to see them, stepping forward to embrace Sumner before turning to Curtis.

'How did it go?'

Curtis turned back, heading towards the bunker. 'Not good.'

*

In the command centre, Billie paced nervously, a quixotic combination of sedate and anxious. Her lungs drew in every last milligram of nicotine from the cigarette she held between her fingers. Smoking was strictly prohibited inside the bunker apart from the service tunnel leading to the underground network.

But on special occasions of high stress, there were exceptions.

This was one of those very occasions where she found herself dancing on the head of a pin.

As Kennedy approached, she stopped in her tracks.

'Anything?'

He shook his head. 'But you should turn on the television.'

She knew instantly from the low-lying eyes of Kennedy that what awaited her would bring pain.

Turning on the television only confirmed it. On every channel: wall-to-wall coverage of the storming of the Museum.

The television cameras made a big deal of the removal of the body bags of the victims while the newscaster addressed viewers sombrely. 'The fire fight at the Reich History Museum has so far cost the lives of eight people – seven brave soldiers of the Reich and one blonde female employee.'

Billie was visibly choked as she turned the television off. Kennedy tried to comfort her but she knew in her bones that the blonde female employee was Elsa.

He held her shoulders. 'It might not be her...'

A voice echoed from the doorway. 'It was her.'

Billie turned to see Curtis before letting out an angry tear.

Curtis stepped towards her. 'She was extremely brave. And I'm very sorry.'

Billie fought to regain her composure. 'She was just doing her job. What did you find out?' she asked, drying her eyes.

'Oh, quite a bit.'

Now it was Curtis's time to pace anxiously, as if he had discovered the Japanese carrier group en route to Pearl Harbor.

'Remember my time travel experiment – well, we were sent in pairs.' He slapped down the blood-stained photograph that he had borrowed from the Museum – of Rothstein and Hess together – on the table. 'There's my pair – Luka Rothstein, stood behind Rudolf Hess in a photograph that was taken over a hundred years ago. Now, either the guy's a vampire and never ages or the little fucker has gone back in time and killed Adolf fucking Hitler.' He pulled the printout from the Roll of the Fallen and handed it to Billie. 'And I know where. And when.'

Billie handled the printout with care. 'Who is this Hitler? Why is he so important?'

Curtis shook his head. 'I can't believe I even have to explain this, that's how fucked up everything is. In my time, this guy is a legend for all the wrong reasons. We had a Nazi Party too, created after the First World War. But it was led by an Austrian fascist called Adolf Hitler. Now, Hitler was a brilliant public speaker. Even his opponents and enemies gave him that.'

He drew a breath.

'After the First World War, Germany was bankrupt. None of the traditional political parties had answers to the problems facing the country. For over ten years, he built up the Nazi Party, gaining more and more support from the disillusioned German people until he – not Göring – became Chancellor in 1933. He – not Himmler – plunged Europe into war in 1939 after faking the Polish takeover of Danzig. But his self-confidence, his audacity, all proved his downfall.'

'How?' Billie asked.

'Hitler wrote this book while he was a political prisoner in jail in 1923. It was called *Mein Kampf*.'

'My Struggle,' Billie translated.

'Right. Now this book was Hitler's personal manifesto, telling the world what he would do if he ever got his hands on the levers of power. Like many Germans, he blamed the Jews for Germany's ills. The blood libel, faked in Russia in the 19th Century about Jews sacrificing Christian children in a ritual, was peddled as the truth to a willing population. So with their tacit approval, he persecuted them, turning them into an underclass. He systematically eroded their rights, stole their property, stripped them of their German citizenship, until he stumbled across the Final Solution. Ever wondered what happened to all of the Jews in your world?'

Billie and Rufus looked at other, without an answer.

'Well,' he continued, 'good old Reinhard Heydrich and Heinrich Himmler concocted the most evil part of it all. Those KZ you guys fear being carted off to – there's a reason people don't get seen again. They're not concentration camps, they're death camps. Six million Jews went to them in my time. He gassed them to death, stole their gold fillings and tried to turn the rest of them into soap.'

Billie and Rufus were disgusted as they recoiled at the thought.

'But this is only half of it,' Curtis continued. 'Hitler hated the Soviets – the Slavs – as much as he hated the Jews. He thought they were greedy sloths, with all this space to expand and no imagination of what they could do with it. He was desperate for what he called lebensraum – living space. What he really wanted was breeding space. Within a year of the start of the war, he controlled all of Europe apart from fascist Spain and Italy, communist Russia and imperial Britain.'

Rufus remained sceptical. 'So if he was such a military genius, how come he lost?'

'Simple. He ignored his generals. He tore up the Non-Aggression Pact he had with the Soviets and invaded them in June 1941.'

'But,' Billie interjected, 'Britain was invaded in June 1941.'

'Not in my history. Hitler had a go at it with the Battle of Britain in 1940. But the RAF – guided from this very room – sent the Luftwaffe packing. Perhaps,' Curtis pondered, 'it was that which forced Hitler to look east instead of west.'

'So, in your time,' Rufus mused, 'in your Britain, you're free?'

Curtis laughed, somewhat inappropriately. 'Nobody is ever free.' Curtis's natural cynicism shone through. 'The government still sucks and all politicians are the same rentaquote morons who've never run a bath but think they can run a country. But we don't have a secret police. We have elections. We're half-arsed members of a trading bloc with the Germans and the French called the European Union, which pisses everyone off but no one knows what better to replace it with. The Americans are our closest allies and the Russians are stuck in the last century. So no change there.'

'Sounds wonderful,' Billie pondered.

'I wouldn't go that far,' Curtis replied, reining her in. 'But it's certainly better than this. And the average life expectancy is a lot longer!'

Billie handed back the printout to Curtis. 'What do you need to make it happen?'

He took a deep breath. 'I need to get back my time bracelet, go back to the trenches of the Western Front in 1918 and stop Luka from killing Hitler.'

He hadn't really thought about it like that but that was what it amounted to.

To save the world, he had to save Adolf Hitler's life.

Rufus didn't understand. 'Why not just go back to 1941 and stop him going to 1918 in the first place?'

'Don't you see – it'll be an alternative 1941. Your 1941, not mine.' Curtis picked up the photograph and held it in front of Rufus. 'Our histories part ways here – in 1918.'

Billie rubbed her head, massaging her temples. 'Mind-blowing.'

Rufus perched on a stool. 'Mind-blown.'

'Personally, I'd like to blow Hitler's balls off. Sorry, ball off.' Curtis corrected himself, recalling that he only had one testicle, though rumours that thanks to his mother the other one was in the Royal Albert Hall proved wide of the mark. 'But knowing that this is the result – it's better that he lives.'

'It's funny,' Rufus smiled genuinely. 'Everybody else wants to get out of the Tower – and you want to get back in!'

Curtis smiled back.

He and Rufus had come a long way in a short time.

As had he and Billie.

It was a love-in destined to be short-lived.

# 23
# THE ENEMY WITHIN

The first they knew was when dust started raining down on them from new cracks in an old ceiling.

Curtis, Billie and Rufus looked at each other quizzically.

Either the tectonic plates had shifted in this alternative world and these were the aftershocks of a nearby earthquake.

Or some serious mechanised artillery was heading their way.

It didn't take long to realise it was the latter.

The first mortars must have burrowed tens of feet deep into ground that had lain undisturbed for eighty years. While not powerful enough to break through in one fell swoop, they made light work of bringing the ceiling of the command centre down on top of them.

The curdling screams of controllers trapped underneath beams and the breathless gasps of those buried under falling masonry echoed throughout the nearby corridors.

When the initial barrage passed, Curtis found himself on one side of a tangled wire mesh with Billie and Rufus marooned on the other.

'You must have been followed,' coughed Billie frantically.

Rufus shook his head angrily. 'You stupid idiot – you've

led them straight to us.'

Curtis tried in vain to move the metal girder that sat between them, to no avail.

Billie was still coughing and spluttering. 'There's no way to get to you.'

Rufus grabbed her arm. 'It's him they're after Billie. There's no point in all of us being captured. You owe it to the Movement to live!'

Billie wrestled with her conscience. Her fighting spirit told her to stay.

But Rufus was right.

They did want Curtis.

She looked at him sadly. 'Sorry Curtis.'

Billie and Rufus backed away, making for the unblocked corridor behind them, with Skunk in tow.

'Billie!' Curtis stepped forward, trying forlornly to follow, but the obstructions were too much and too many. Insurmountable. Another shell landed and the corridor was blocked, with Billie, Rufus and Skunk on the other side. Even if Curtis could traverse the wreckage, he couldn't follow them now.

He was on his own.

And it was probably for the best, given the death and destruction he had wrought upon them.

He looked down at the floor. The photograph, battered but still intact, lay next to the printout. He grabbed them both before turning to find Kennedy stood behind him.

Kennedy extended his arm. 'I know a way out. Come with me.'

Curtis felt reassured not to be on his own. He grabbed his arm and clambered over the carnage as stoßtruppen entered the base.

Other resistance members put up a spirited fight, with some success, but the sheer numbers were against them. As one stoßtruppler fell, another almost immediately replaced them, taking full advantage of dwindling ammunition to take their prey.

Curtis and Kennedy bounded down a corridor. Curtis stopped dead. A dying Sumner lay reaching for him. Before he could make it to him, a fresh hail of bullets finished the job.

'Halt!'

Curtis turned to reveal a stoßtruppler, gun trained on him. He raised his hands slowly as the stoßtruppler smiled, knowing he had netted his Ace of Spades. As he did, another barrage of shells landed, loosening the ceiling above the stoßtruppler. Before he had time to move, a huge chunk of the reinforced concrete ceiling had landed on top of him, squashing him to a pulp.

A relieved Curtis sighed. 'Thank God for German efficiency.'

Curtis and Kennedy emerged through a porthole into the sewers underneath Uxbridge. The putrid air filled his nostrils but it was their only chance of escape.

Kennedy reached for a rusty ladder. 'This way Curtis.'

Curtis closed the porthole behind him. 'Above ground will be swarming with SS. We'll be safer underground.'

'I'm afraid I must insist,' Kennedy interrupted him. Curtis looked down to see Kennedy holding a tranquiliser gun, pointed straight at his torso.

'You!?'

'Me,' Kennedy nodded. 'Rufus was right about one thing – they only want you.'

Curtis was incredulous. He had suspected Sumner, Rufus, even Elsa at one point.

Never Kennedy.

'But you're, you're...' He stumbled across his words.

'What?'

'You're black!' Curtis blurted.

Kennedy was incensed. 'And?'

'The Nazi hate blacks!'

'And blacks hate the Nazis,' he barked back. 'But a deal's a deal and I can't stand living like a rat in the sewers any longer. They'll send me home to my family in Ghana. With the reward money, I can set up my own surgery and look after my own people.'

'These are your people!' Curtis spat back angrily. 'Billie trusted you!'

Kennedy smiled. 'And she still will. It's you she thinks led them here – not me.'

Curtis lunged at Kennedy but it was never going to be in time to avoid the tranquiliser dart flying through the air towards him. He grasped at his torso as the sedative took hold. Kennedy looked on smugly but before he could take advantage of his incapacity a blade tore through his chest from behind.

Gutted, the tranquiliser gun fell limply from his hand, splashing into the polluted pools surrounding his feet.

A look of stunned surprise was etched into Kennedy's face as he dropped to his knees, before falling face first into the sewage. Behind him stood Skunk, wiping his bloodied blade clean, flanked by Billie and Rufus.

Billie stepped onto Kennedy's corpse, squelching it into the excrement. 'That's for Elsa, you lying bastard.' She looked down at Curtis, eyelids fluttering as he fell unconscious. She turned to Rufus. 'Come on, we haven't much time.'

It was probably for the best that Curtis was unconscious when she produced the penknife and carved the identity implant from his arm.

An implant that had secretly been a tracking device all along.

*

With the gaps between bursts growing shorter, the tracking machine's signal was growing stronger.

'Zehn Meter links und dann geradeaus,' the SS signal finder watched the signal, directing the squadron traversing the tunnels cautiously and in flanking formation. At their rear followed Schultz, hunting for rats indeed in the sewers below Uxbridge.

A rat came across Schultz's path. The SS chief drop-kicked it out of his way, its squeals coming to an abrupt halt upon impact with the blown Victorian brickwork.

As the party arrived at the tunnel where Kennedy had confronted Curtis, they saw at the foot of the rusty ladder a man on his knees, from behind looking almost as if he was praying.

Schultz smiled with confident satisfaction as the squadron approached ahead of him.

The signal bursts became constant. The party cantered forward to find the man was Kennedy. The signal finder looked perplexed until he saw, in the palm of his bloodied hand, the identity implant Billie had removed from Curtis's arm.

None of the party could have known that he was laden with proximity charges.

And that they had just set them off.

Seeing the firestorm ahead, Schultz dived into the sewage as the blast above tore through the tunnel, consuming his elite troops.

*

Down a distant tunnel, two canoes ambled slowly away, unmoved by the obvious death and destruction elsewhere.

Rufus and Skunk aboard one.

Billie and an unconscious Curtis in the other.

# 24
# GHOST OF CHRISTMAS PAST

The wind howled all around Curtis as he stirred from slumber. His eyes took some time to adjust to the extremes of dark and light, a darkness punctuated by narrow beams of natural light coming from a distance.

As his eyes struggled to adjust, he sensed a silhouette shuffling in front of him, hopping and skipping.

It was only when his eyesight fully returned that he realised that the silhouette was in fact a young girl. She must have been about six years old, of Asian descent, with pink ribbons tied in her hair and an infectious grin.

She was very, very thin.

She held out a daisy, handing it to Curtis before skipping away towards the light.

He wondered if he was dead and this was purgatory.

As he tried to get to his feet, feeling every millimetre of his butchered arm weeping underneath a soiled bandage, he realised he was still in hell.

And memories of the raid on the bunker at Bomber Command came flooding back.

Kennedy.

He felt his arm. That made sense. If Kennedy was the inside assist – the mole – he would have been in a unique position to control his identity implant, effectively turning it into a tracking device. That was how they found him at the Museum and at the bunker.

They knew exactly where they needed to look.

Curtis stood and followed in the direction of the girl.

Into the howling wind.

Into the light.

As the light grew closer and closer, the salty sea air filled his nostrils. But it didn't feel fresh and pure, the fresh air that he would expect from the coast.

It felt polluted.

Toxic even.

As he clambered up the side of the cliff, all became clear.

This was an old gun battery, etched deep into the white cliffs of Dover.

Dating back to the Second World War, the Fan Bay Deep Shelter was a series of tunnels set twenty-three metres into the white cliffs at Fan Bay, near the Port of Dover itself.

It housed the Fan Bay artillery battery, a last line of defence against any invasion fleet approaching the Kent coastline.

It obviously hadn't worked.

Despite the failure of the Luftwaffe to gain superiority over the RAF during the summer of 1940, Hitler's Directive 16 – authorising the invasion of Britain, if necessary – had remained in effect. The directives were instructions or strategic plans, issued by the Führer himself, covering a wide range of subjects from authorisation of military units on all fronts to invade enemy territory to the governance of occupied territories.

Under the Nazi system of government, the Führer's directives were binding, superseding any other law – even one made by the Reichstag, Germany's nascent parliament – and to be followed to the letter.

With Directive 16 remaining in effect from July 16th 1940 throughout the remainder of the war, the southern coast would stay on high alert.

Lined with corrugated steel arching, the tunnel complex originally included five large chambers offering storage for small arms and a field hospital with its own subterranean medical stores, along with a generator and washroom amenities.

In Curtis's time, the shelter had been abandoned in the Fifties, its significance as a monument to the war lost on those using it for landfill soon after. Only when the National Trust took ownership of the White Cliffs did extensive restoration work begin, starting with the removal of over a hundred tonnes of rubble.

All too quickly, people forget, Curtis thought.

Above ground, as far as his eyes could see, were row upon row of tents. This was a refugee camp, set in the shadow of seven old power stations, filling the air – and the refugees' lungs – with the exhaust fumes of the Reichskommissariat's energy production. The power stations were in full throes, churning out $CO_2$ and toxic pollutants without care or concern for the local inhabitants.

But there was clearly some kind of party going on.

To Curtis it looked like the Notting Hill Carnival had decamped to the south coast.

Of course, he thought. It must almost be Christmas.

The camp was made up of everyone – and everything – that would be most unwelcome in a Nazi society. Gypsies and

Roma. The disabled. Gays and lesbians. Jews and Muslims. Afro-Caribbeans and mixed race. All of these disparate groups, hate figures for the Aryan purist, appeared to exist in harmony.

It was like a microcosm of the London he had known and loved.

All around him, children from all ethnic groups played everything from cricket and hopscotch to cowboys and Indians. In the background, grown-ups – their parents, presumably – prepared a banquet of sorts, despite the modest temperatures.

Among the sea of colour and diversity, he saw Billie holding court with a group of younger children, sat on the laps of their parents, listening intently. She saw Curtis and gently nodded.

For now the children had her undivided attention. She was telling them a story.

Curtis knew it straight away, as Billie prowled like a tiger on all fours before jumping up onto its hind legs and gobbling up all the food.

The children giggled.

They were too young to realise that the book, *The Tiger Who Came To Tea*, was rumoured to be an allegory about Nazis.

Nonetheless, this act of normality, in a world far from normal, made Curtis smile.

Hearing the footsteps crunching into the frosty ground behind him, Curtis turned to find a scouting party returning. Amongst their number were Rufus, Skunk and Stoltz. Rufus stopped as the others continued past, in need of sustenance.

'How are you feeling?' Rufus was being unusually nice.

'I'm pretty sure James Bond never got knocked out this much.'

'James who?'

'Never mind.' Curtis sighed. Yet another cultural casualty of Trans-Animate Displacement.

007.

Rufus faux smiled. 'What hurts more – being knocked out or waking up to all of this?'

Curtis ignored the question. 'How many made it out of the bunker?'

Touché. 'Five. Including you.'

Curtis sighed. 'Fuck.'

Rufus placed his hand on Curtis's shoulder, pointing with his other hand to the pumping chimney stacks of the nearby power stations. 'You know, you're almost as bad for everyone's health as those things.'

Rufus laughed and coughed in almost equal measure as he followed after Skunk and Stoltz in search of food.

He left Curtis feeling dreadful.

*

The band of log-jammers made for one hell of a party. Despite freezing temperatures and squalid conditions, the refugees were clearly determined to enjoy themselves. Amongst them, Billie, her hair braided. She looked unusually pretty for a warrior princess.

But one of their number was not celebrating.

Curtis sat alone at the edge of the chalky white cliff, looking pensively across the English Channel at the barely visible flickering lights of northern France just twenty miles away.

'Room service.'

Curtis turned to find Billie, stood holding a bowl and some bread, smiling down on him. She sat next to him, placing the bowl between them, looking out to sea for herself.

'Thanks.' Curtis studiously avoided eye contact. 'But I'm not that hungry.'

'Make the most of it,' she blurted testily, the real Billie never far from the surface. 'I don't make a habit of waiting on sulking men. Especially those about to leave without saying goodbye.'

'I'm not sulking! I'm feeling extraordinarily guilty about the death and destruction I've brought to your world!'

'You've brought!?' Billie hopped up. 'You've not caused any of this. Those butchers in Berlin and their lapdogs in Hessburg have done this.' She placed her hand on his shoulder. 'Not you.'

Curtis stared ahead into the dark night. 'Tell that to the parents of those children when the SS crash the party.'

'Oh, they won't waste their bullets. The fumes from those things,' she pointed to the chimney stacks, 'are poisonous. Deadly. They know they'll eventually do their work for them.' She sighed. 'Besides, none of these people officially exist. They're all the children of Originals or undesirables exiled by the regime. Once you're classed as undesirable, your implant is removed and you're banished from Hessburg. No implant, no entry to Hessburg, no job, no home, no healthcare, no education. The regime expects them to starve – eventually.' She crouched down next to him. 'Which is why you've made such a difference.'

Curtis didn't understand. 'What kind of a life is that?'

'You've given us the first hope ever that there is a better life for all of us somewhere out there. That's why we're with you.'

James Curtis – the beacon of hope. Jesus Christ…

He turned to Billie. 'You know what I have to do.'

She looked at him with uncharacteristically doleful eyes. 'Yes.'

'It's going to be extremely dangerous.'

'Yes.'

'Whether I make it or not, I won't be coming back.'

Billie clenched his lapel. 'Yes.'

'So why?' he asked.

'Because I'm not the kinda girl to wait at home for bad news.' She pulled him towards her and kissed him full on the mouth. It was a kiss you don't get away from, tender yet not rabid in passion or intensity. Perhaps it was the family audience nearby.

Her lips left his but their eyes remained shut. 'But we don't know where the bracelet is. It could be halfway to Berlin by now.'

Billie's eyes opened. 'I know exactly where the bracelet is.'

She removed a folded newspaper sheet from her own back pocket. It was today's edition of Der Times. On the front page, next to a spread about the US President's visit to Hessburg, was a picture of von Braun saluting at a memorial service for the Hess Square victims.

On his wrist: Curtis's time bracelet.

'Son of a bitch.' Curtis snatched the newspaper sheet. 'Where is von Braun now?'

'At his official residence on the outskirts of London, Castle Saxe-Coburg.'

'I don't know where that is.'

'Maybe you know it under its old name: Windsor Castle.'

Of course he lives in Windsor Castle, Curtis thought.

Billie retreated a step. 'We'll leave in three hours.' She knelt to collect the bowl of soup and the bread. She handed them to Curtis. 'So now is the time to eat — and rest.'

*

How on earth could Curtis rest after that kiss?

They say that we have different loves as we meander through life. The first. The romantic. The mind fuck. The one.

Which one was Billie?

For sure, in a different time and certainly in a different place, he would like to get to know her much better.

But not in this time.

It didn't stop him from being entirely distracted by the scent of her hair or the taste of her mouth, still lingering on his palette.

He had barely touched his meal.

Curtis had taken to some light bedtime reading to distract himself from his more animalistic urges.

The book he had bought in the Reich History Museum, *The History of the 20th Century.*

Despite the poor reception underground in the shelter, for company he had managed to find Sounds of the Free World on the wireless radio.

It was clearly Love Hour, belting out the King, which hardly helped matters.

'And still wishing you a very Merry Christmas,' the DJ announced. 'That was Elvis Presley with *Love Me Tender*. It's hard to think that this guy was still going strong and singing into his eighties.'

Only in this world could Elvis have lived!

'Coming up on Sounds of the Free World,' the DJ continued, 'we have Billie Holliday, Ella Fitzgerald and a classic from Frank Sinatra.'

Even taking into account its overt Nazi revisionism, the book was an engrossing read, particularly the history of Windsor Castle – Castle Saxe-Coburg. It was the seat of the Nazi King, Edward VIII, who returned to the throne after Britain was invaded and his brother Bertie fled to Canada. Edward had reigned until his death in 1972. Without an acceptable heir, the monarchy was abolished, allegedly as a mark of respect.

And the spoils of monarchy now rested with the Reichskommissar, Erich von Braun.

He looked the type to savour all of the pomp and ceremony that went with such a role.

He was looking forward to meeting him in the flesh.

Billie stepped gingerly into the bunker, her braided hair now loose, flowing evenly across her Amazonian shoulders. 'This doesn't look much like resting to me.'

Curtis didn't look up. 'Before all else, be armed.' He waved the book at her.

'Profound,' she stepped into the alcove, letting the plastic sheet drop behind her. It afforded them at least some privacy.

'No, I think it was Machiavelli.' He looked up and smiled, closing the book. 'Sorry. Benefits of a private education and a tutelage in the fine art of politics by my Dad.'

'Your father was a politician?' Billie sat at the end of the makeshift bed.

'God no,' Curtis laughed heartily. 'He was a businessman. But business is politics behind closed doors.'

'Clever man.' She pulled out a sparkling metal whisky flask.

'He had his good days.'

She offered him the whisky. He gladly accepted.

'I never met my father.'

'Was he...?' Curtis asked before taking a swig.

'Black?' Billie finished his sentence for him. 'No – I get my genes from the dark continent from my mother.' She paused, then said nonchalantly: 'He was a German officer.'

Curtis nearly choked on the whisky.

He wasn't expecting that.

'My mother was in the resistance in the Eighties,' Billie continued, 'back when it was a pacifist movement. She was there for the first Hess Square Massacre back in 1989. After that, everything changed. Peaceful methods went out the window. They showed no mercy. Neither did we. It was brutal. The resistance intercepted a death march to the woods. Killed everyone bar one officer who they took prisoner. It was her job to interrogate him. He was only a young man then, a conscript from Switzerland. She fell in love with him. I was the result.'

Curtis had heard of Stockholm Syndrome, where the captive fell in love with their captor, but not the other way around. 'Fairy-tale stuff.' He handed her back the flask.

'Not exactly.' She took a swig to steel herself. 'No fairy-tale ending. When I was very little, she went on a mission to Hessburg. She never came back.'

Curtis held Billie's hand, sensing the faintest sign of a tear emerging in the corner of her eye. On the radio in the background, Billie Holliday's *All Of Me* began playing.

Billie smiled as she pinched the bridge of her nose, blocking her tear ducts with her fingers, ever so slightly embarrassed. 'My mother used to play this kind of music to me all the time when I was little.' She sensed his next question. 'And yes, I'm named after her.'

Curtis smiled. Good taste all round. 'My favourite's *God Bless The Child*.'

Billie's head bobbed gently. 'I love them all. But this one's my favourite.'

Curtis stood up, pulling Billie up with him robustly, their bodies tantalisingly close to each other. He pulled her body close to his, cheek to cheek, soft body parts against hard body parts. He found it peculiar dancing with this warrior princess.

She nuzzled in close too, comforted by the warmth of his body next to hers. 'What do you think I'd be doing if I was in your world?'

He smiled. 'Kicking ass, most probably.'

'I think I'd be a singer. Like Billie. Playing in the old jazz clubs.'

He grinned. 'I'd pay good money to see that.'

She pulled away a little, bringing her face to face with him as their feet boxed around on the dugout floor. 'Would you now...?'

Billie kissed Curtis a second time, more passionately and ravenous than their earlier locking of lips.

There wasn't much time left.

As they settled into the bed, through a break between the plastic modesty drapes a furious Rufus spied. He wasn't happy as he moved off, leaving Curtis and Billie alone as the full moon rested low in the clear night sky.

Beneath them, the Dover Straits shimmered.

# 25
# A WINDSOR KNOT

The river Thames shivered in the moonlight, obscured only by the footprint of Castle Saxe-Coburg.

A royal residence dating back to the Saxon kings of the 8th Century, the castle stood supreme on the chalk ridge above the town of Windsor.

The sprawling fortress sat in thirteen acres of high ground on the north bank of the river, its two convoluted, quadrilateral-shaped building complexes flanking the enormous Round Tower, an elevated stone construct built on an artificial mound by Henry II to replace a stockade originally built by William the Conqueror himself.

The Round Tower sat dominant above all other buildings within the castle's Middle Ward. To its east, in the Upper Ward, sat the State Apartments – the private residential quarters of the monarch and their visitors – including the Waterloo Chamber, St. George's Hall and the Grand Reception Room.

First converted by Edward III, they were later reconstructed by Charles II upon the restoration in 1660, a statue of the third Stuart monarch maintaining a watchful and suitably suspicious gaze to this day. The apartments sat alongside the royal library, home to priceless works by da Vinci, Michelangelo, Raphael, Holbein the Younger and other Old Masters.

Hitler would have certainly approved.

To its west sat the Lower Ward, a collection of buildings which included St. George's Chapel, a perpendicular gothic-style construct dating back to the Tudor Century, ranked second only to Westminster Abbey as a royal mausoleum. Within it resided the remains of Henry VI, Edward IV, Henry VIII and his short-lived third wife Jane Seymour, the beheaded Charles I, Edward VII and George V.

And now the remains of the last King of England, Edward VIII and his Queen Wallis.

When Edward died in 1972, the Reichskommissariat Groβbritannien was still in the throes of the First Uprising, an initially minor industrial dispute that began in the shipyards of Belfast that had spread as far afield as Bangor, Berwick and Brighton on the mainland.

The name Saxe-Coburg was not entirely alien to Curtis. After all, the House of Windsor had originally been called the House of Saxe-Coburg Gotha after the dynastic name of Queen Victoria's consort Prince Albert, Sachsen Coburg und Gotha. With Victoria's death in 1901, her House of Hanover had made way for the House of Saxe-Coburg, giving rise to four monarchs across five separate reigns.

During the frenzied anti-German rhetoric of the Great War, in 1917 George V declared by royal proclamation that all male British descendants of Queen Victoria would adopt the surname of Windsor instead.

It was ironic that its original name change had been for such noble cause.

The military presence in this fort town was visible everywhere, overwhelming in anticipation of the US President's visit. Troop carriers crossed the bridges over the river as reinforcements travelled from across the south-east to join the garrison already in situ.

It was as much about protecting the gathering as projecting military might to the travelling statesman.

Star-spangled banners flapped, unfurled from lampposts, interspersed with Reich flags.

Further downstream from the castle, to its north-east, stood a lonely, secluded jetty.

A patrol guard ambled back and forth down the jetty, keeping moving to keep warm. In one hand was his sub-machine gun, strapped around his neck. In the other he held a packet of American Camels, the strongest cigarettes available in the Reich, albeit contraband ones.

A sign of the new markets open to the United States once the Treaty of Hessburg was signed by the two superpowers.

The guard pulled a protruding cigarette from the packet with his clenched teeth before shuffling the packet back into an easy access pocket in his uniform. He cupped his lighter, which sparked up on the fourth attempt, and lit the cigarette. He took a long, deep drag.

In the guardhouse behind him, etched into the hill upon which the castle was stood, sat two other guards watching late night television.

Christmas television.

Bad German Christmas television at that.

*Strictly Come Dancing* Swiss-style with yodelling and lederhosen.

With both feet up on the desk and their chins resting in their hands, the two guards were both thoroughly bored, disenchanted to be working over the festive season. But with the last-minute state visit, all leave had been cancelled at short notice, leaving many disgruntled loyal soldiers of the Reich this Yuletide.

One of the guards reached down for a bottle of Schnapps, placing it on the desk. This provoked a flicker of life in the eyes of his colleague, who himself reached down and grabbed three shot glasses, placing them alongside it on the desk. They smiled at each other.

It could be worse. They could be outside patrolling, like Rolf.

Rolf came to the end of his cigarette. As he flicked the dying embers into the shallow water of the river, he fully expected it would be a matter of minutes before he sparked up again.

Rufus had other plans.

As the butt landed in the water, a bamboo shoot emerged, firing a dart without any warning. The dart landed squarely on Rolf's neck. The paralysis induced by its venom was almost instantaneous as Rolf dropped to his knees and then his face flat on the wooden jetty.

Within the guardhouse, the two guards were too busy chinking shot glasses to notice Rolf's unconscious body being dragged off the jetty, seemingly into the water, by two shadowy figures in black wetsuits.

Feeling guilty, one of the guards poured a third shot for Rolf, walking slowly to the door to give it to him. He walked out of the guardhouse without looking, expecting to see him. He stopped in his tracks when he wasn't anywhere to be seen.

'Rolf?' he shouted in German. 'Wie gehts du?'

There was no answer. And no sign of Rolf. The guard turned around, walking back towards the guardhouse, sharing an anxious look with the other guard. As soon as the second dart hit him, the shot glass dropped from his hand, bouncing along the wooden planks of the jetty a moment before he did.

The remaining guard reached immediately for the alarm. But through a small gap in the window flew a third dart.

His head soon rested on the desk, alongside the bottle of Schnapps.

*

The three guards, bound to each other and gagged, wrestled as they came to be sat on the cold stone floor of the storeroom behind the guardhouse, in a circle facing outwards and in just their undergarments.

On the other side of the door, Rufus smiled sweetly as he pulled one of their caps over his head. He locked the storeroom door, snapping the handle after locking it for good measure.

In the guardhouse, Stoltz sat alert, looking lovingly at the Schnapps bottle.

On the jetty, Skunk – conspicuous with his unlikely disguise of being a black disabled man in a Wehrmacht uniform – blended into the night as he patrolled its wooden boards.

Two shadowy figures stepped onto the jetty and walked towards Rufus outside the guardhouse: Billie, in a figure-hugging black wetsuit, followed by Curtis, dressed in the uniform of a Sturmbannführer (Major).

Billie stopped and turned to Rufus. 'Shame you can't come with me.'

He laughed. 'What – with this face?' drawing a circle with his finger in the air.

Billie looked down at her watch. 'If I'm not back in thirty minutes...'

'Come and rescue you,' Rufus cut across her.

Billie's face turned stern. 'If I'm not back in thirty minutes, I'm dead. So leave and regroup – that's not a request.'

'Jawohl mein Führer,' he mock saluted.

Billie motioned forward, planting a painfully platonic kiss on Rufus's cheek. 'Thank you.'

He knew this could very well be the last time he saw her. It was probably the time he should have told her he loved her. But with Curtis approaching, it felt inappropriate. Rufus turned to his love rival. 'Go change the world.'

Curtis nodded reluctantly, shuffling past Rufus with Billie in tow. Before them was a hatch etched into the rock.

It led to a concealed priest's hole in the castle high above them, built to allow escape from the castle.

Not the other way around.

*

The State Apartments of Castle Saxe-Coburg were pristine and ornate in their decor, none more so than the King's Rooms used by King Edward VIII during his second reign as the final monarch of the British Isles.

All that spoiled it were the liberal sprinkling of garish art pieces hanging from the walls, including a rather severe portrait of a by then elderly Edward and Queen Wallis, the chiselled playboy looks hidden under world-weary eyes and sagging skin.

The look of an old man or a guilty man, Curtis wondered as he emerged into the room through a hidden side panel behind the late monarch's portrait.

It was well after midnight but Curtis remained vigilant, having removed the panel quietly. Silenced handgun at the ready, he cautiously stepped into the audience chamber, Edward's antique desk preserved at its centre. As he edged towards it, he stopped in his tracks, catching a glimpse of himself in the ten-foot, gold leaf edged wall-mounted mirror.

Not the first person in a Royal palace to wear a Nazi uniform, he mused, though the sight of it did make Billie wince as she followed after him.

Assuming that von Braun was vain enough to use the late monarch's Audience Chamber for his own office, he hoped that the time bracelet would be hidden in the desk. But given the scarcity of paperwork to be found on the desk and its largely empty drawers, he sighed as it appeared to be essentially ceremonial.

Then came the sound of a toilet flushing. Curtis and Billie looked at each other anxiously, both dropping back to lie flat against the wall next to the bathroom door before it opened. Curtis readied his hand to come down on the back of the neck of the occupant. The door unlocked and creaked open. As the figure emerged into the room, his hand came down sharply.

His victim was a young woman, slender in her silk nightgown, now splayed unconscious on the floor.

Curtis smiled as he admired von Braun's chutzpah.

The smile was soon wiped from his face.

'In here, Herr Curtis.'

He recognised the voice from the television bulletins, though he now spoke in perfunctory English with a heavy German accent. Guns held between their hands, Curtis and Billie inched cautiously towards the adjacent bedchamber.

Von Braun sat alone atop his bed, wearing an extravagant dressing gown, Luger in hand. 'Come in, come in,' the Reichskommissar beckoned. 'I was expecting you before this.'

Curtis hated being predictable. 'Well, I've been busy,' he barbed, almost closing the door behind them.

'You have indeed.' Von Braun looked upon him admiringly. 'You, how do you say, scrub up well in a German uniform.' He beamed. 'I approve!'

Curtis ignored the faint praise. 'Get them in all the fancy dress shops where I come from. They go down a bomb.'

Von Braun turned to Curtis's companion. 'And you must be Billie, the infamous freedom fighter.' Billie's eyes widened, a picture of pure hatred, coming face to face with evil. 'You've come for this, I imagine.' He hoisted his sleeve to reveal the time bracelet, secured firmly around his own wrist.

'Yes,' Curtis snarled, gun pointing at von Braun. 'You can keep the newspaper as a souvenir.'

'You've risked a great deal to get this back.' Von Braun rotated the time bracelet on his wrist. It seemed to have the same alluring effect on him as it had on Luka Rothstein. 'Why?'

'It has strong sentimental value.'

Von Braun raised an eyebrow. 'When Herr Hiltz here —'

Click. The sound of a Luger being readied as a hidden Hiltz emerged from behind a curtain, dimly lit by a reading lamp. The Luger was trained on Curtis's back. Now it was two on two with the Nazis holding the advantage. Curtis and

Billie lowered their weapons to the floor, slinking down onto their knees, resignation coupled with despair.

This wasn't part of the plan.

The Reichskommissar suppressed most of his smugness. 'When Herr Hiltz here told me your time travel story, I was fascinated.'

'I thought you were adamant I was a terrorist, a member of the Freiheit Movement, the Bomber of Hessburg?'

'So you do read the newspapers?' Von Braun smiled. 'Good God no, I arranged all that. You just happened to be in the right place at the right time.'

'You what?' Billie was incredulous. 'You killed hundreds of people, including your own troops?'

'I did,' the Reichskommissar boasted. He was almost proud. 'In fact, I did a better job of resistance than you!'

Her mouth was dry with anger. 'Why would you do that?'

'To make it look like you did it.' The Reichskommissar rose from the bed to circle them. 'You see, every hero must have a nemesis – a villain. Your resistance is weak. Pathetic. Doomed. But I could not get anyone in Berlin to take eradicating you seriously. Not until I upped the ante, so to speak. Now, everyone in Berlin is taking you seriously, especially with the American President arriving tomorrow. It is my duty to foil your attempt on his life – just in time, of course.'

Billie's heart sank. She had been played like a fiddle.

'The resistance is over.' The Reichskommissar was circumspect. 'With this time bracelet, I can go back and reverse any defeat. I, along with my heirs, will reign supreme as leader of the Reich. Unchallenged. Insurmountable. I will be the next Führer, going down in history as the indisputable leader of the world.'

'Up there with Caesar, Genghis Khan and all the other despots,' Billie barked.

Von Braun honed in on her. 'You know, you're the spitting image of your mother.' Billie shuffled uneasily. 'Beautiful, for one of your lot. I remember her well, her long black hair below the waist. A spirited fighter, even at the end.'

Billie's eyes grew angry and emotional. 'My mother died in an ambush on a KZ.'

'Oh, she died in a KZ all right – but not before my men took her to the Tower. Once they had all had a go on her, they brought her to me. A broken animal. I promised to make her death a quick one, if she told me the location of the resistance's secret base. She refused, obviously. So my men went at her, again and again and again, until she begged me for mercy. She died in my arms in fact.'

Von Braun relished retelling his disgusting story, which had reduced Billie to painful, angry streams of tears down her cheeks as she desperately tried to control her emotions in front of this monster.

The Reichskommissar ran his lecherous fingers over a lock of her hair. 'It's a fate, I'm afraid, that awaits you too.'

A shiver ran down her spine.

'Herr Hiltz,' von Braun called to his loyal servant.

Hiltz stepped forward, cocking his Luger and placing the gun to Curtis's temple.

So this was it. The world was to be left with this evil, crazed tyrant in charge.

And thanks to Curtis, now he had the means to change history.

Curtis closed his eyes and Hiltz emptied his magazine.

Into the Reichskommissar.

# 26
# BLOOD AND WATER

It was hard to imagine who was more surprised at Hiltz.

Curtis.

Billie.

Von Braun.

Or Hiltz himself.

Curtis opened his eyes just in time to see von Braun's dying expression, a face of stunned surprise, a venomous scowl of disappointment and betrayal towards his supposedly loyal lieutenant.

Why would have to wait, as the silence was soon punctuated by the Reichskommissar's ever-present adjutant bursting into the room, only to meet the same fate as their liege.

Hiltz rushed to the door, locking it. He dared to glance across at Billie, who was equally stunned, and probably a little resentful that she hadn't pulled the trigger herself. 'There isn't much time. The SS will be coming.'

Hiltz bounded into the study, returning with von Braun's mistress, dragging her body to where he had been standing. He wiped the butt and trigger of his gun with a handkerchief before placing the Luger in her hand, the barrel pointing into her mouth. He tilted his head away as he pulled the trigger, blowing her skull open and redecorating the regal curtain behind. He released the mistress's body, letting it slump naturally to the floor.

Driven and seemingly unmoved, Hiltz stepped over her corpse towards the late Reichskommissar, removing the time bracelet from his wrist.

'This won't fool them but it will stall them long enough to get you out.'

*

The alarm in the Reichskommissar's private quarters, in the north-eastern corner of the castle in its Upper Ward, would have sounded in SS barracks up to ten miles away.

The first to the scene docked with the jetty, making their way with haste towards the guardhouse.

It was deserted.

As the first stoßtruppen arrived in its doorway, all that remained was an empty bottle of Schnapps with three soiled shot glasses. One of them heard the muffled kicks coming from the storeroom behind.

The door being locked and the lock being jammed, an industrious cadet kicked at the wooden door. It burst open to reveal the guards, panicked and sweating, with a beeping sound nearby.

The stoßtruppler looked behind one of the guards to find a heavily concentrated explosive attached to a timer. He tilted his head and squinted to read the red LED display.

0:02...

0:01...

There was no time for him to react. The explosion gestated in the store room, building to an unstoppable eruption as it billowed out onto the jetty, consuming the guardhouse along with the SS detachment and setting fire to their landing craft.

The ball of flame could be seen rising into the sky, momentarily turning night into day.

*

In the King's Rooms, Curtis and Billie heard the explosion. Billie ran to the blood-splattered curtains, drawing it to see the top of the explosive stack poking out above the high tree line of the forest between the river and the castle two hundred and fifteen feet below.

'Oh no...' Billie covered her mouth, grief stricken.

'Don't worry,' came the familiar cocksure voice of Rufus from the adjacent Audience Chamber, where he stood with Skunk and Stoltz. 'We're not dead. Well, not yet.' His smile evaporated as he saw Hiltz stood holding the time bracelet over von Braun's limp body. He raised his gun to shoot before Billie jumped in the line of fire.

In the nick of time.

'No! He helped us. I don't know why but — ' She walked forward and placed her hand on Rufus's gun, gently lowering it as she turned back to face Hiltz. 'Just no.'

Hiltz nodded in sober acknowledgement. He walked briskly towards Curtis, time bracelet in his hand. 'I love my country, Herr Curtis. But some things —.' He handed him the time bracelet. 'Some things are more important.'

Curtis couldn't quite believe it. His first thought was that Hiltz had murdered von Braun to take the time bracelet for himself. He took the time bracelet and returned it to his wrist, back where it belonged, before turning to Rufus. 'Escape route?'

'Blocked, indefinitely,' he sighed. 'First priest hole used to get into a dangerous situation.'

'There is a way,' Hiltz interjected, looking straight into Billie's eyes. 'But you'll have to trust me.'

*

Sturmbannführer Karl Strasser's detachment of SS stoßtruppen were the resident security force at Castle Saxe-Coburg, based in barracks opposite the Military Knights' Lodgings on Castle Hill. They were first into the State Apartments, fanning out up the Grand Staircase towards the Grand Vestibule. The door to the Waterloo Chamber creaked open and the stoßtruppen trained their sights – and their formidable arsenal – on them.

'Hold your fire!' Hiltz shouted from behind the door. 'It's Gauleiter Hiltz! I'm coming out with prisoners.'

Silence ensued as Hiltz emerged, frogmarching Billie and Skunk – the two non-Caucasians of the party – out of the Chamber.

As prisoners.

Flanking him were Curtis, Rufus and Stoltz, playing their part by virtue of their German officers' uniforms and the plausibility of their white skin.

Strasser broke ranks with the other more deferential and unquestioning members of the detachment, outstretching his arm. 'Where are you going?'

'Herr Oberst, I'm afraid the Reichskommiserar is dead. Murdered. I found these rebels trying to escape from the castle via a secret passageway from his quarters. I am taking them back to the Tower for interrogation.'

Strasser's eyes darted between the two prisoners. 'I'm sorry Herr Gauleiter, but Herr Schultz has given express orders that no one is to leave the castle.'

Hiltz sought to disarm him with sophistry. 'My dear Herr Oberst...'

Strasser interrupted him. 'That included you, mein Herr.'

Hiltz was visibly incandescent. 'I am the Gauleiter of Hessburg. I do not take orders from a Major in the SS!'

'I'm sorry Herr Gauleiter, but I must insist.'

Strasser's fingers ran over the back of his Luger, still in its holster. As he did, Curtis took matters into his own hands, kicking him in the stomach. The wounded Strasser doubled up as Rufus and Stoltz opened fire on the detachment.

Billie and Skunk parted with the group, running for cover in the nearby Lantern Lobby. The others backed away into the Lobby one by one as the return volley began in earnest.

'Untie me for fuck's sake!' Billie screamed. 'If one of these bastards is going to get me, at least let me take some of them with me!'

Hiltz untied her bindings. 'You are spirited. I wonder who you get it off...'

Rufus bounded in and the door slammed shut. 'We can't hold these off for long. If your new best friend has a plan B, now's the time to share!'

Hiltz peeked through a crack in the door. 'The doors to the staircase will be shut. Part of the security protocols of a lockdown.'

Curtis ran to the window. The courtyard to the Upper Ward was empty, apart from a solitary surviving SS stoßtruppler running past the King Charles II statue.

Reinforcements would soon be upon them. He sighed. He looked down at the time bracelet.

He could get himself out.

But the others would be lambs to the slaughter.

Then he saw Stoltz's crossbow hanging from his belt. He turned back to Hiltz. 'Can you get us up to the roof?'

'Now's not the time for flying lessons,' Rufus intervened abruptly. 'The roof is a dead end.'

'Yes,' Hiltz replied functionally.

Then there was a chance. 'Rufus — smoke.'

Reluctantly, Rufus threw a smoke grenade down into the Grand Staircase, to obscure the line of sight of any stoßtruppen. The party made their way down from the Lobby into St. George's Hall, headed for the Brunswick Tower and the roof. A single brave stoßtruppler burst in from the Waterloo Chamber, a survivor of the earlier fire fight. As he fumbled with his jammed gun, Skunk put him to bed with short shrift from his blade.

In unison, reinforcements snaked through the Lobby, the Waterloo Chamber and the Grand Reception Room. As the last of the group to make it to the stairwell headed through the Brunswick Tower for the roof, Curtis and Rufus gave covering fire. Billie rolled a smoke grenade between them, followed by a real one, setting the confines ablaze.

To block their access to the roof from the foot of the Tower, Billie threw another grenade down its spiralling staircase, setting the fabrics ablaze.

It was the roof.

Or bust.

*

The sound of the grenade exploding in the stairwell of the Brunswick Tower, in the far north-eastern corner of the castle, echoed across the wards.

As the roof of the State Apartments gently flamed in the distance, a canopy-roofed car sped up Castle Hill towards St. George's Gateway. The gatehouse – along with the Henry VIII Gate and the George IV Gate – made up the three official entrances into the castle. It was heavily fortified. A Sturmbannführer approached the car officiously, indicating that its occupant should wind down the window. He checked himself, saluting immediately, when he realised that inside the car was Schultz.

'Report, Major,' Schultz barked.

'Gunshots were heard in the Reichskommissar's private quarters, Herr Schultz. My men sealed off the State Apartments and went to investigate. Herr Gauleiter Hiltz was stopped trying to leave with prisoners.' The Sturmbannführer leant in. 'Originals.'

Schultz suppressed his delight. 'Major, alert all forces that an attempt has been made on the Reichskommissar's life by Gauleiter Hiltz, who is working with Freiheit separatists. Your orders are to shoot to kill.'

The Sturmbannführer was taken aback. 'Does that include Gauleiter Hiltz, mein Herr?'

'Especially Herr Hiltz, Major.'

'Yes sir,' he replied sadly. The Sturmbannführer saluted once more.

As the car motioned through the gate, Schultz smugly imagined the spoils to come.

'Fantastic!' he exclaimed to himself, slapping one hand with his leather glove.

*

The fire door from the Brunswick Tower burst open and the rebels filed out onto the roof.

'I want the fire doors mined, now,' Rufus barked to Stoltz and Skunk, who fanned out. There were four towers leading to the roof of the Upper Ward – running clockwise, the Brunswick Tower that they had travelled up, the Prince of Wales Tower next to it, the Queen's Tower in the south-east corner and the Edward III Tower in the south-west.

Skunk began adding explosives to the Brunswick Tower exit while Stoltz took the adjacent Prince of Wales Tower, before taking off for the Edward III Tower. Rufus ran ahead to the Queen's Tower.

It wouldn't stop their would-be assassins making it to the roof, especially given the value of the lives of their own soldiers meant so little to the Nazi authorities, but it would slow them down.

It might even give them a chance.

Billie ran along the roof, staying away from the edges and line of sight, with Curtis and Hiltz in tow. They crouched low at the edge of St. George's Gateway, watching grimly as the military build-up continued below.

'We're trapped,' Billie sighed forlornly.

'Not yet.' Curtis reached for Stoltz's crossbow. He pointed to the Lower Ward, beyond the Round Tower. 'There's St. George's Chapel, just along the tree line.'

'You're not serious?'

Curtis smiled. 'I'm always serious. All of the troops are marshalling around the Upper Ward. If we can get across to the roof of the Deanery, we can get into the Chapel through the roof. I'd bet there's another priest hole that'll take you down to the river.'

Billie looked down. There was a reason why the Round Tower had been built where it was, standing hard and fast in the castle's grounds for a millennium. 'That must be a hundred foot vertical drop. We'll never make it.' She placed her hand on the time bracelet. 'Just go.'

'Not until I get you off this roof. I have to give you a fighting chance. I owe you that, at least.'

Curtis scurried across the top of St. George's Gateway onto the roof of the Round Tower. Billie noticed that Hiltz had been smiling as he observed them together.

'He's a good man.' Hiltz paused. 'There's something I need to...'

The fire door behind them burst open, knocking Stoltz out of the way as he was positioning charges atop the Edward III Tower. A sharpshooter dropped to his knee, raising his gun. He fired at Billie. Hiltz dived to block the bullet. It ripped through Billie's wet suit, flesh-wounding her arm. The sharpshooter reached for a stick grenade to finish the job but Stoltz came to and lunged for him, both of them hurtling down the stone stairwell of the Tower until the stick grenade exploded on impact. The Tower collapsed on top of them.

Curtis scuttled back across the Round Tower, reaching for Billie.

'It's just a flesh wound,' she protested, clearly in pain.

Hiltz stumbled. Only then did Curtis and Billie notice the matting of blood on his uniform. The bullet had gone through him, deflecting before hitting Billie. He'd saved her life, again. He dropped to his knees. Despite the pain, Billie instinctively moved to catch him, cradling his head in her lap.

Curtis's heart sank. If it wasn't for Hiltz, none of them would be there.

Billie ran her hand towards the wound.

Hiltz stopped her, holding her hand gently. 'Don't. It's ok. It's my time.'

Billie was strangely distressed. 'You were going to say something. Before, I mean.'

'Yes.' Hiltz's voice was curtailed. 'I'm your father.'

Billie's face contorted, belying repulsion and non-acceptance coupled with grief, but she continued to cradle him.

Hiltz began to cough blood. 'Your mother... I knew she was pregnant but she told me she had to have an abortion, as the other members of Freiheit would never accept the half-child of a Colonial.'

Billie struggled for sense. 'I... I...'

Hiltz began to feel the pinch, his body tensing up. 'You must go. Now. Before it's too late.'

Billie's eyes began to mist up for her mortal enemy. 'But what about you? I can't just leave you here...'

Hiltz smiled. 'There's no need for that. Not now.' He squeezed her hand. 'I don't expect you to forget what I was part of, Billie. But I hope in time that you can forgive...'

A massive seizure took Hiltz. He passed abruptly, mid-sentence.

Billie was shell-shocked, unknowing, unsettled.

'Billie?' He called to her but she was in a daze. 'Billie – we have to go.'

She ran her hand over Hiltz's face and closed his eyes.

Now there were only four of them left.

Curtis took her hands and began to pull her away as the sound of German infantry marching their way grew ever louder. They scurried onto the Round Tower roof. They didn't have much time. Curtis got the measure of Stoltz's crossbow. He looked at the length of cord, which he estimated at a hundred and fifty feet.

At a push it would get them to the Deanery – just.

He aimed and fired. The bolt shot across the Middle Ward, the grappling hook landing on the roof of the Deanery and scraping across its surface. Curtis secured the crossbow at his end, wrapping it around the stonework to make the cord tense.

There was enough of a gradient for them to make it.

He hoped.

Skunk went first as Rufus placed a bag of grenades above St. George's Gateway before running towards them.

Rufus followed him across the chasm, wheezing through the winter air.

An infantryman below realised the change of tactics and called for reinforcements from the Upper Ward. The massed infantry inside about turned and ran from the State Apartments across the Upper Ward, filing past Charles II.

Billie watched from a concealed vantage point above the Gateway as they headed towards them. 'Time to go!' she shouted to Curtis as she pulled a pin out of a grenade, throwing it onto the bag of grenades Rufus had left behind.

Curtis hadn't allowed for two at a time, but he was left with little choice as he and Billie jumped from the roof of the Round Tower into the crisp night air, the wind whistling past their ears as they gathered apace.

A hundred feet.

Sixty feet.

Thirty feet.

The grenade detonated the bag of grenades. The roof of the Round Tower and the Visitors' Apartments nearby erupted in a cataclysmic explosion, decimating the Gateway. Splinters from centuries-old wooden beams joined masonry in deadly flight through the night sky.

With just ten feet to go, the masonry around which the cord was secured gave way from the wall, leaving Curtis and Billie in free-fall.

They slammed into the side of the wall of the Deanery, dropping to the ground below, dazed and stunned.

Rufus and Skunk used the cord to abseil down the side of the Deanery to join them.

An approaching detachment of infantry began to open fire on their position.

As the blanket fire grew closer, Skunk charged the approaching infantry with two blades, slaying a body of them before being hit between the eyes by a long-distance sniper. He dropped to the ground, to Rufus's horror, but having bought valuable time for the others.

Curtis, Rufus and Billie burst into Chapel, shutting the door and slamming the wooden barrier bar down across it.

But it offered only brief respite.

If they weren't trapped on the roof of the Round Tower, they were now.

Outside the Chapel, waves of infantry swelled as they enclosed the space.

Schultz minced towards the Chapel, characteristically remaining behind the cannon fodder.

'Herr Curtis!' he shouted. 'Herr James Curtis! You are

completely surrounded on all sides. There is no escape. Come out with your hands above your heads and I promise I will make your deaths swift.'

Curtis slumped, his back against the heavy wooden door, seemingly with the weight of the world on his shoulders. Billie stood before him, her arm bleeding through her wet suit. Alongside was Rufus, hands on his thighs, catching his breath and mourning Skunk and Stoltz.

'I'm sorry,' Curtis blurted.

Billie looked up. 'For what?'

'That I couldn't get you out,' he replied sombrely. 'All I've given you all is death.'

Rufus stepped forward. 'You've done better than that. You've given us hope. Even if nothing you've said comes true, we've taken out the Reichskommissar!'

Billie smiled. 'Some things are worth dying for.' She looked across at Rufus, knowing that this was the end of their road.

Rufus extended his hand to Curtis. 'See you on the other side.'

Curtis shook it with warmth, tinged with the painful memory of Luka Rothstein uttering the same words to him in 1941.

That felt like a lifetime ago. Not days.

Curtis cupped Billie's face in his hands as she leant in and kissed him.

It was a tender kiss with an air of finality to it.

'Go make it right,' she whispered in his ear before stepping back.

Curtis sighed as he activated the time bracelet, the date on the display going further and further back until he came to January 26th 1918.

He looked up for one last time.

Billie smiled. 'Look me up in your world.'

'Definitely.'

The time bracelet beeped. The familiar blue hue enveloped Curtis and in a moment he was gone. Seeing him evaporate was a comfort for Billie and Rufus, knowing for sure that he had been telling the truth all along.

Rufus reached out for her hand.

What they would face on the other side of the wooden door, they would face together.

*

Schultz was getting agitated.

'I'm not renowned for my patience!'

The Chapel doors swung open, creaking with the wind. Billie and Rufus emerged, hands on their heads, fingers interlinked. Schultz snarled sadistically, knowing full well that he had no intention of affording either of them a quick death.

Particularly Billie.

After von Braun and Hiltz, he was next in line to become Reichskommissar and he intended to squeeze every drop of information – and blood – out of them before they succumbed in the torture chambers of the Weiss Tower.

The infantry stepped forward to take them into custody.

Billie and Rufus looked at each other in unison.

In each of their hands lay detonators for the explosives covering every party of their bodies.

They turned back to the approaching infantry, smiling contentedly as the closed their eyes.

'Freiheit!'

It was the last thing that Billie, Rufus, the infantry in front of them and Reinhard Schultz would see or hear in this lifetime.

# 27
# FLYING VISIT

'May those that God unites never be torn asunder. You may kiss the bride.'

The cavernous lungs of the organ exhaled the Wedding March at full blast as the creaking grand oak doors to St. George's Chapel flung open.

But it was a St. George's Chapel unscathed by the calamitous explosions at the hands of Billie and Rufus, instead bathed in the crisp freshness of a winter's day.

The coy young bride – in vintage, shoulder-covering white lace and accompanied by her groom, in naval dress and replete with Edwardian moustache – stepped nervously out into the throng of well-wishers lining the steps. A shower of confetti and white petals obscured the low-lying sun for them momentarily.

It was clearly the grandest of high society weddings.

A garrison of wedding guests, from in-laws and invited guests to hangers-on and flunkeys, left the Chapel behind them in a caravan of hope, snaking across the Lower Ward for the reception in the State Apartments on the other side of the castle.

This was very much the business end of the castle.

As the last guest passed, a familiar blue hue illuminated the Chapel's arched stain-glass windows.

And a familiar face stepped through its doorway, still wearing his SS Major's uniform.

As he made his way tentatively down the steps out of the Chapel, Curtis felt like he was home.

Home in the past.

But home in his past.

As the marching caravan disappeared into the distance, Curtis found himself remembering all that had just happened on this very ground.

'I see they put you back together,' he muttered to himself.

For a moment he dared to reminisce, mourning fallen comrades.

Stoltz.

Skunk.

Hiltz even.

And though he didn't see it, he assumed Billie and Rufus. They had sacrificed their lives so that he could be here.

His reminiscing, which could easily have developed into a melancholy, was punctuated by the unexpected roar of a small biplane – the Royal Postal Service – passing overhead. In the distance, the wedding party looked up in awe, applauding loudly. Curtis clapped to fit in, while looking around for someone to ask where it had come from.

He didn't fancy the trek to France by boat, not with the mining of the English Channel and the intense U-boat activity from the German Navy.

Suddenly the oak doors closed behind him, a portly Bishop in all his pomp and regalia brushing him aside as he locked up. He too was headed for the wedding breakfast of Kings, Queens, minor Royals and their loyal servants.

'I say.' Curtis carried off an effected upper class English accent a little too well. It was certainly better than his American Harry Holder. 'Excuse me Bishop, but I wonder if you could tell me where that plane took off from?' The off sounded more like owf. Curtis fitted in beautifully.

'Ridiculous contraptions.' The Bishop was animated. 'They'll be the death of us all!'

'Well,' Curtis smiled, 'it's progress like that which won the war!' The Bishop was bemused by Curtis's poor turn of phrase. He quickly corrected himself. 'Will win us the war, I mean.'

The Bishop overcame his own suspicions, while removing a whisky flask hidden surreptitiously beneath his cloak. For the habitual quelling of performance nerves, no doubt.

'Heston, my boy. There's a new airfield down there.' The Bishop felt the collar of Curtis's uniform. 'Tell me, this is a peculiar uniform. Which side are you on?'

Curtis was unnerved, speechless until the Bishop clarified. 'Bride or groom?'

Curtis was relieved. 'Oh, the bride Bishop,' he smiled. 'Always the bride.'

'Thank the Lord for that,' the Bishop boomed as he took a generous swig of his flask. 'The groom's family are all bloody Germans, no matter what they call themselves these days!'

It was a good job Curtis had done away with the Iron Cross with Oak Leaves en route.

The Bishop brushed past Curtis with haste, seeking to catch up with the wedding party. Realising Curtis wasn't walking with him, he looked back.

'Aren't you coming my…?'

His voice trailed off as Curtis was nowhere to be seen.

*

It had been barely fifteen years since the Wright brothers turned the four centuries' old dream of Leonardo da Vinci's "flying machines" into a reality at Kill Devil Hills, North Carolina.

But the transition from their rather primitive flying craft into the killing machines now dominating the skies above the Front was no less remarkable.

The exigencies of total war and the increasingly toxic effect of stalemate on the ground had forced both sides to think outside the box.

For the British, this centred predominantly on the development of the tank, first used in battle in 1916. Their emergence into the sodden trenches during the First Battle of the Somme had driven fear into the hearts of the German ranks.

But if the mechanised artillery on the ground was coming to be dominated by the British, the Germans dominated the skies above.

Aerial superiority oscillated between the two sides as new designs were constantly launched into service. Britain's response to the German Fokkers was the Sopwith Camel. The best and most famous of three designs developed to regain the initiative in the air war, the Camel was responsible for the downing of 1,294 enemy aircraft in the Great War, more than any other allied fighter.

Though similar to its predecessors the Tabloid, the Pup and the Triplane, when the first Camel rolled out in December

1916, it was a revolutionary and trailblazing machine. Its Twin Vickers machine guns, mounted side-by-side in front of the pilot's cockpit, became a standard design feature of British aircraft for the next two decades. The compacting of the pilot's controls, the engine and armaments to the front of the aircraft gave it its phenomenal performance.

But the bi-product was that it made the plane extremely difficult to fly, bestowing it the curious honour that more pilots died learning to fly it than in actual combat. Coupled with the fire hazard posed by its wood and fabric construction and a lack of fire protection for the fuel tank, the parlous state of pilot training in 1917 saw the life expectancy of a pilot in the Royal Navy Air Service or the Royal Flying Corps plummet to just two weeks.

Despite this frightening statistic, the Camel was deployed across the Western Front, with some of the earliest additions to the fleet deployed by the Royal Navy from cruisers and battleships. They were also employed as night fighters and balloon busters, with a variation fitted with eight Le Prieur air-to-air rockets proving an effective menace to German Zeppelins as well as long-range bombers.

It was this variation that sat on the modest airfield in the shadow of Windsor Castle, part of the homeland defence. The airfield was hardly a flurry of fevered activity. Its clubhouse sat at the end of a grassy runway flanked on all sides by farmland. Aside from a solitary mechanic tending his master's Camel that winter's morning, the airfield was deserted.

Curtis approached the airfield with care, having learned from his run-in with the Bishop. His jacket was now draped inside out over his shoulder, obscuring the distinctive

German shoulder flashes, while his tie sat loose below an unbuttoned collar.

He now looked more like a philandering nobleman executing a walk of shame than someone up to more nefarious skulduggery.

He had intended to bribe the mechanic with the gold sovereigns from his belt. They would be more use to him, albeit a little in the future, than for Curtis where he was going.

The mechanic was desperately trying to get to grips with the biplane's engine, growing increasingly frustrated with it. It was unfortunate that Curtis coughing to catch his attention caused him to let the wrench slip, cutting his hand open.

'Bejesus!' he cried in a distinctive southern Irish lilt, shaking his hand violently as the wave of pain enveloped him. He reached for an oily rag to stem the blood, acting as a tourniquet as he scuttled towards the clubhouse, leaving his winter flying jacket with its fleece collar dangling from a hook against a workbench.

When the mechanic finally emerged from the clubhouse, hand securely bandaged, it was just in time to see the Camel – his Camel – taking off in front of him. Though his shouted words at the perennially unlucky mechanic were wholly drowned out by the roar of the Camel's prop, it was clear what Curtis – sat in the cockpit, wearing the mechanic's winter flying jacket buttoned up to his chin – meant.

'Sorry!'

The mechanic's cheeks grew redder and angrier, as he watched the biplane heading directly into the low-lying sun as its wheels broke contact with the shards of grass beneath.

That is, until he saw the fifty gold sovereigns from Curtis's belt laid out atop the workbench.

Whistling the opening bars of *It's A Long Way To Tipperary*, he calmly collected the sovereigns into every available pocket before returning to the clubhouse for a restorative whisky or two.

Curtis smiled as he grappled with the stick. It was every inch the bastard to fly that its reputation suggested but, as the wind lapped his ears, he felt for himself the rush that the pioneers of early aviation had clearly grown addicted to as they sought to build on the accomplishments of Wilbur and Orville.

The plane banked, turning so that the sun rested behind him in the winter's afternoon sky.

He was headed east, for the blood-soaked fields of Flanders and northern France.

He had a date with destiny.

He couldn't afford to be late.

*

As the sun reached its golden hour in the sky behind him, Curtis crossed over the white cliffs of Dover below, finally above the English Channel.

Just yesterday he had been dancing to Billie Holliday, in the Fan Bay Deep Shelter hidden within its cliff-face, before spending the night with her namesake.

The biplane handled like a fragile bird, a fleeting pinprick against the chalk white cliff top below.

His thoughts wandered to think of Billie, a woman whose grandparents may not even be alive yet.

And who, if he succeeded in his mission, may be destined to never even exist at all.

*

It was almost dusk as the Camel crossed the threshold into French airspace. With the winter chill beginning to bite, he looked down from the cockpit at the impact of mass mobilisation on the hitherto agrarian Nord-Pas-de-Calais department below. Its natural landscape was now peppered with manmade features – roads, railway lines, field buildings set back from the layer upon layer of trenches – all illuminated by what from the sky looked like a beautiful arrangement of candles.

Welcome to the Western Front.

With the battle alive below, it was imperative that Curtis landed on the German side of the lines.

Staying alive that long was going to be the most challenging part of his mission.

In the dying sunlight, Curtis could barely distinguish the shadowy object rapidly approaching him in the cloud cover settling. He squinted before suddenly realising that it was a Fokker Dr.1 triplane.

A German plane.

On a collision course.

He banked hard to avoid it, succeeding by the narrowest of margins as the two aircraft averted a mid-air Glasgow kiss.

Clearly shaken, he levelled off.

The Fokker was nowhere to be seen.

Perhaps it had better things to do with its time.

No such luck.

As the Fokker settled into the Camel's slipstream, its pilot began to empty its magazines. The air around Curtis was live with the tinkling metallic bullets gently puncturing its serenity. He had no idea how to activate the Le Prieur air-to-air missiles. Besides he was in front of his adversary.

He banked hard, flipping the Camel momentarily onto its back as he spun to avoid the Fokker's volley, dropping out of its field of destruction.

Curtis smiled, feeling triumphant as the adrenalin rush of the encounter coursed through his veins.

'You'll have to do better than that, you cheeky Fokker!' he shouted into the wind, audible to nobody other than himself. 'I've had people shooting at me all week and I'm still…'

His words trailed as a hail of bullets rained on the engine, shattering the glass of the dashboard. Curtis had ducked instinctively in time but there was no longer any doubt.

His Camel was going down.

And fast.

*

The Camel's descent was rapid and merciless. It dropped onto a bank of snow-drizzled trees like a brick, the remaining fuel on-board providing ample encouragement to the burgeoning fire already afoot, let alone the Le Prieurs.

As the fire plumed into the crisp night sky, an innocuous and flimsy parachute descended all too quickly towards the icy ground below.

Attached precariously to its canopy, Curtis hit the ground with a bump that would have broken bones on a less resilient man. The canopy enveloped him as he wrestled with it, finally overcoming it and reigning it in.

*

The parachute safely packed beneath the freshly driven snow, by the time anyone found it Curtis would be hell and gone.

As he broke from the woods into a clearing, his heart sank. Ahead of him, obscured by the dark, was a lonely wooden post sunk deep into the frozen ground.

Slumped at its base, a German army deserter, a private, bound, blindfolded.

And recently deceased.

Curtis shook his head gently in disgust at the brutality of man to his own, this senseless taking of a life, before reaching in for the dead soldier's identity tags still dangling around his neck. He gently pulled at them, snatching them from his body.

Helmut Gorst, 1st Supplementary Regiment.

Moments later, Curtis was walking down a country lane wearing Private Gorst's ill-fitting uniform. As he trudged in the crunching snow-flecked soil at the roadside, a sign grew ever closer.

Cambrai. 2km.

The home of the German 2nd Army.

# 28
# ALL QUIET ON THE WESTERN FRONT

The night sky was unusually clear of cloud cover, making for a brisk night at 2nd German Army Field Headquarters in Cambrai.

A gentle sheen of frost had already bedded in across this battle-worn stretch of northern France. In the distance, shells could be seen erupting indiscriminately without focus, almost a bombardment for the sake of it.

Cambrai had had more than its fair share of new sheriffs in town.

Originally called Camaracum when Gaul was part of the Roman Empire, its bishops had later been made Counts by the German king Henry I in the 10th Century.

But that did little to settle its allegiance, and throughout medieval times control had oscillated with depressing regularity between the countries of Flanders and Hainaut along with the Holy Roman Empire before eventually being assigned to the Kingdom of France by the 1678 Treaty of Nijmegen.

Almost two hundred and fifty years of relative peace and prosperity followed and by 1914 Cambrai had developed a burgeoning textile economy based on a fine cloth called cambric. But that economy could not withstand the simple reality of being a frontline town, lying on the river Escaut and occupied throughout the entirety of the Great War.

The town was used to lending its name to significant events. The League of Cambrai – an alliance against Venice formed by Pope Julius II, Louis XII, Ferdinand II of Aragon and Emperor Maximilian I – was signed there in 1508, as was the treaty between the Holy Roman Emperor Charles V and Francis I of France in 1529.

And on November 20th 1917 the First Battle of Cambrai marked the first large scale, effective use of tanks in warfare.

In an offensive led by the British 3rd Army to relieve pressure on the Western Front, nineteen British divisions – including 476 tanks – attacked a ten-mile section of the German Hindenburg line just west of Cambrai. Attacking with complete surprise, the British tanks took advantage of the rolling chalk downland and ripped through German defences, taking nearly 8,000 prisoners. But Mother Nature was not on the British side and bad weather stunted the opportunity for British cavalry to take advantage of the breakthrough. With inadequate infantry reinforcements, in just over two weeks the offensive had been halted after an advance of six miles before twenty German divisions counter-attacked to drive the British back, almost to their original positions.

With casualties of 45,000 apiece and no change in the status quo, the battle epitomised the stalemate that had bedevilled the Western Front since the very outset of war.

By January of 1918, the fledgling Bolshevik government in Russia had sued for peace, bolstering the Central Powers in their drive to break the stalemate. The remaining Entente powers – France and Britain – had only entered the war in support of Russia due to treaty obligations and would not have been able to sustain the campaign without the belated entry of a reticent United States of America into the war nine months earlier.

But America's military build-up had taken time. Boots on the ground numbered just tens of thousands when the final German offensives were taking place in the spring of 1918.

Offensives yet to come.

German field headquarters consisted of a variety of commandeered buildings, from village huts to makeshift constructs and easy-up field tents. Temporary telegraph wires connected these separate entities and the army battalions they aimed to control.

Four transports arrived outside headquarters without fanfare. They were laden with reservists from The List Regiment, mainly injured frontschwein being returned to active duty as the German Army struggled to replace the fallen. They cut forlorn, often pathetic figures as they disembarked back to a hell they believed would be over long ago.

Ambling down the icy steps to the crunching soil beneath his boots was Oberstleutnant Frauherr von Tubouef. Intemperate in the winter cold as he was all too often in the warmth of his own quarters, this was a duty von Tubouef lamented and frequently cursed.

Leading the new arrivals was a young Second Lieutenant, cap bowed across his forehead. But his chiselled jaw was all too familiar.

'The List Regiment,' saluted Hess, 'reporting to the Front, Herr Oberstleutnant.' The other members of The List Regiment fell in behind him.

Von Tubouef was far from impressed as he lazily saluted back. He knew all too well that the best had already fallen in this war. The depleted ranks in front of him represented merely the rest.

Unlike his more familiar later incarnation, Hess was a young man, those youthful features masking bravery and trauma experienced at the Front in almost equal measure.

Born into a wealthy merchant family, the young Hess had showed little interest in taking over the reins from his father Fritz. His grandfather Christian Hess had emigrated to Egypt in 1865, setting up the trading company Hess & Co. But the Hess family had originated from the town of Wunsiedel, sixty miles north-west of Nürnberg deep in the Fichtelgebirge. Despite bringing up young Rudolf and his two siblings in the Alexandrian suburb of Ibrahimieh, Fritz maintained a house in Reicholdsgrün, on the outskirts of Wunsiedel, which became the Hess family's summer retreat.

By 1914 the population of the Second Reich had hit 68 million, more than double that at unification in 1870. With its economy booming and unemployment low, the German Empire had become a military giant, with a well-equipped army and a modern navy.

But its covetous eyes, salivating over the overseas imperial possessions of the British and French, rang alarm bells in the Palaces of Westminster and Élysée.

War was widely regarded as imminent, inevitable and in some ways desirable.

When it came, it was ironically behind the fig leaf of the tripartite treaties that had been struck to avert war, the Triple Alliance of Germany, Austria-Hungary and Italy facing down the Triple Entente of Britain, France and Russia.

The assassination of the disliked Archduke Franz Ferdinand of Habsburg-Este, heir to the dual monarchy of Austria-Hungary, along with his consort Sophie Chotek, the duchess of Hohenburg, in the Bosnian city of Sarajevo on the morning of June 28th 1914 altered the destinies of many millions of Europeans.

Nobody more so than Rudolf Hess.

After leaving the École Supérieur de Commerce at Neuchâtel in Switzerland, Hess had begun an apprenticeship in Hamburg. A career in business in the Fatherland beckoned.

In August 1914, as the belligerents mobilised, the Hess family were in their summer residence at Reichsholdgrün. All apart from Rudolf. Against Fritz's wishes, twenty year-old Rudolf had left his apprenticeship in Hamburg and travelled to Munich to join the ranks as a volunteer. He enlisted in the 7th Bavarian Field Artillery Regiment and after a brief period of initial training Private Hess was posted to the Western Front.

Stationed opposite the BEF on the Somme, Hess didn't have to wait long for action. In response to Belgian inundation of large swatches of both sides of the Yser between Nieuwpoort and Bikshote, at the end of October the Germans withdrew and took stock before attacking again on a narrower front between the Messines Ridge and Gheluvelt, just outside of Ypres.

Amongst the German infantry were patriotic volunteers, many of them students burning with idealistic zeal but ill equipped to go up against the British regulars. They sang beautifully patriotic songs as they were mown down in their thousands.

The losses on both sides were colossal. In a matter of days, the British lost fifty thousand men to death, injury or missing in action. Their French allies to the south lost a similar number. German losses, though never published, must have been greater, leading to this First Battle of Ypres being dubbed Der Kindermord von Ypern (the Massacre of the Innocents at Ypres).

Hess had been lucky to survive the battle.

On November 9th 1914, Hess had been transferred to the 1st Company of the 1st Infantry Regiment, stationed near Arras in the occupied Artois region of north-eastern France. Soon after the move from the Supplementaries came his promotion to Gefreiter in April 1915, along with the award of the Iron Cross Second Class for bravery in the field.

In the summer of 1915, he had left the Front to train at the Army Training School in Munsterlager, rising again in rank to Visefeldwebel (Lance-Sergeant), and receiving the Militarisches Verdienst Kreuz from the Kingdom of Bavaria before returning to Artois in time for Christmas in the trenches. The turn of the year saw the intense battles for Neuville St. Vaast, which was decimated.

But it wasn't battle that would prove the first threat to Hess's life. On February 20th 1916, a throat infection took him behind the lines to a military hospital for two months, dodging by a day the many bullets as the Germans sought to subdue the fortress towns along the French border as part of the Battle of Verdun. In Hess's absence, the Germans had met with significant success east of the

Maas, but with a stiffening of French resistance it became a costly folly of a campaign, a campaign of attrition with unsustainable casualties on both sides. Even by the time Hess returned from the Reservelazarett, despite the ruin of the fort of Douaumont, the German General in charge – von Falkenhayn – had realised the Verdun campaign was turning into a failure.

Nonetheless, as was the way with generals on both sides, the campaign continued with further pointless attacks. On the outskirts of Douaumont on June 12th 1916 came Hess's first brush with death on duty. An exploding shell sent splinters into his left hand and upper arm, sending him back to the Reservelazarett for a second time. By the time he returned to his unit a month later, von Falkenhayn had called it a day in an offensive that had cost the lives of a third of a million soldiers apiece for the Germans and the French.

Almost six months later on Christmas Day 1916, Hess was posted to the 18th Bavarian Reserve Infantry Regiment, serving as platoon leader of the 10th Company on the by then fractured Eastern Front in Romania.

Seeking territorial gain in Transylvania, the Romanians had cheekily declared war on the Central Powers – what was left of the Alliance after Italy chose to align itself with the Entente instead – in August 1916. But the combined might of German, Bulgarian and Turkish forces attacking from the south had checked their poorly officered troops. By Hess's arrival, the Central Powers held most of the country, including its capital Bucharest.

Hess was never far from battle in Romania, taking part in the Battle of Rimnicu Sârat seventy-five miles north-east of the capital. On July 23rd 1917, while at the Oituz Pass, his left arm once again took a hit from a shell splinter. This time the wound didn't require a visit to a Reservelazarett.

But just two weeks later he came within millimetres of his own mortality. During the storming of the Ungüreana, a small hill in the Carpathians near Focsani north of Bucharest, Hess took a bullet through the body of a Romanian soldier.

Hess had been rushed to a Kriegslazarett in the Hungarian town of Bezdivasarhely the next day, where they found that the bullet had entered at the front of his chest near his left armpit, leaving a "pea-sized" hole surrounded by puckered skin. It had passed through his lung, exiting the body near the spinal column of the 4th vertebra beneath the shoulder blade, leaving a "cherry stone-sized hole".

It was clear to the medics that Hess had been shot with a small calibre rifle but, by some miracle, the bullet had missed his heart and bones by a fraction.

Given his convalescence would not be short, he was returned to Germany on a hospital train in September, commissioned as a Leutnant der Reserve until he could be discharged as fit for active service.

This latest brush with death had clearly focused Hess's mind. Rather than returning to cannon fodder duty on the Front, Hess wanted to quench his pre-war thirst for mathematics and science in the fledgling Air Service.

When he put in a formal application to be transferred from his new unit – the 1st Supplementary Infantry Leib Regiment, Munich – he claimed that he had expected to be posted to the Air Service in August 1917, had he not been wounded in battle.

Having spent more than three years in the infantry, much of it on the front line, Hess had been wounded three times while many of his comrades had fallen.

He must have felt like he had been living on borrowed time.

And while his life expectancy could hardly be enhanced by joining the Air Service, where as many seemed to die by accident as from hostile action, it had to be better than the constant shelling, the squalid conditions, the stench of death and the appalling malnutrition of the Front (though at least they didn't have to endure the introduction of ersatz food replacements, unlike the civilian population back home).

The Air Service could also give him another thing he craved.

Recognition.

Hess, while fascinated by the rapid advance of technology and the sheer thrill of flying, was not the first to realise that all pilots were held in high esteem by the general public, with fighter aces amongst their number becoming folk heroes.

So after escorting the List Company to the Front in early 1918, he would return to Munich for aptitude and medical tests before beginning ground instruction at Flieger-schule 1 at Schleissheim.

Little did he know that, by the time he was fully trained to be behind the stick of a Fokker D.VII, widely regarded as Germany's finest fighter of the war, just four weeks of hostilities would remain.

And he – along with all of the other poor frontschwein – would return to Germany to live the lives of the vanquished, not the victorious.

'Thank you Lieutenant,' von Tubouef nodded to the young officer, retaining an air of diplomatic nicety with Hess before turning to the assembled Regiment.

'Men,' he barked, 'welcome back to the Front. Many of you will have already played a role in this war, a war which is a battle for the very future of our nation against the savages of the east and the imperialists of the west.'

'After a long and bloody war of attrition, in which many lives have been lost, the end is finally in sight. The Bolsheviks have sued for peace — at a heavy price. And soon it will be the turn of the British and the French and their benefactor Wilson across the Atlantic in America's White House.'

'Nobody believed we could beat the Russians into submission. But at Tannenberg we did!' Von Tubouef beat his chest like a drum, hand clasped like a fist. 'We took 125,000 Slav scoundrels prisoner in one day, while fighting on two fronts. Imagine what we can do with only one front!'

The reservists chanted in hubristic, patriotic approval. It was a speech von Tubouef had given many times over, a tub-thumper to rally the troops to go over the top for the Kaiser. He smiled smugly before turning away to his adjutant standing nearby.

'They'll be lucky if they see tomorrow night,' he whispered. 'They'll be sending us men in wheelchairs next!'

Von Tubouef turned back to the reservists.

'Dismissed!'

Von Tubouef spun on his heel and was en route back into headquarters as the reservists filed out, kit bags slung over their shoulders. Hess approached von Tubouef's adjutant.

'Corporal,' Hess enquired of the adjutant, 'the wife of one of my men is expecting their firstborn any time now. He is anxious to hear news from home. If possible, could he use your telephone to call a relative?'

The adjutant turned to face Hess.

It was a young Adolf Hitler.

'I'm sorry Lieutenant but…' Hitler wanted to decline.

Detecting an imminent rejection, Hess interjected. 'It would mean a great deal to him and his family – Austrian aristocracy – especially if he is to go over the top tomorrow…'

Hitler relented. 'Alright — but we'll have to be discreet…'

'Thank you Corporal,' Hess smiled back warmly before turning back to the line of reservists marching past. At the back of the group stood a straggling infantryman.

Hess called out to him.

'Herr von Rothstein?'

Luka Rothstein looked up at Hess and smiled warmly.

*

Hitler marched into the office, full of nervous energy and impatience for the favour to be taken. Rothstein followed in his wake, cold, methodical and dispassionate in his demeanour. Hitler reached for the telephone receiver as the door shut.

'You'll have to be…'

Click.

Hitler's words trailed off as he looked back in horror at Rothstein, standard issue Luger in his hand, pointed directly at him.

'Allo? Allo?' The operator was talking to himself as Rothstein waved the Luger to an agitated Hitler to replace the receiver.

Hitler looked at the gun and then into Rothstein's angry eyes. 'What, what, what do you want?'

Rothstein smiled.

*

With every step, Hitler's boots seemed to sink further and further into the increasingly thick layer of snow smothering the field. His fingers intertwined, his hands behind his head, the future Führer stumbled nervously, frequently losing his footing.

It was a sight that Rothstein, following behind with Luger in hand poised to shoot at any opportune moment, thoroughly relished.

As the 2nd Army Headquarters became a distance sight, Hitler's agitation grew.

'There must be some mistake,' he rambled. 'I've not done anything to hurt you!'

'No, not yet you haven't.'

'Then why?' he dared to turn his head back a little. 'You are Austrian, like me!'

'I am NOT Austrian,' Rothstein began in German before putting the fear of God into Hitler by switching to English mid-sentence. 'And I am nothing like you!'

Hitler fumbled, his lip trembling as it became obvious to him. 'You're… you're a spy!'

'That'll do.' Rothstein grabbed Hitler's shoulder, stopping him abruptly. He was startled a little by his slight frame. 'Now, on your knees…'

'You don't have to do this!' Hitler's voice had an increasing air of desperation.

Rothstein could almost have felt sorry for him, were it not for the vision of those yet to die similarly ignominious deaths at this quisling's whim. 'Oh yes I do.'

The visions stiffened his resolve.

He was doing the world a favour.

Hitler refused to drop to his knees, so Rothstein kicked them out from underneath him. He fell into the snow, his weasly body making a remarkably insignificant indentation. He whimpered pathetically as Rothstein hoisted him back up by the scruff of his neck.

'You – you are a monster!' Rothstein bellowed in Hitler's ear, making him visibly shudder. He imagined that, if he looked, he would find a patch of yellow snow below the feet of "Mein Führer". He cocked the Luger and put it against Hitler's temple. 'And only I can stop you.'

Hitler closed his eyes, his face creasing in fear of the coming pain, an agony prolonged by Rothstein's inner turmoil at taking a life in such cold blood.

Even this life which would return the favour many million times over in the decades to come.

A turmoil unexpectedly punctuated.

'Hello Luka.' Rothstein heard Curtis's voice before he saw him stride confidently towards him, emerging from the fog. His gaze edged up from the job in hand. It was a mixture of relief to see a friendly face, albeit with cropped dyed locks, coupled with unease as to what he was doing there.

'James – you shouldn't be here.'

'That makes two of us.'

'What do you want?' he asked, his head indicating his prey. 'I'm kind of busy.'

'I'm here to stop you making everything worse.'

Rothstein was incredulous. 'How can this possibly make anything worse?'

Curtis was calm. It was as if he was dealing with a hostage situation. In a way he was, though he knew all too well that more than one life was at risk.

It was a whole way of life that was at stake.

'I know you think that this is the right thing to do.' Curtis's tone remained level, his stride reducing to baby steps. 'And I know why you're doing this. For your family. How is your great-grandfather Luka? Seen him recently?' Curtis held up the photograph of Rothstein and Hess that he had purloined from the Reich History Museum, still stained with Elsa's blood.

'My, my, you have been busy.' Rothstein seemed surprised to have been found out. 'Then you know why this bastard has to die.'

'Luka,' Curtis's tone imbued fraternity. 'I've been to the future. And as much as all of this makes sense, what you do – what you create – is a million times worse.'

'Worse than the genocide of six million Jews, Gypsies, the disabled, twenty million Russians?' Rothstein spoke impassively, betraying his fanaticism.

'Yes, worse than all that.' Curtis knew this was the hardest sell of all time, so he had to make it personal for it to register with Rothstein. 'Luke – you don't save your great-grandfather's life. He still dies. Just younger. And these guys win.'

'Well, I don't believe you.' Rothstein was in denial. 'There has to be a time when all this works.'

Rothstein's eyes studiously avoided Curtis's gaze as the cogs turned slowly but inevitably to the terrifying import of his words.

'You know? You KNOW what this does because you've been there! You've seen the future you create!'

Rothstein didn't reply or acknowledge, hiding any shame deep inside.

Curtis was incandescent. 'How many times have you killed him before Luka?'

'A few,' he replied abruptly. 'And I'll keep killing him until I get it right.'

Curtis's own Luger was already in his hand before Rothstein could place his own back at Hitler's temple, the Austrian corporal who had managed to survive the horrors of the trenches only for it to come to this.

'What?' Rothstein smiled menacingly. 'You want to do it this time?'

'No Luka. I have to stop you.'

'James,' Rothstein snarled, 'I promise you. Not even God can stop me.'

Before Rothstein could make good on his promise, the bullet hit him. But it wasn't a bullet from Curtis.

It had come from behind.

Three armed German military policemen approached, shouting inaudibly towards them. As the bullet floored Rothstein, Curtis took a knee and fired. The three MPs were dead, the last falling as a calculating Hitler took advantage of the opportunity to break free. He ran back towards the headquarters, shouting frantically.

'English spies! English spies in German uniforms!'

Curtis grabbed Rothstein's Luger from the ground, spinning it through the air like a boomerang at the future Führer's head. Hitler's eyes swivelled in their sockets as he slumped unconsciously to the ground.

In the distance, the alarm was raised at field headquarters. Curtis could hear the sound of leather and metal colliding en masse.

He didn't have long.

He reached for Rothstein, pulling him to rest his head on his lap. His old friend was badly hurt and losing blood.

But moreover, he was crestfallen and bitter.

'Do you…' Rothstein gasped wispily. 'Do you realise what you've done? Do you…?' His eyes lolled as he passed out.

Curtis looked at the photograph. Rothstein was gone. As was Elsa's blood.

He pulled the printout from his pocket, the extract from the Roll of the Fallen.

It was now but a blank sheet of paper.

He could almost have cried.

The nightmare was over.

Finally.

But not if they stayed there.

Curtis reached for Rothstein's time bracelet. He synchronised the date on it with his own before sending him on his way.

*

As the soldiers approached the bracken with caution, all they could make out in the eerie silence of the night were two brief blue flashes ahead.

By the time they reached the flashes, all that remained was an unconscious corporal lying next to an unfired Luger in the snow.

If only the night could talk.

# 29
# JOURNEY'S END

The shards of grain fell like tenpins under the deadly rotor blades of the tractor snaking along the field on the outskirts of Cambrai. Despite the glorious sunshine the air remained chilly, but inside the tractor's sun-kissed cabin it felt like a greenhouse.

The silver-bearded farmer behind the wheel took off his cap and wiped the beads of sweat stationed above his eyes, hidden within voluminous brows comprised of more than fifty shades of grey.

Finally able to see ahead for fear of raindrops of sweat stinging his eyes, he squinted in disbelief. Taking his foot off the gas pedal of the tractor, he leant out of the side of the cabin to see for himself the small fire burning ahead of him.

And the young man in nothing but his undergarments carrying another, presumably unconscious. Possibly even dead.

They looked like they had been in a warzone.

In the flaming corn stack behind them, their German uniforms spanning a century burned bright but brief.

*

Rothstein slept soundly in the single wooden bed, under the watchful gaze of a young girl's doll collection residing on a shelf above him. Nearby, the young girl – Coralie, Curtis assumed from the montage of letters affixed beneath them, made from dried petals of flowers grown in the farmhouse garden – helped the doctor to stitch the entry and exit wound of the single shot that the MP had fired at him.

In the doorway, as the dying embers of the spring day outside shone through the thick netted curtains, Curtis stood watch over his old friend.

The bullet had missed bones and organs by millimetres, instead leaving his body with two "cherry stone-sized holes".

Just like great-grandfather Rudolf.

Rothstein had been lucky.

Luckier than his three unwitting assailants, though Curtis mused that if that was the limit of the unintended casualties of Rothstein's misguided vendetta, he could bear the guilt of killing them.

The silver-haired farmer, clearly Coralie's father, rested his own shoulder against the other side of the doorframe. Curtis looked across. He was always fascinated at the lengths that human beings would go to for strangers in crisis situations. Perhaps it was the lack of time to think, to rationalise the risks and the dangers, that allowed innate humanity to assert itself and override all other considerations.

Whatever it was, Curtis was grateful.

'Merci beaucoup.'

The farmer raised his eyebrows gently. 'You're welcome.'

Curtis was surprised. 'You speak English?'

'So do you,' the farmer replied blithely.

The doctor had finished packing his bag, putting his hat and coat on to leave. As he passed between Curtis and the farmer, he stopped. He looked into Curtis's eyes.

'Your friend is very lucky,' he ventured in French. 'Whatever hit him missed all of his vital organs and arteries and passed right through him. But he lost a lot of blood. He needs to rest.'

The doctor tipped his hat at the farmer and was gone.

'Your friend,' the farmer offered. 'He can stay a few days.'

Curtis smiled. 'Thank you. I'm sure he won't be any trouble.'

'Well, if he is, I have a gun too. And I'm a better shot than whoever shot him.'

Curtis didn't doubt it. He offered his hand and the farmer shook it.

A fisherman does indeed know another fisherman from afar, he thought as he made for the stairs. He almost forgot to ask the one burning question.

'By the way…' Curtis turned back. 'Who won the war?'

The farmer looked at him incredulously, as if he needed to call back the doctor. 'We did, obviously!'

Curtis smiled, tapping his head. 'Just checking.'

'Do you need a doctor too?' the farmer chided him as he walked down the stairs, to no response. 'Crazy English.'

# 30
# THE DEVIL YOU KNOW

Begun in 1160 under Arducius de Faucigny, prince-bishop of the Diocese of Geneva, Cathédrale St. Pierre was a peculiar fusion of styles.

Starting life as a squat Romanesque construct, it was completed a hundred and fifty years later with Gothic flourishes before its columned neoclassical façade joined it almost six hundred years after the first stones had been laid.

A religious site as far back as the 4th Century, between the 8th and 10th Centuries it was just one of three cathedrals to co-exist on the same site prior to Christianity's arrival in Geneva.

The modern-day cathedral grew from the one devoted to ecclesiastical use and an early Christian funerary cult, subsuming the other constructs that had been devoted to public sacraments and church teaching. Its Chapelle des Macchabees was added in 1397.

Originally the Catholic Cathedral of St. Peter, in the reformation that swept Western Europe in the 16th Century it was transformed into a Protestant church. John Calvin preached at St. Pierre from 1536 to 1564, during which time the cathedral quickly rose to become the seat of Protestantism.

Behind the 15th Century choir stalls sits the 19th Century tomb of Duc Henri de Rohan, leader of the French Protestants after Calvin. The Calvinists, like reformers across Europe, had no time for religious idolatry and stripped it of its altars, statues, paintings and furniture. Even its famed murals were whitewashed. Only the cathedral's stained glass windows survived the inferno of religious purification.

A hundred and fifty-seven narrow winding steps led from the nave to the spectacular panoramic view of Geneva visible from the summit of the cathedral's north tower, its bell tolling for midnight mass.

It was Christmas Eve.

The cathedral was full, almost to breaking point. For latecomers, it was standing room only – if they were lucky. But sat amongst the congregation, enjoying the choristers' rendition of *Alleluia*, was Ida Schildberg.

She looked deep in conversation with her maker.

*

The candles flickered silently in stepped ranks for those already gone from this world. Christmas was a time for reflection as well as for family. As the Bishop of Geneva bid the last of his flock goodnight, Schildberg stepped forward to light two candles.

'I do hope one of those is for me.' The voice came from the shadows, as well as her past.

Curtis stepped out of the shadows. Schildberg was startled but at the same time pleasantly surprised to see him.

'James. We were beginning to wonder…' As Schildberg turned around, her beaming smile disappeared when she found him alone. 'Where is Luka?'

Her voice betrayed her anxiety. Curtis smiled wryly before stepping forward to light two candles of his own. 'Now now Dr Schildberg.' Curtis sparked up, his hand hovering close the flame. 'There's no need to call him by his full name. Just call him what he is — your grandson.'

Schildberg's immediate thought was to protest her innocence but she knew Curtis was too wily for that. He was always going to work it out eventually. Any further misinformation was futile.

Her perambulation around the cathedral began with mincing steps. 'How long have you known?'

'Oh, around the time your grandson abandoned me to go off on some secret solo mission for you to kill Adolf Hitler to try and save the life of your father – Rudolf Hess.'

Schildberg almost looked relieved.

That the lie was over.

'You know, Luka said you would figure it out. He said that it would be better if we told you. I counselled against. We couldn't afford for you to not come on board.'

'Because that was Crombie's price for funding you when you had your little accident.' Whenever he said the man's name, he felt a poisonous taste in his mouth.

Schildberg was embarrassed. 'Yes.' She took a deep breath. 'Is Luka dead?'

Curtis took a deep breath too. 'No.'

'Then where is he?'

'Safe.'

'Can I see him?'

'Not without one of these.' Curtis pulled up his jacket arm to reveal both his own and Rothstein's time bracelets on his arm.

Schildberg swallowed deeply. 'What do you want James?'

'Burn the programme.'

The words send a shiver down her spine. 'I can't do that.'

'You don't have a choice.' Curtis stopped in front of Schildberg, blocking her way. 'Killing Hitler doesn't kill the Nazis. It makes them stronger. Beware the hydra. Cut one head off and another grows in its place. For another thing, there's no way the military are going to let this stay a scientific experiment. That's not the way they roll and you know it. History proves time and again that scientific development can and is always misused by those with power. Do you think Oppenheimer intended for his work on the atom bomb to risk the future of mankind? Some battles are meant to be lost — for the greater good.'

Schildberg was agitated. 'That's easy for you to say. Hitler didn't betray your father!'

'No – the Allies betrayed your father and it was wrong. He was a Cold War pawn. But history has a habit of correcting itself. They know him to be a man of good intentions, who tried in vain to end the war and saved many Jews. Crikey, even one of the Popes was a member of the Hitler Youth! I don't doubt your honourable intentions Doctor – but this is the way it has to be.'

Schildberg sighed pensively. 'If I accept, I can't just go in there and resign. There's no way they'd let me do that.'

Curtis cupped Schildberg's hand in his own and smiled. 'I did say "burn" the programme, Doctor.'

Curtis let go of her hand gently, backing away to leave. Schildberg turned on her heel and shouted after him.

'Why didn't you go back and save your father, make things right?'

Curtis smiled. 'Because that would make me a hypocrite, Dr Schildberg. The past is a foreign country. They do things differently there. And none of us should live there anymore. Besides, you can make things right in other ways.'

Schildberg nodded.

Here endeth the lesson.

'Merry Christmas James.'

'Joyeux Nöel, Dr Schildberg. I hope your grandson makes it home in time.'

# 31
# A PROMISE IS A PROMISE

The tourists snaked through the subterranean confines, eagerly following their somewhat over-enthusiastic tour guide. She was clearly a gap year student from the American south, her Texan drawl peculiar as it went into exquisite detail about a place so integral to British history.

'This room played host to one of the defining moments of the Second World War,' she pronounced.

That was an understatement, Curtis thought.

The truth was that everyone owed the men and women that had worked there a debt of gratitude that would – could – never be repaid

RAF Uxbridge had the twin honour of not only being the original home of the Royal Flying Corps – which merged with the Royal Naval Air Service to form the Royal Air Force in April 1918 – but also of being headquarters to 11 Group, responsible for the aerial defence of London and the south-east of England during the Battle of Britain.

But its history had only relatively recently taken a military turn, having originally been built as a hunting lodge in 1717 by the Duke of Schomberg, a German-born general knighted for his role in the 1690 Battle of the Boyne by William of Orange (later King William III).

Formerly known as the Hillingdon House estate, it was bought by the British government in 1915 with the intention of turning it into a prisoner-of-war camp, not dissimilar to the likes of Princetown at the summit of Dartmoor, which before becoming part of the British prison network housed French and American prisoners during the Napoleonic Wars.

However in one of the earliest examples of organised nimbyism, the locals protested and it went on to house the Canadian Convalescent Hospital instead.

For the two years up to 1917, it was home to injured troops evacuated from the front line. But in November of that year, it was joined by the embryonic Royal Flying Corps Armament School, moving into Hillingdon House itself with 114 officers, 1,156 men and a dowry of £2,289 12s 9d for the Canadian Red Cross to sweeten the pill.

As the Great War increasingly took to the skies to break the stalemate in the trenches below, the hospital soon shut its doors.

And on April 1st 1918, it began its new life as RAF Uxbridge.

In 1926, the Air Ministry chose it as the new base for the ADGB – Air Defence of Great Britain – from where home defence would be conducted. It was chosen because of its unique position, located close to the corridors of power in Whitehall but far enough away from them to make it difficult for any enemy to identify and bomb it successfully.

But the original wooden Operations Room was only fit for purpose during the summer, as maintenance of the signalling and communications equipment became difficult in the wet winter months.

As early as January 1933, before Hitler had even come to power in Germany, plans to take the Operations Room to safety below ground were already being mooted.

With German rearmament and territorial adventurism dominant themes of the late 1920s and early 1930s, the preparation and operational readiness of Britain's air force became of increasing importance. The defence of the UK's airspace within RAF Fighter Command was divided into four groups: 10 Group (which covered Wales and the West Country), 11 Group (which looked after London and the approaches to it across the south-east), 12 Group (defending the Midlands and East Anglia) and finally 13 Group (taking care of the north of England, Scotland and Northern Ireland – as well as Deputy Führers on fanciful missions to meet Scottish Dukes).

Formed in 1936, 11 Group was naturally headquartered at RAF Uxbridge, and the following year planning began for its new underground Operations Room.

What would go down in history as the Battle of Britain Bunker.

Initially designed to rest sixty-six feet below ground level, London's impermeable clay forced its construction at sixty feet instead. But it could still withstand a direct hit from a 500-pound bomb.

The Bunker was finished just ten days before the outbreak of the Second World War. On September 2nd 1939, the new underground Operations Room reached war readiness.

In the months of phoney war that followed, RAF Uxbridge was the staging post for despatching personnel to and from northern France as well as providing air cover for sea convoys in the English Channel. But following the execution of Operation Dynamo – the evacuation of the British Expeditionary Force from Dunkirk after the fall of France in June 1940 – the war came much closer to home.

Hitler had never wanted to invade Britain. Having sent the BEF packing, first in Norway and then in France and the Low Countries, he had seen the English Channel as a natural border between the Third Reich – stretching from the Bay of Biscay to the Baltics – and the British Empire. He saw no distinction between what he was doing in continental Europe and what the British had been doing for centuries with its own imperial conquests the world over. He convinced himself that the British government, pragmatic and with no selfish strategic interest in mainland Europe, would agree a negotiated peace, as Chamberlain already had at Munich before the war.

But the disastrous Norway campaign, coupled with the routing in northern France, had cost Chamberlain his job.

There was a new man in 10 Downing Street.

Winston Churchill may have been a pragmatic politician during peacetime. But in war he was a soldier, a ferocious defender against the actions of aggressors. After years of being a lone voice counselling against appeasement, in its darkest hour Britain had turned to him.

Under no circumstances was this most immovable objects going to budge.

Rejecting all overtures from the German government, Churchill promised that Dunkirk was merely the beginning, not the end. He pledged to the people of occupied France that Britain would be back.

His steadfastness incensed Hitler, who on July 16th 1940 issued the forces of the Wehrmacht with Directive 16: ordering the preparation for the invasion of Great Britain.

Operation Sea Lion required that, given Britain's strength on the sea and in the air, at the very least air superiority had to be achieved before the amphibious craft carrying invasion forces would make their short but perilous journey across the English Channel.

All that stood in the Wehrmacht's way was the Royal Air Force.

Göring's Luftwaffe were tasked with destroying them and their Fighter Command structures. Throughout July and early August 1940, his Stukas targeted convoys in the Channel with the occasional foray into the RAF's airfields and southern ports.

But with faulty intelligence underplaying the strength and morale of the RAF, on August 2nd 1940 Göring issued the Eagle Day Directive, a plan of attack against the south-east of England that was intended to deliver a series of knockout body-blows to British defences and infrastructure in anticipation of the start of Operation Sea Lion.

Eagle Day – Adlertag – would be August 13th, with a massive onslaught against RAF airfields.

Though Göring's intelligence woefully underestimated the RAF's strength, the British were nevertheless outnumbered four-to-one. Six hundred British frontline fighters squared off against thirteen hundred German bombers and dive-bombers, supported by nine hundred single- and three hundred twin-engined fighters.

As they stared across the Channel at an arc stretching from the Cherbourg Peninsula to the fjords of Norway, the odds were heavily stacked against the British.

Göring clearly fancied his chances.

On August 8th, the battle moved inland and the most intensive phase of operations began. Fifteen hundred German aircraft filled the skies, targeting fighter airfields and radar installations.

While air threat warnings were filtered by nearby RAF Bentley Prior to avoid duplication, doubt or confusion, it was 11 Group's Operations Room at RAF Uxbridge that, through its plotting table, allocated resources and issued orders to the airfields.

11 Group personnel numbers doubled to 20,000 in 1940 alone.

They needed them.

Between August 8th and August 13th, 145 German aircraft were lost at a cost of 88 British fighters. Losses that were unsustainable for either side. But believing that the RAF were down to their last three hundred serviceable fighters, Göring rolled the dice with an audacious bombardment that would become known as The Hardest Day.

On that single day, the Luftwaffe flew 970 sorties over Britain, countered by 927 from the RAF. Every aircraft in their respective fleets flew at least once, some as many as five times, in a battle that waged over twenty-four hours.

The Luftwaffe ruthlessly targeted 11 Group's airfields in the south-east. RAF Biggin Hill, Kenley, North Weald, Gosport, Ford, Thorney Island, Hornchurch – all came in for a battering alongside Liverpool docks and the Poling radar station, crucial to the effectiveness of the Chain Home radar system.

But in part due to their effective use of radar, a system that was the most advanced and operational in the world, the British had enough notice of where to direct their finite forces to best repel the Luftwaffe's bombers.

On that single day, the Luftwaffe lost 71 aircraft to the RAF's 68. But the momentum was with the defenders, not the aggressors.

Göring had peaked.

By the time of the fiercest day of fighting – September 15th 1940, later dubbed Battle of Britain Day – the RAF had lost nine hundred fighters. A colossal figure, but just half of the seventeen hundred losses sustained by the Luftwaffe.

The Germans were losing bombers faster than Willi Messerschmidt could replace them.

Despite Hitler's fury at the temerity of the British bombing Berlin in return, for which he retaliated against London and other English population centres like Coventry and Liverpool, it was by now clear even to the German hierarchy that the Luftwaffe could not gain the ascendancy in the skies above the British Isles.

Unternehmen Seelöwe was postponed.

Indefinitely.

And though Hitler's bombardment from the skies continued well into the following summer with the Blitz – where 10,000 sorties between March and May 1941 decimated London – Germany's lack of a systematic plan in the previous summer had blown an unique opportunity never to be repeated.

The Battle of Britain epitomised all that didn't work about German warmongering. One day the Luftwaffe would be blockading Britain by destroying its ports, the next it would be hitting the Command and Control installations of Fighter Command and Bomber Command, which it would follow-up with morale-sapping raids on the civilian populace.

Were it not for Germany's divided aims and seeming lack of focus, coupled with a lack of planning and fighters flying at the very limits of their range, the Battle of Britain could easily have become the Battle for Britain.

A battle which Curtis alone knew the consequences of losing first-hand.

As the group of tourists moved on, Curtis paused to reflect. His hand gently snaked along the top of the plotting table, which was just as it was when he first met her.

It felt like only yesterday that he was in this very room, scurrying around with the other rats in the underground tunnel, watching the brave members of the Freiheit Movement fighting for the freedom of the British people in the same way as the heroes of 11 Group had on The Hardest Day.

They too would be unsung heroes.

People like Skunk and Stoltz.

Elsa.

Rufus.

And Billie.

Curtis kissed his fingers before placing them on the plotting table.

Now he knew what was going through Churchill's mind when, leaving the bunker with General Ismay on one of his many tense visits, he uttered those immortal words.

'Never in the field of human conflict was so much owed by so many to so few.'

*

Curtis sat in the booth drinking root beer while picking at long-cold fries.

He was far more interested in the news unfolding on the television in the background.

He watched intently as the bulletin reported the full extent of the carnage of a devastating fire at CERN.

'Once a decade, disaster seems to befall this close-knit scientific community.' The reporter's overlaid commentary was suitably grave and exaggerated in tone. 'In 2008, it was the damage to the Large Hadron Collider that many thought would be its undoing. Now, more than a decade later, it is man's more common foe: the freak accident. In the early hours of Christmas Day, fire engulfed the complex, causing many, many millions of pounds worth of damage. But what is incalculable is the loss of irreplaceable scientific data. CERN's data backup facilities were maintained onsite and the damage is reported to be so extensive that all are believed to have been destroyed. Thankfully as the holiday season was underway, all staff were on leave. Including this adorable cat.'

Curtis smiled as he watched Dr Schildberg's cat Rudi circling the reporter before taking another sip of root beer.

'In a separate development,' the reporter continued, 'the director of CERN's Special Projects Division – retired Colonel Arnold Crombie of NATO – has been arrested after fresh evidence surfaced on YouTube of a secret meeting between him and that other famous Colonel, Muammar Gaddafi, in April 1988. The previously unseen footage of the meeting appears to contradict Colonel Crombie's earlier evidence at the trial of the late John Curtis, a legitimate arms dealer whose company LEIN Holdings had been accused by authorities here and in the US of breaking an arms embargo with Libya. Curtis committed suicide before a jury could reach a verdict. Following the arrest, its posthumous conviction is now very much in doubt.'

Curtis smiled even more, toasting the television. As he did, the waitress turned the television off. 'Hey, I was watching that…' he jumped up in protest as the waitress walked away towards the jukebox.

'It's New Year's Eve!' she replied over her shoulder. 'That's no time for watching the news! It's time for something more peaceful.'

The voice was familiar.

As was the tone.

And as she selected *All Of Me* from the jukebox, there could be no doubt.

The waitress was Billie.

Curtis couldn't quite believe she was there in his world. He looked at her name badge for reassurance.

Billie.

She looked down. 'Yes, I'm named after her…' before Curtis could say anything.

Same old Billie.

'But what would they have called you if you were a boy?' he asked cheekily.

Billie faux frowned.

Curtis sought to recover the situation. 'My favourite's *God Bless The Child*.'

'I love them all,' Billie said, tapping her fingers against the jukebox, 'but this one's my favourite.' She looked quizzically at Curtis. 'Have we met before?'

Curtis smiled. 'In another lifetime, perhaps.' Curtis extended his hand. 'I'm James.'

Despite him already knowing from her badge, Billie felt the need to reiterate it.

'Billie.'

'Billie.' He held her hand just a little longer. 'I know we've just met and all but — would you like to dance?'

The neon-lit sign flickered from open to closed.

Curtis spun a laughing Billie around the diner, replete with twirls.

It was like they had never parted.

*

'Coralie?' Her father's voice reverberated throughout the farmhouse, but he knew exactly where she was.

She was in with the young man.

Again.

The time would come when the young man would be well enough to leave. Until then, he would have to keep a watchful eye on his daughter's obsession with him.

She stood over his sleeping frame, smiling as she placed the fresh rose on his chest. She let out a little sigh, the sigh of a young girl in love.

'Coralie!'

That was her last warning.

'Coming Papa,' she shouted as she scurried out of her bedroom for the kitchen table.

On her way, she passed the young man's few belongings.

His Omega Seamaster watch.

His boots.

And his spare time bracelet.

THE END

# ABOUT THE AUTHOR

Ben Pickering was born in London in 1979 to Welsh parents passing through. Growing up in the South Wales city of Swansea, he longed to be an astronaut before settling on an even more difficult ambition: becoming a successful filmmaker. In a career spanning almost a quarter of a century (he started young), he has directed feature films including TWO DAYS IN THE SMOKE and WELCOME TO CURIOSITY and produced half a dozen others including most recently ELECTION NIGHT. A single father of two young children, he splits his time between Cornwall and London. FREIHEIT is his debut novel.

Printed in Great Britain
by Amazon

32676258R00196